Dear Reader,

The thinking behind the PEOPLE OF THE PLAINS series is that truth is not only stranger than fiction, but also more exciting. The traditional "Western" gave us gripping tales of gunslingers, cattle barons, clean-cut heroes, fierce Indian horsemen collecting scalps, and the U.S. cavalry racing to the rescue. But, with some notable exceptions, it concerned a frontier as mythic and romantic as Camelot.

Thanks to the work of historians, we now know that what was happening on the western frontier was far more complex than the myths, and far more interesting to today's reader. In the middle years of the 19th century the rules determining who owned that "sea of grass" and the mountains which surround it were being formed. The horse was revolutionizing Indian cultures, tribes were jostling with tribes over hunting grounds, the Spanish frontier was collapsing, and the new Americans were trickling westward looking for their fortune, their freedom, or simply adventure.

Ken Englade is best known for books focused on notable criminal trials. In this PEOPLE OF THE PLAINS series he taps a lifelong fascination with the history of the American frontier to give us a series of novels of this era as it really was. I hope you enjoy this as I have, and look for future titles in the series, coming soon from HarperPaperbacks.

Sincerely,

Tony Hillerman

BOOKS BY KEN ENGLADE

Hoffa

TONY HILLERMAN'S FRONTIER

People of the Plains

The Tribes

The Soldiers

*Battle Cry**

NONFICTION

Hotblood

To Hatred Turned

Blood Sister

Beyond Reason

Murder in Boston

Cellar of Horror

Deadly Lessons

A Family Business

*coming soon

ATTENTION: ORGANIZATIONS AND CORPORATIONS

Most HarperPaperbacks are available at special quantity discounts for bulk purchases for sales promotions, premiums, or fund-raising. For information, please call or write:
Special Markets Department, HarperCollins*Publishers*,
10 East 53rd Street, New York, N.Y. 10022.
Telephone: (212) 207-7528. Fax: (212) 207-7222.

TONY HILLERMAN'S

FRONTIER

PEOPLE OF THE PLAINS

The SOLDIERS

Ken Englade

HarperPaperbacks
A Division of HarperCollins*Publishers*

HarperPaperbacks
A Division of HarperCollins*Publishers*
10 East 53rd Street, New York, N.Y. 10022-5299

If you purchased this book without a cover, you should be aware that this book is stolen property. It was reported as "unsold and destroyed" to the publisher and neither the author nor the publisher has received any payment for this "stripped book."

This is a work of fiction. The characters, incidents, and dialogues are products of the author's imagination and are not to be construed as real. Any resemblance to actual events or persons, living or dead, is entirely coincidental.

Copyright © 1996 by HarperCollins*Publishers*
All rights reserved. No part of this book may be used or reproduced in any manner whatsoever without written permission of the publisher, except in the case of brief quotations embodied in critical articles and reviews. For information address HarperCollins*Publishers*, 10 East 53rd Street, New York, N.Y. 10022-5299.

ISBN: 0-06-100945-8

HarperCollins®, ®, and HarperPaperbacks™ are trademarks of HarperCollins*Publishers* Inc.

Cover illustration by Steven Assel

First printing: December 1996

Printed in the United States of America

Visit HarperPaperbacks on the World Wide Web at
http://www.harpercollins.com/paperbacks

❖ 10 9 8 7 6 5 4 3 2 1

For Heidi

PEOPLE OF THE PLAINS

The SOLDIERS

Lieutenant Jason Dobbs rose awkwardly to his feet, gingerly unfolding his gangly, six-foot-two-inch frame a segment at a time.

Grimacing like a man in considerable pain, he slowly straightened his back. Then he raised the skinny, stooped shoulders that never properly filled the blue, one-size-fits-all uniform shirts the Army churned out in total disregard for corporeal reality. Finally, he lifted his head, a massive appendage that looked far too heavy for the willowy stem on which it rested. "The only thing worse than getting old," he groaned in proper Bostonian English, running his thin, reedlike fingers through hair the consistency and color of corn silk, "is the alternative."

Dobbs's deliberateness resulted partly from respect for the physical frailties that he perceived as becoming more numerous the closer he got to his thirty-fifth birthday, but mainly it was because he had been crouching for hours over the leather bound ledger that stood open on the rickety table in front of him, black ink still glistening wetly in the late afternoon light.

Warily, mindful of the consequences of not allowing cramped muscles to be awakened slowly, he went into his stretching regimen, first bending backwards, hands over kidneys, until he could hear the vertebrae click, then forwards, forcing the blood to rush to his head. Lastly, he stretched his long arms over his head and strained vainly to touch the ceiling. Rising on his toes, he tried again, this time successfully grazing the rough, pine planks.

"Goddamnit!" he exploded, grabbing his hand where a long, dark splinter had imbedded itself in the tip of his right middle finger. Wincing, he yanked on the sliver of wood, swearing again when a large drop of blood popped to the surface. "You clumsy fool," he berated himself, thrusting the finger in his mouth.

Crossing the room in three long strides, he grabbed a cloth off the shelf that held the few basic culinary utensils he shared with the compartment's other occupant, his friend and fellow officer, Jean Benoit, and wrapped it tightly around the wound.

"It's a good thing Jean isn't here," he whispered in the tone that those accustomed to solitude use when talking to themselves. "He'd be ridiculing me unmercifully for my ineptitude."

After peeking at his finger to make sure the bleeding had been stanched, Dobbs took down a battered, blackened pot and filled it with water from a nearby jug. Opening the door of the stove, he threw in a few lengths of fresh wood, jabbing vigorously with a broken cavalry sabre that served as a poker until the fire blazed.

While waiting for the water to boil, Dobbs strode to the narrow window and looked out. The room was the smallest in the entire Bachelor Officers' Quarters, the building referred to as Old Bedlam by everyone at Fort Laramie, military and civilian alike. There was barely enough space for two cots, the table that also served as a desk, and the potbellied stove. Although the

Washington bureaucrat who designed the building obviously intended it to be used as a storage space, it was pressed into service as living quarters when the soldier population grew unexpectedly. If it had not been for the window, obviously added as a sop to the unfortunate junior officer quartered there, the small room would have been as unbearable as a jail cell.

As post surgeon Dobbs was entitled to better accommodations, but the choice had been his. When George Teasley, the district's new Indian Agent, arrived ahead of schedule with his quarters not yet ready, Dobbs voluntarily surrendered his room. Supposedly, it was a temporary arrangement designed to last only until a small adobe could be erected for Teasley. But with one thing and another the weeks had stretched into months and Teasley was still in Dobbs's room. Not that it mattered much to Dobbs since he spent most of his waking hours, and a good deal of his sleeping ones, too, in the infirmary.

As the post surgeon, Dobbs was not only responsible for the 150 officers and men at Fort Laramie and the post's half dozen resident civilians, but he also was charged with examining and administering to the five women who lived in the whorehouse just to the south, the facility that had been dubbed the Hog Ranch by a cynical trooper. In addition Dobbs also cared for members of the wagon trains that passed through heading west, *plus* the odd Indian who straggled in needing medical care.

Although the room was at the back of the building, the side that faced the rugged bluffs that lined the fort's western rim instead of the clear, cold Laramie River that ran along the eastern edge of the post, there was a visual advantage because Old Bedlam was the only two-story building in the compound. When the sun reached a certain angle, usually just before noon, Dobbs could see the glint of its reflection off the Laramie, but the mile-wide North Platte was too far around the bend to be visible.

By leaning slightly out the open window, Dobbs could see a section of the empty parade ground and the westernmost of the two enlisted men's barracks that marked the northwest quadrant of the post's rough oval. As he watched, a single soldier came into view: a dusty, tired-looking private walking off a sentence handed down by a court-martial board. Strapped to the private's sagging shoulders was a knapsack Dobbs knew was filled with bricks, and around his neck hung a crude sign displaying a single word: "THIEF."

Before Dobbs himself had decided to call it a day, the bugler had sounded Recall, so the troops were free to entertain themselves until First Call for Retreat at 7:45. The men were using the two hours and forty-five minutes to gamble, sleep, wash their clothes, or do absolutely nothing. A group of a dozen or more had unbuttoned the heavy wool uniform shirts they wore winter and summer and were lounging in front of the barracks, smoking and retelling the same jokes they all had heard a hundred times or more. Despite this, they still laughed at the punch lines and poked each other jocularly on the shoulder.

It's curious, Dobbs thought idly, that none of them are paying the least attention to the private marching off his punishment. Maybe thievery is such a common occurrence that no one gives it a second thought except the one who gets caught. I'll bring this up to Grant; maybe there's a growing problem the officers aren't aware of.

Shifting his attention back the troopers who were roughhousing like a group of schoolboys (which, in fact, many of them were young enough to be), Dobbs could not resist smiling himself. Despite his frustration with the bureaucracy and his sometimes seemingly overwhelming anger at Washington politicians, most of whom knew nothing about "the situation on the frontier" although they tried their damnedest to formulate policy to correct "the Indian problem," the Army was his home. It had been for years, ever since he joined up soon after graduating third in his class from Harvard Medical School the year before war was declared against Mexico. That conflict had been his first real test, both as a physician and a man.

Marching with Jebediah Briggs from Veracruz westward to Mexico City, Dobbs had been in the thick of the action. It was during that campaign that he built a solid reputation as a surgeon and decided to make the military his career. Not that things had been easy; it was never easy watching men suffer and die. He vividly recalled the torn bodies that came before him in a never-ending stream; their screams still haunted his dreams. But the minute-to-minute crises forced him to dig deep within himself and he was surprised at his own inner strength. He lost a lot of soldiers, many of them simply because he had not been able to be everywhere at once, but he saved a lot of them, too. And along the way, he honed the skills that made him one of the best battlefield surgeons of the campaign.

There was more to war than fighting and marching, Dobbs quickly learned. There were some good times, like the twelve-course dinners with excellent French wine, liberated from the Mexicans, of course, that he was privileged to share with Briggs, then a colonel, and his staff. Certainly not least was the camaraderie, the feeling of brotherhood that germinated and took root among men who shared common dangers and delights.

Dobbs also learned another valuable lesson: the real horror of war was not the fact that men were killed and maimed, since that was expected. It was never known who would be struck, but it was assumed by every soldier that *someone* would be. The true terror of fighting in a foreign land was the inability to control events at home. While death was a commonplace among an army in the field, it was much more of a shock when it involved a loved one who was supposedly safe at home.

It was soon after one of the fiercest skirmishes in which Dobbs was involved that the letter arrived from Boston. Dobbs had not even had a chance to strip off his bloody clothes when the sergeant handed him the envelope. That's strange, Dobbs remembered thinking, studying the neat penmanship he recognized immediately as that of his father-in-law. Why is he writing?

Near exhaustion after sixteen straight hours in surgery, Dobbs's instincts told him to open the envelope immediately. "Dear Son-in-law," it began in Dr. O'Brien's typical formal way, "I know that you will want me to get immediately to the point." Closing his eyes, Dobbs could still see the letter as plainly as if it were on the table in front of him. "Your wife, Colleen, succumbed this morning of Asiatic cholera, an epidemic of which is sweeping the city. Her death was quick and relatively painless."

When he recovered sufficiently from the shock to read the rest of the letter, Dobbs learned that his two children, a daughter and a son, had been sent to the country to live with his late wife's sister and her husband. Although he briefly entertained thoughts of having them rejoin him, he soon realized that such action would be ill-considered. Mary Margaret, now almost 10, and Patrick, nearly 7, were well established with Sean and Agnes and it would be to their benefit to remain in

Massachusetts. "God," Dobbs mumbled, suddenly feeling old and tired, "it's been forever since I've seen them."

In actuality, it was only a little more than a year. Just before leaving for Fort Laramie, he had taken his accumulated leave and travelled to Boston for what he knew would be the last visit he would have with his children for a long time.

Rubbing his chin, Dobbs struggled to bring their faces into focus. It was difficult because he had not been seeing things too clearly at the time. After being assigned to Washington following the war, Dobbs quickly grew bored with peacetime garrison duty. And, as happens to many soldiers in such circumstances, he began looking for a way to relieve the tedium. Some men, Dobbs knew, turned to cards and dice. Others to whoring or brawling. But his transgression had been even more serious. Suddenly left with nothing to do except feel sorry for himself and brood about his wife's death, Dobbs had become addicted to dilaudid, a mixture of alcohol and opium. In his sober moments, as a physician, he knew he was not only ruining his own body but endangering the lives of his patients as well. But he had no incentive to stop. At least not until he was summoned to General Briggs's office. Thank God for Briggs, he thought.

More astute than Dobbs had given him credit for, Briggs had spotted the surgeon's problem early on and decided to take drastic action. The old soldier had not exactly been understanding, Dobbs recalled, but he had been forthright. In an attempt to save Dobbs's skills for the Army, Briggs had banished him to the frontier. "If I hear that you've fucked up out there I'm goin' to be mighty pissed off," Briggs had told him gruffly. "If you go to Fort Laramie and men start dyin' because of *your* problem, I'm not going to take it lightly. I have a long reach. If men suffer and die because of your incompetence, I can arrange it so you become an unfortunate casualty of 'an Indian attack,'" he had added threateningly. The threat wasn't necessary. Dobbs knew he had to straighten up or resign his commission; take control of his life or spend the rest of his days as a worthless tramp. He chose to straighten up.

Now, Dobbs sighed in relief, there was no reason to believe Briggs would ever have to carry through on his warning. He had gone cold turkey and had not touched a drop of dilaudid since he left the capital. By the time he had returned from visiting his children, he had been through the worst of the withdrawal and when he joined up with Benoit for the overland journey to Fort Laramie, he was virtually symptom free. Neither Benoit nor anyone else at Fort Laramie knew about Dobbs's lapse. It was his secret. And that's the way he liked it.

Startled by a loud sizzling, Dobbs spun on his heels, his reverie broken. "The water," he said aloud. "I forgot all about the damn water."

Hurrying across the room, he yanked the pot off the stove and set it on the shelf. Although he was hardly indecisive in carrying out his professional duties, Dobbs paused, thoughtfully considering his next move. He had watched Benoit countless times but for some reason known only to a perverse Cajun god, the surgeon who could handle any medical emergency with skillful aplomb had never been able to master the art of making decent New Orleans–style coffee.

Routinely, he carefully mashed the beans sent West by Benoit's family in his own prized mortar. Just as carefully, he measured the grounds into the appropriate receptacle in Benoit's long-necked coffeepot. And, exactly as he had seen Benoit do, Dobbs placed the pot in a heavy iron skillet whose bottom was covered to a half-inch depth with hot water. Then he carefully spooned the water from the skillet into the pot until he had five or six inches of thick dark brew. As Benoit had shown him, Dobbs then poured a bit of that concoction into a cup, topping it off with more hot water. The procedure was unvarying and, as with any well-performed chemical process, the result should have been just as predictable. When Benoit did it, the coffee was wonderful almost beyond description: strong, aromatic, bracing, and flavorful. But with Dobbs the result was the opposite. Whenever he tried to imitate Benoit's expertise, the coffee tasted like horse piss. But one day, he was confident, he would turn the corner.

"This time I think I've got it," he said optimistically, delicately lifting the cup with his index finger and thumb, extending his splinter-punctured middle finger outwards. Slowly he lifted the cup to chin level and inhaled. "Ahhhh." He sighed. "It smells just like Benoit's."

In anticipation, he eased the cup to his lips, blowing gently across the dark liquid. With a loud slurp, he drew in a tentative mouthful. It was all he could do to keep from spitting it on the floor.

"God*damn*it!" he grumbled loudly, all but gagging as he forced himself to swallow the bitter liquid. "Why *can't* I make a simple pot of coffee? Damn you, Benoight," he said to the empty cot, deliberately bungling the name that his friend was continually reminding everyone was pronounced Ben-wah, "why don't you get the hell back here and take over the coffee making, you miserable, inconsiderate frog bastard."

Banging the cup down in disgust, Dobbs went back to the work table and settled himself in the wobbly, straight-backed chair. Angrily flipping back a dozen pages, he began rereading what he had spent most of the afternoon composing:

June 18, 1855

Finally, almost six weeks after the massacre at Blue Water Creek, I have time to sit down and semi-rationally consider the sequence of events that led to that terrible debacle. Notwithstanding the letters that Kemp is getting from Washington pointing to the incident as a prime example of the correct way to solve the "Indian problem," the memory of what happened continues to enrage me almost beyond description. To the day I die I will never understand why that butcher Harney felt it necessary to try his best to wipe out most of the Wazhazha band of the Brulé Sioux and a band of Minniconjou. Granted, some of the tribesmen had participated in the killing of Lieutenant Grattan and his men, but by the Indians' account, which we must rely upon since no soldiers survived, the attack was not entirely unprovoked. And even if it were, that would be no excuse for wholesale slaughter by the Army, certainly not when the leader of the band, by his own sworn testimony to Kemp, begged for leniency for his people. Harney claims that he was only following orders, that the Department had commanded him to seek revenge against the Indians and "teach the bastards a lesson they will not soon forget." But was it necessary for Harney to strike with such vehemence? Did he have to mercilessly murder women and children? The official count has settled at eighty-six Indians killed, many of them women. But God knows how many others were wounded and died later of their injuries.

Dobbs stopped reading, staring at the huge blot of ink that stained the page, remembering how his anger had been so great that he had jammed the quill into the paper in frustration. Feeling himself about to be enveloped anew with rage, Dobbs changed subjects, turning instead to Benoit's mysterious disappearance. His eyes again picked up the narrative.

Poor Jean, an excellent soldier-in-the-making who nevertheless has the misfortune of attracting bad luck wherever he goes. I remember how he was wounded by that crazed trooper at Fort Kearny before we even got to Fort Laramie. Then he reinjured himself during the Indian attack on the wagon train. Now I wonder what he has gotten himself into? According to Roaring Thunder, Jean was taken from the battlefield by two Brulé warriors, ironically the same two young men I treated after they were wounded in a fight with the Crow. God, all these events get incredibly commingled. Although Roaring Thunder has not himself seen Jean, he told Kemp he had heard from messengers that his condition is not life-threatening. The Indian told Kemp that Jean was being nursed back to health by the wife of one of the warriors, the one that calls himself Red Horse, the very same young warrior who sat on the floor of my infirmary for days without speaking while waiting for his friend, called, I believe, White Crane, to regain consciousness. The damn fool damn near starved himself to death to boot, refusing all of Holz's excellent dinners. Anyone who turns down Holz's cooking deserves to starve, I say. I digress. Roaring Thunder says he understands Jean suffered some sort of chest wound during the fight. Ironically, the wound supposedly came not from an Indian fighting for his survival but from one of our troopers, a well-known troublemaker named Darcy Connors. Unfortunately, Connors also is dead so he can't confirm the report. His was one of four soldier's bodies recovered from the field and his wounds clearly were of Indian origin. What could have happened out there? I have seen enough of war myself to know that the truth often belies the apparent evidence and I pray to God that Jean recovers, not only because he is my dear friend but because his testimony is needed to set the record straight. It would be . . .

"Jace," an agitated female voice called from nearby. "What's wrong with you? Why haven't you answered my knocks?"

"Jesus, Inge, I apologize," Dobbs said, looking up in surprise. "I was so involved in what I was doing I didn't even hear you. Come in, please. Take this chair," he said, rising.

"No," Inge said, shaking her head, her blond pigtails swinging rapidly. "I can't stay. But you gave me a fright, Jace. I couldn't find you in the officer's room and no one has seen you all afternoon. I feared maybe you had decided to take matters in your own hands and gone off looking for Jean."

Dobbs made a face. "No, I didn't do that, but it's not a bad idea. I think we've been patient long enough. Kemp said initially that he had to wait until Harney and his men left for Fort Pierre before he could do anything about Jean. Said the general would consider it a sign of weakness to turn the whole fort upside down for just one soldier, a mere brevet second lieutenant at that."

"A *mere* . . . " Inge began, her cheeks reddening.

"Hold on," Dobbs said, raising his hand. "Those are Harney's words, not mine. I know for a fact that Kemp has a lot of respect for Jean. He wants to help but there was not much he could do with a brigadier general looking over his shoulder."

Inge stamped her foot. "That's a big mound of buffalo shit," she flared. "Harney left three days ago."

"That's precisely my point," said Dobbs. "Now that the general's gone, Kemp doesn't have any more excuse. I plan to start pressuring him about a rescue mission this evening."

"If you're just trying to humor me, Jace, it won't work. If you don't know by now that I'm a *very* strong-willed woman . . . "

"I'm not trying to humor you, Inge. Believe me. I know what you can do when you get your mind set. Both you and your mother. You and Holz are definitely cut from the same cloth; there's *nobody* at Fort Laramie that doubts that."

Inge's anger disappeared as quickly as it erupted. "Goddamn it, Jace, you sure know how to get me quieted down. Maybe I ought to forget about Jean and set my sights on you."

"Now who's trying to humor whom," Dobbs laughed. "You've had your eyes on Jean ever since you first met him. Back in Missouri, when the train was just starting out."

"God, that seems like such a long time ago."

"I know." Dobbs nodded. "I thought so too until I started writing in my journal again today and I was reminded it was only a little more than a year ago. In fact," he said brightly, "it was exactly ten months ago today that I had to amputate your mother's leg. Don't you think she's done well?"

" 'Well' is a marvelous understatement." Inge chuckled. "She's done marvelously. She's even more intimidating now than before she was wounded. I mean, who in his right mind is going to try to cross a tough old German frau with only one leg? She'd use that stump to kick anyone who dared from here to Independence and back. And she could do it, too."

"Speaking of her," Dobbs asked, frowning, "are you sure she doesn't mind that we call her 'Holz'?"

"There's nothing wrong with that," Inge said firmly. "Holzbein is a perfectly respectable German word."

"But it means 'Wooden Leg.'"

"So?"

"So, don't you think she might think it sounds just a tad disrespectful?"

"No!" Inge replied emphatically. "Not to me and not to Mutter. She wears the name proudly. In her mind, the loss of the leg proves that she has bought the right of citizenship with her blood. Hers," she added softly, tears building in her eyes, "and Vater's."

"Do you still miss him?" Dobbs asked. Before Inge could reply, he brushed the air with his hand. "Forget that! That was a stupid question! Of course you still miss him. Hardly a day goes by that I don't think of my wife and she's been dead more than five years. I don't think we ever stop missing someone we truly love."

"What I think," Inge said, wiping her eyes with the hem of her smock, "is that we're going to miss dinner, if we don't get going. You *are* planning to eat dinner, aren't you?" she said with a smile. "I mean," she said, lifting her nose and pretending to sniff like a hound, "you've probably been drinking coffee all afternoon and maybe it's killed your appetite."

Dobbs's face dropped. "I don't want to talk about it," he said resolutely.

Inge began laughing. "You still can't do it, huh? The best surgeon west of the Missouri still can't make a cup of coffee."

"I was wondering how long it was going to take you to get around to asking," Kemp said, pushing his plate aside.

"You mean that's all you were waiting for, colonel?" Dobbs asked, annoyed. "You were just leaving it up to me?"

"No," Kemp said, shaking his head. "That wasn't the only thing. I've been giving it a lot of thought myself. I even brought it up to the general."

"So I heard. I also heard he wasn't keen on the idea."

"True enough," said Kemp. "Naturally, he said no or you would have been gone by now. Said we had better things to do than waste time looking for a man who's probably dead anyway."

"That's about what I figured he'd say," replied Dobbs. "At least I didn't read him incorrectly. Do you feel the same way?"

The colonel did not answer at once. A heavyset man with Santa Claus cheeks and a pug nose that betrayed his Irish ancestry, Kemp had been commander at Fort Laramie since the previous September, sent as a replacement for the hapless Captain Samson Granger, recalled in disgrace for exhibiting incredibly bad judgment in allowing a young bully named Johnny Grattan to walk into an Indian camp and try to pick a fight. Instead of routing the Brulé, as Grattan predicted would happen, the Indians fought back, killing Grattan and all his men: twenty-seven privates, two noncoms and a French interpreter. It was this incident that precipitated the revenge raid by some six hundred soldiers under General William Harney. That had been in May. Now Harney and his troopers were marching overland to Dakota, virtually daring the Indians to attack them enroute. Everyone at Fort Laramie knew that that was not more than a remote possibility. The Brulé were scattered, trying to recover from the blow that Harney had levelled against them.

Harney's prey had been a large contingent from the Wazhazha band led by Roaring Thunder, which had been camped just north of the Platte about a day's march southeast of Fort Laramie, along a creek called Blue Water. Because most of their food supply had been exhausted during the preceding winter, which had been particularly severe, Roaring Thunder's people were hunting buffalo, not preparing for war, when Harney arrived. They were targeted because Roaring Thunder had ignored an edict from the Indian Agent, Teasley, to move south of the Platte as a demonstration of their peaceful intentions. Roaring Thunder had mistakenly believed that the soldiers would easily see that he and his people were interested in food, not fighting, and thus would pass him by.

A few days after the attack, a shell-shocked Roaring Thunder, wearing his best finery and singing his war song, had ridden into the fort to surrender, certain he would be executed on the spot. Trailing behind him, also anticipating that they would be hanged, were two of his wives.

In a move that surprised Dobbs, Harney simply moved Roaring Thunder and his women under guard to Fort Leavenworth, where presumably they would be imprisoned. Just what for, Dobbs was unsure since Roaring Thunder had not precipitated the attack and, in fact, had his offer to surrender rejected by Harney.

Although Dobbs had disagreed with Kemp on various issues, the surgeon had considerable respect for the post commander, a man whose bravery had never been questioned and who believed in the principle that he would never ask his men to take on a task that he himself would not assume. In Dobbs's view, Kemp was tough but fair. Sometimes, Dobbs felt, he was too easily influenced by Teasley, who had served as his adjutant before the war, but basically he was an honest man trying to do an almost impossible job: keeping the Great Plains safe for emigrants headed toward California and Oregon.

In essence, the men at Fort Laramie were police entrusted with bringing order to an area that stretched from Fort Union on the south to the Canadian Border on the north; from Fort Kearny on the east to Fort Hall on the west, a humongous expanse of mountains, valleys, vast forests, and scorching deserts inhabited by more than a dozen major tribes and countless bands of Indians, all of whom were constantly fighting with each other. When the white man showed up, as far as most of the Indians were concerned, he was just another enemy. Although eight of the tribes had signed a treaty at a meeting near Fort Laramie in September 1851 promising safe passage to emigrants, agreeing to a pact was one thing, seeing that it was adhered to was another. Already, many of the bands were exhibiting growing hostility toward the whites and attacks on the emigrant trains were becoming more frequent.

Not that Indian resistance had slowed the stream of adventurers heading westward. In 1852, thanks mainly to the discovery of gold in California and the offer of free land in Oregon, sixty thousand emigrants passed through Fort Laramie. The number of wayfarers decreased slightly after that but it was still incredibly heavy, severely taxing the resources of the seven thousand soldiers delegated to control events in an area encompassing two million square miles.

As Dobbs knew well, the Indians were not the only

danger. Disease accounted for thousands of lives each year, especially among the Indians who seemed particularly susceptible to the white man's ailments. Wild animals killed their share of travelers, too. Even the weather was hostile. In 1847, a half dozen years before, a succession of blizzards entombed an entire wagon train in California's Sierra Nevadas, forcing the emigrants to turn to cannibalism to survive.

Because of all these factors, Dobbs realized, Kemp, as did the other commanders scattered throughout the West, had to be very selective in deciding how to appropriate manpower.

"Let me make sure I understand this," Kemp said, producing a long black cigar from a pocket in his blouse. "You think we ought to send a detail out looking for Benoit? Just as the emigrant travelling season is building toward its peak?"

"That's right, sir," Dobbs replied stubbornly.

"Hmmmmm," Kemp mumbled, leaning forward to light his cigar off a flame instantly proffered by his chief aide, a serious-looking captain named Jonathan Harrigan. "And what if something untoward occurs while this detail is out combing the hills? What if I need every man I can get to counter an Indian attack?"

"Sir," Dobbs said patiently. "I'm not suggesting a large detail. Just send me and Legendre."

"What if I need a surgeon to treat men wounded in a fight with the Indians? What if I need an interpreter?"

"As far as the interpreter goes, sir, you still have Ashby."

"Somebody's going to have to do some hunting. The post needs meat."

"Let Erich handle that."

"You think young Schmidt is capable?" Kemp asked in surprise. "He's only sixteen."

"But a very *advanced* sixteen, sir. He's been apprenticing under Ashby for the last year and Jim tells me he's been an exceptionally fast learner. Besides, we won't be gone that long."

Kemp blew a cloud of dark smoke into the air, pondering Dobbs's argument. "How long?"

Dobbs shrugged. "Four days. A week at most. It isn't as if we're going to be scouring the whole territory. Roaring Thunder has given us a pretty good lead on where Benoit is being held. We just need to go there, get him, and come back as quick as we can."

"How do you know they haven't killed him? More importantly, how do you know they won't kill *you*?"

"I don't think that's likely, sir. The group that Roaring Thunder says is holding Benoit wants peace, not war. They had already complied with Teasley's order to move south of the Platte."

"That was before Harney's attack."

"That makes it even better," Harrigan interjected. "Now they can see what happens if they kill soldiers."

Kemp swivelled to face the captain, shooting him an icy glare with eyes the color of obsidian.

Harrigan flushed. "Sorry, sir. I didn't mean to interrupt. I just thought it was pertinent."

"The captain has a point," Dobbs conceded grudgingly, unwilling to attach any positive results to the Harney massacre.

"How about your duties?" Kemp asked. "Can you leave for a week?"

Dobbs sighed, knowing the fight had been won. "Yes, sir!" he answered enthusiastically. "My only patient right now is Private Fletcher, recovering from a broken bone in his foot suffered when his horse stomped him."

"Okay," Kemp said slowly, knocking ash into his

dinner plate. "Leave tomorrow. Take Legendre. Be back in no more than a week. Am I clear?"

"Absolutely, sir." Dobbs beamed.

"Now," Kemp said, turning to Harrigan, "let's talk about escorts. The first group of emigrants will be showing up pretty soon and we need to map out a schedule for getting them through here and on the way west."

Dobbs caught Inge's eye as she and her mother bustled about clearing the dinner table. "See," he mouthed, winking broadly.

Inge turned her head so Kemp wouldn't see her broad grin. "Isn't that wonderful, Mutter?" she whispered. "It will be so good to have Jean back."

"Ja," Fraud Schmidt replied in German. "I just wish Colonel Kemp took as much interest in seeking the return of poor Wilhelm and Werner."

2

It was still dark when Dobbs and Etienne Legendre saddled their horses and rode out of Fort Laramie, heading northwest, toward the Big Horn Mountains, a two-day ride away.

"You think that's the place to look?" Dobbs had asked somewhat dubiously. "You know we don't have a lot of time. Kemp wants us back by Monday."

"Who knows?" Legendre said with a shrug. *Les peaux rouges* are . . . are, I don't know in English. In French, *sans prévision*. No one can say for fucking sure."

Dobbs grinned. The words "fucking sure" had become Legendre's favorites, something he had learned from the troops and used frequently in various, sometimes highly amusing, permutations. A simple "Good morning" to the Canadian might draw the response: "*Bonjour*, it is a beautiful day, that's for fucking sure." Dobbs had forgotten how rudimentary Legendre's English was. Although the trapper spoke at least a half dozen Indian languages fluently, English was not his long suit. But, since no one at Fort Laramie wanted to dampen his enthusiasm for increasing his proficiency in the new language, no one had the heart to tell him that "fucking sure" was an expression not ordinarily used around the dinner table.

"They could be after the *bison,*" Legendre continued, unable to see Dobbs's smile in the dark. "Or maybe a raid by the *Corbeaux.*"

"Who?" asked Dobbs. "Who are the Corbeaux?"

"Ahhh," sighed Legendre. "I forget. You call them Crow." He spit into the dust. "The Corbeaux are *odieux.* How you say, 'nasty'? Of the tribes, nobody much likes the Corbeaux."

"I remember Ashby saying the Crow call themselves *Apsaruke,* which translates as 'We,'" Dobbs said. "Why do you call them Corbeaux? What does that mean?"

"A corbeaux is *un oiseau,*" he said, lifting his arms and moving them rapidly up and down in a flapping motion.

"A bird?" Dobbs asked, surprised. "A corbeaux is a bird?"

"*Oui,*" Legendre replied, nodding vigorously. "Like this," he said, thrusting out his hand with the index and middle fingers spread.

"A forked tail," Dobbs said brightly. "Like a magpie."

"*Oui, oui.*"

That's curious, the surgeon thought, making a mental note to explore the etymology of the word to see why the Crow were called forked-tail birds by the French. "But you think the Brulé will be camped in the Big Horns?" he asked.

"I do not know for fucking sure," Legendre replied, "but Roaring Thunder, he say go there first."

"Then that is where we will go," said Dobbs. "Roaring Thunder is the best authority we have."

As they rode, Dobbs studied his companion, still

somewhat indistinct in the semidark. A tall man with a thick chest, Legendre was not as old as Dobbs had figured the first time he had seen him. Of course, the conditions then had not been ideal. Seven months previously, Jim Ashby, the chief scout at Fort Laramie, and Erich Schmidt, Holz's son and Inge's younger brother, had brought Legendre in on a travois more dead than alive. The Canadian had been with his wife, a southern Cheyenne named White Woman, and his son, David, when they were caught by a blizzard while moving from a northern Cheyenne camp to spend the winter with his wife's people. Seeking shelter, they had run into a cave, only to find it already inhabited by a grizzly who had decided to use it for his winter den. Irritable at being disturbed, even though grizzlies really didn't *need* anything to make them irritable, the bear had attacked White Woman, pregnant and almost ready to deliver, while Legendre had been gathering firewood. Although he came running when he heard White Woman scream, Legendre had arrived too late. By the time he shoved David up a tree and ran into the cave, the grizzly had ripped White Woman to shreds.

Legendre killed the bear, but not before suffering severe wounds himself. Luckily for him, Ashby and Erich had not been far away when they, too, heard the commotion. When they got there, the bear was dead and Legendre was laying on top of the animal, almost dead himself. The animal had torn off the tip of the trapper's nose, bitten off his left little finger and most of the ring finger, and almost severed his ear. When Dobbs first saw him, it was barely hanging by a thread. There was nothing Dobbs could do, but take it all the way off.

As a result of the mauling, Legendre, who was

known among the tribes as Buffalo Shoulders because of his massive upper body, was a fearsome-looking man indeed. The wounds had all healed by now but some of the scars still ran like pink strips down his muscled forearms and across his right cheek. Instead of braiding his long, black hair Indian fashion, as he apparently had done before the incident, Legendre now let it hang free on the sides, the better to cover the earless side of his head. Nothing could be done about camouflaging the nose, though; it still remained the feature that most people could not resist staring at. To Dobbs, Legendre looked like a man who always had his face pressed against an invisible pane of glass.

At first, Dobbs had figured Legendre was in his mid-thirties, but once he got him cleaned up and the wounds sewn, he could see that he actually was several years younger. Although he had never asked, figuring it really was none of his business, the physician judged Legendre was about thirty-one, maybe thirty-two. It was much easier to judge the age of his son, a half-Minniconjou born of his first wife, who also had died tragically. Known among the Indians as Plays-with-His-Toes, the boy was now spending the season with the northern Cheyenne.

"Do you think he's doing well?" Dobbs asked, breaking the not-uncomfortable silence.

Legendre gave him a puzzled look. "Benoit?"

"No," Dobbs replied. "Sorry. I was thinking about your son. Do you think David is well?"

"Oh, yes." Legendre smiled. "Da-vid enjoys the *Tsis-tsis-tas*. They let him do whatever he wants. It is the way they raise the children."

Dobbs decided to broach a subject that was very sensitive around the fort, especially in front of Holz. "Do you think they're equally solicitous of the German children?" he asked carefully. "Les enfants de . . . de . . . les allemande," he struggled in his own fractured French.

"So . . . so . . . so-less . . . ?" the Canadian mumbled.

"Solicitous," Dobbs said. "It means 'concerned, eager.' Do you think the Cheyenne are treating the two German boys as well as they treat David?"

"Oh." Legendre nodded. "*Mais oui.* Children are children to the Cheyenne. They will not be harmed."

"Its been almost a year now since they were captured by the raiding party," Dobbs said, speaking more to himself than to Legendre. "If they're still alive I imagine they're speaking Cheyenne pretty well."

"Speaking, *oui.* Thinking, *aussi.* I wager a night with my next wife that they no longer remember much the whites."

Dobbs could understand that. He had to strain to remember himself what the children looked like. Werner was the older, he recalled, a tow-haired, bright-eyed boy of about four. His brother . . . what the hell was his name? Dobbs thought, furrowing his brow in concentration. Wilhelm. That was it. Wilhelm. With the w's pronounced like v's they sounded like a book title: Verner *und* Vilhelm. Wilhelm had been two years younger, a chubby, happy-go-lucky little fellow with darker hair and eyes, more like his mother, Johanna. She and her husband—goddamn, what was his name? Dobbs asked himself peevishly. Heinrich! he recalled. With a silent h. Both parents had died in the attack, along with Heinz Hartmann and his daughter, Emmi. Plus, of course, Holz's husband, Hans. Goes to show how senile I'm getting, Dobbs thought. I spent almost three months with that train and now I'm having trouble remembering the people's names.

"Do you think we'll ever get them back?" he asked soberly. "The children, I mean."

Legendre swiveled. "Only if the tsis-tsis-tas want us to," he said bluntly. "If they decide they want to keep, they will do so."

"Hmmmm," Dobbs mumbled. "I guess you're right. If you want to be analytical about it, I guess there's nothing really wrong with it. If they're being well taken care of, it's probably as good for them to be living with the Cheyenne as it would be for them to be living in Fort Laramie."

"*Les Indiens*, their way of life is *admirable*," Legendre said solemnly. "They are not, as you think, all *les sauvages*."

"Don't jump on me," Dobbs said quickly. "I certainly don't think they're savages. Different from us yes, but their culture is extremely sophisticated and they have many qualities that any man, white, black, or yellow, would envy."

"That's for fucking sure," Legendre replied. "I like *les Indiennes*. I have married two," he said, raising two fingers. *Aussitôt que possible*, I will marry another. First, I visit White Woman's people."

Dobbs looked surprised. "Why her people?"

"White Woman's *soeur*." Legendre smiled.

"*Soeur*?"

"*Soeur*," Legendre repeated. "Sister."

"Sister?" Dobbs asked in surprise. "By God!," he said, slapping his forehead, "I forgot. Many of the tribes practice sororate, the custom of marrying a wife's sister. So you have your eye on White Woman's *soeur*, eh?"

Legendre grinned crookedly. "And why not?" he asked. "It is more good than *le mouton, c'est pas vrai*?"

Dobbs laughed heartily. "Anything is better than a sheep," he agreed.

Both men were still chuckling when, as if by agreement, they suddenly reigned their horses to a halt and stopped, staring at the mountain in front of them.

"*Regarde ça*!" Legendre murmured. "*C'est magnifique*!"

Fifty miles to their west, although it seemed much closer in the clear air of the high desert, Laramie Peak jutted majestically into the sky. Behind them, the sun was beginning to poke over the foothills and the day's first rays were bathing the mountain's face, turning the snowcapped summit a bright pink that stood out against the sky like a rose on a piece of blue satin.

"Absolutely breathtaking," Dobbs concurred.

There was not a cloud in the sky, nothing to detract from the peak's singular wondrous presence. The middle and foot of the mountain, where the fir and spruces grew in thick abundance, had not yet been touched by the sun but even in the shade, they were a dark emerald green. The part of the mountain above timberline that had been blown free of snow was as black as the inside of a coal bin.

"Incredible," Dobbs added, trying to burn the sight into his memory, a precious thing to carry with him when he eventually went back East where the horizons were defined by trees and tall buildings and not the majestic Rockies.

For the next hour neither man spoke, each was so captivated by the splendor unfolding before them. As they rode silently toward the mountain, the sun inched higher, gradually illuminating the entire range as it stretched pristinely before them in a long, humpbacked line running northwest to southeast.

Hours later, with darkness approaching, they camped along a bubbling creek that flowed out of the forest and sliced through the grassy plain that sloped off toward the east. Without uttering a word, Legendre raised his arm and pointed toward the horizon.

Dobbs squinted to see what he was pointing out, but all he could make out was a dark smudge against the green.

"*Bison*!" Legendre said softly. "If *bison, les peaux rouges aussi*. Tonight, no fire."

Dobbs groaned. On the plains, even in June when the days were hot and dry, the temperature dropped thirty degrees after dark so it was cold sleeping at a fireless camp. "I'm glad I brought an extra blanket," he mumbled, unsaddling his horse.

"I take," Legendre said, leading the two horses into the trees where he affixed hobbles to keep the animals from wandering.

"How long have you lived in the West?" Dobbs asked, chewing on a tough hunk of buffalo jerky.

"A long time," Legendre said. "I was *douze*," he said, signalling twelve with his fingers, "when *mon père*, he brought me to this place. *Mon mère*, she die of disease, so *mon père* he decide to be a trapper. When he die, I stay. I take for a wife a Minniconjou and together we have David. She die of disease so then, after a short time, I marry White Woman. She was *un èpouse de bien*," he said sadly. "That is why I think of her sister. If one is good, the other also is good, *non?* I think," he added, grinning, "that's for fucking sure."

Shortly after noon the next day, as they wound through the forest on a barely discernible trail, Dobbs looked up. Blocking their path were a half dozen warriors. Dobbs gasped, reaching for his pistol.

"*Non*! *Non*!" Legendre said excitedly, lifting his hands in the air. "Friends. Friends. This is the group we seek," he said happily. "That warrior," he said, pointing, "that is White Crane, the *kola* of the man you desire."

Dobbs looked closely. Indeed, the Indian Legendre was pointing at was the one who had lain unconscious in his infirmary for several days while recovering from his concussion. "I know him!" Dobbs said in recognition. "He looks a hell of a lot better now than he did the last time I saw him."

With the warriors acting as escorts, they broke off from the trail and rode for two hours before the forest opened up and the Brulé village lay before them. Since White Crane had sent a messenger ahead to notify the villagers of Dobbs's and Legendre's imminent arrival, every Brulé in the group was waiting to greet them. Not all of them, Dobbs realized, looked overjoyed at seeing a white man in a blue uniform.

"Are we in danger?" the surgeon whispered to Legendre. "Should I prepare to fight?"

"*Non*." The trapper laughed. "If they wanted, we would be already *mort*. These are my brothers. No *abus*."

On the ride through the trees, Dobbs wondered about White Crane. The Indian had looked at him with total indifference when they met on the trail, as if he had never seen the surgeon before. The least he could have done, Dobbs told himself, knowing he was being illogical, was give some sign of recognition. This feeling was quickly forgotten when they reined to a stop in front of a lodge that looked to Dobbs like any other in the village. But standing in front of the tipi was Benoit, grinning like a man who just learned a rich uncle had left him his fortune.

"Jean!" Dobbs yelled, leaping off his horse.

"Hello, Jace!" Benoit replied enthusiastically, throwing his arms around his friend and hugging him tightly.

"Heh!" Legendre called loudly, also grinning

broadly. *"C'est plus qu'il n'en faut*! You keep up the *embrassement* and *les peaux-rouges*, they will think you are *les homosexuels*."

"And hello to you, too, 'Tienne," Benoit said joyfully, sticking out his hand. "*Comment allez-vous? Comment ça va?*"

"*Bien! Bien!*" Legendre said, grabbing Benoit's hand in both of his. "And you?"

"I am *wonderful*," Benoit replied, tears running from his eyes. "I have only this," he said, lifting his shirt, "to show for my adventure."

Dobbs looked closely. On the left side of Benoit's chest, just below the nipple, was a small scar.

"Is that it?" the surgeon asked in surprise. "That is the result of your grave wound?"

"Oh, it was very bad at one time," Benoit gushed. "I thought surely I was going to die. Try as I might, I could hardly breathe. But my medical history can wait. Right now you have to sit and relax, smoke some *shongsasha* and tell me what's happening at Fort Laramie. Tell me especially about Inge. Is she well? Does she miss me?"

"She is well," Dobbs laughed. "As beautiful as ever. And she misses you, although I'm not sure why. I was hoping for a while a romance would develop with Teasley so you could get your mind off her and on to work, but no such luck."

"You bastard!" Benoit replied jovially. "I want to know about Teasley, too, the son of a bitch. But first, come with me. We have to wash and get ready for the feast."

"The feast? What feast?"

"You don't think I would let my friends arrive without arranging something special for dinner, do you?" He grinned. "Look!" he said, pointing to a middle-aged woman standing on the sidelines, "Black Swan is about to prepare the banquet."

The woman beamed at him. Lifting her arms so Dobbs could see, Black Swan proudly exhibited the raw material for the day's repast: two plump puppies, one black and one a pale yellow, both of which hung lifelessly from her fists.

"Hooray," called Legendre, using another of his newly learned English words. "*Chien*! It is much better than *biftek*, even more tasty than *foie de bison*."

"Now there's a man who knows his food!" Benoit laughed. "Buffalo liver is definitely hard to beat."

"Jesus Christ!" Dobbs replied in mock horror. "Have you gone completely native?"

"What can I say?" Benoit asked, raising his palms upwards. "Is it my fault that I've learned to appreciate an entire new lifestyle?"

"I can see we have a lot to discuss," Dobbs replied. Turning to Legendre, he asked, *sotto voce*, "Do I really have to eat the dog?"

"But it is *èclatant*," he whispered back. "Trust me. It is good."

"Besides," interjected Benoit, "if you refuse, you will hurt everyone's feelings. And," he added, winking at Legendre, "I say in all sincerity, you don't want to get the Brulé angry with you."

"*Mais non*!" Legendre added, winking back. "You do not want to do that. That's for fucking sure."

"Where's White Crane's friend?" Dobbs asked. "The one with the limp. What's his name? Crooked Leg?"

"It's not Crooked Leg any longer," Benoit replied. "He's now called Red Horse."

"Red Horse?" Dobbs asked, raising his eyebrows. "Why is that?"

"It's a long story," Benoit replied. "I'm not sure I

understand it all, but now that Legendre is here we can get it straight. To answer your question, Red . . . Crooked Leg . . . whatever, is out hunting. He and his wife are calling a feast tomorrow as part of the ceremony for his son's ear piercing. It's a major event for them and they have to have plenty of fresh meat. At least that's the way I understand it. I could be wrong since the lines of communication are somewhat blurred."

"How *have* you been communicating?" Dobbs asked. "Sign language?"

"It's a little more sophisticated than that, but not much. One of the women in the village was married to a Frenchman until he was killed by the Crow. But over the years she picked up a smattering of French. She's been my interpreter."

Dobbs shook his head. "It's a wonder you haven't gone batty. But before we get onto the Indians, tell me what happened at Blue Water. Your disappearance from the battlefield is a great mystery at Fort Laramie."

"It isn't a pretty story," Benoit said, his mouth forming a tight line. "Where should I begin?"

"You don't have to tell me about Harney's attack. That's all documented. Begin with what happened to you. The last time anyone saw you, you were riding off into the camp alone, apparently on a mission to help the wounded."

"That's right," Benoit said. "The slaughter was terrible. And so goddamn unnecessary. For the soldiers, it was nothing more than target practice with live targets. Totally disgusting. That bastard Harney—"

"Harney's gone," Dobbs interrupted. "Marching to Fort Pierre. He's a hero in Washington. If you try to blacken his image it will just reflect on you. My advice is to try to forget it."

"Forget it, hell! You weren't there! You didn't see what happened."

"It doesn't matter whether I was there or not," Dobbs said soothingly. "It doesn't matter whether Harney was right or wrong. It's over with. There's nothing you can do to change it, and the less you mention it the better. But what happened to you?"

Benoit rose from his place in front of the fire and began pacing back and forth across the interior of the lodge. "I went into the camp," he said, agitation still evident in his voice. "I found a wounded woman so I carried her to a more sheltered location, just so those riflemen wouldn't shoot her again. I went back to see if there were any other wounded I could help when I heard a noise behind one of the lodges. Thinking it was another wounded Indian I went to investigate. Instead, what I found was a soldier committing a terrible atrocity."

"What kind of atrocity?" Dobbs asked.

"He was raping a girl!" Benoit replied, his cheeks reddening at the memory. "Worst of all, I think the girl was dead. That son of a bitch was committing . . . what's the word? What's that called when you have sexual relations with a dead person?"

"Necrophilia," Dobbs said softly.

"That's it! That trooper was a necrophiler."

"Necrophiliac," Dobbs corrected.

"Whatever. I should have shot the bastard right there."

"But you didn't."

"No. I ordered him to come forward under gunpoint."

"Well, what happened?"

"He tried to minimize his guilt. Said he wasn't *raping* her, he was only scalping her privates. Jesus, I thought I was going to vomit."

"Do you know who he was?"

"Oh, yes," Benoit. "At least I know what he told me. He said his named was Connors, attached to H Company."

"That makes sense," Dobbs said, rubbing his chin. "One of the dead was a Corporal Darcy Connors. I examined his body. He had two arrow wounds in his body and his throat was slit with a vengeance. He was almost decapitated."

"That would have been White Crane," Benoit said. "I remember him running to the soldier after he and Red Horse shot him with their arrows."

"His penis and testicles were cut off, too," Dobbs added. "And, naturally, he was scalped."

"I didn't see that," Benoit said. "But I lost consciousness for awhile."

"How did you get wounded?" Dobbs asked.

"Pure stupidity," Benoit confessed. "I let Connors get the drop on me. He produced a knife from somewhere and stabbed me in the chest. He was getting ready to shoot me with my own pistol when White Crane and Red Horse showed up. If it weren't for them, you'd have buried me, too, and it would have looked like I was killed by an Indian."

"Sit down here and take off your shirt," Dobbs ordered. "I want to examine that wound."

Obediently, Benoit stripped to the waist.

"You've lost some weight," Dobbs commented dryly. "But I guess I would too if I were on a steady diet of dog."

A tall man only a couple of inches shorter than the scarecrow-like Dobbs, Benoit had a deep chest and a short, thick neck that made it look as if his head rested directly on his shoulders. His skin was a creamy off-white and, since he had not been out in the sun much while recuperating in the Brulé village, he still had his winter pallor.

"Dog is the good part." Benoit smiled. "You should be here on the day we have raw buffalo brains."

Dobbs shuddered. "Are you serious? You really eat raw buffalo brains?"

Benoit grinned. "I'll never tell. My advice to you, since you seem to have a nervous stomach, is not to eat *anything* that isn't cooked."

"You know, Jean," Dobbs said, leaning over to examine Benoit's wound, "we've been friends for more than a year and I *still* never know when to believe you. Hmmmm," he added in his professional tone, "it must have been a small knife because there's not much of a scar. It sure healed nicely, though. What did you put on it?"

"Damned if I know," said Benoit. "The medicine man kept rubbing something dark and gooey on it. About the consistency of mud. Within a couple of days it scabbed over, though, and it never gave me any problem after that."

"You're a damn lucky Cajun," Dobbs chuckled. "The knife probably had a blade long enough to let air into the chest, but not long enough to puncture the lung."

"Is that good?"

"Yeah, you could say that. If that blade had been a half inch longer or the wound a half inch to the left, you would be dead."

"And I always thought the Irish had all the luck."

"Don't be blasphemous," Dobbs smiled, thumping Benoit hard on the chest. "You talk badly about God's Chosen and you could end up in a peck of trouble."

"God's chosen, eh?" Benoit said bitterly. "And I could have sworn Connors was an Irish name."

"I didn't hear you running out in the middle of the night to puke your guts out, so you must have survived the dog," Benoit teased his friend.

"Actually, it was pretty good," Dobbs replied. "But if you ever tell anyone I said that, I'll call you a liar. Don't you think we ought to get ready to go?"

"Didn't you say we don't have to be back until Tuesday? It's only Thursday and I'd like to stay at least until tomorrow. The ear-piercing ceremony is this afternoon and Red Horse and his wife have been so good to me. I'd like to see it. With the Brulé, it's an important ceremony."

"You mean just getting the baby's ears pierced?"

"That's the end result, but it has much more significance than that. The way I understand it, it is more akin to our Baptism or a Jewish circumcision."

While waiting for the ceremony to begin, Benoit, Legendre, and Dobbs sat outside in the sunshine, enjoying the parade of villagers as they went about their business. Legendre, who occasionally hailed old friends he knew from the days when he was a frequent visitor among the Brulé because of his first wife, would explain the band's customs to Benoit in French, who would then translate into English for Dobbs's benefit.

"See the man in front of the lodge there," Benoit said, pointing with his chin, "the one with what looks like a sheave of branches at his feet. Legendre says he's the village's chief arrow maker and he's very busy right now because this is the season when arrows are most needed, both for hunting and for raids against the Crow."

"You mean they have a special arrow maker like we have, say, a blacksmith?" Dobbs asked.

"That's right," explained Benoit. "Although every warrior can make arrows if he has to, the arrow maker is the one who turns out the best product and it is his arrows that all the warriors would like to have."

"What's so special about the art?" Dobbs probed. "It looks fairly straightforward to me. All you would need, I assume, is a fairly straight branch, a piece of metal for the head, and a few feathers."

Legendre laughed uproariously. Rising to his feet, he walked over to the man, whose name was Lame Elk, and spoke to him for a few minutes. When he returned, he had a shaft in his hand.

"See this," Benoit translated, holding up the piece of wood. "This is cherry, which, Legendre says, along with Juneberry, make fine shafts but not nearly as good as gooseberry. And see here," Benoit said, conducting a running translation, "these small marks made by the arrow maker's knife? They will be completely obliterated when the finished product is smoothed. That," he added, "is accomplished by pulling the shaft through a piece of sandstone which has been especially grooved for the process. And once that is done, Lame Elk will carve a number of zigzag lines in the shaft."

"Is that for decorative purposes?" Dobbs asked.

Benoit looked at Legendre.

"Not entirely," the trapper said. "It is also believed that the carvings, which to the Brulé symbolize lightning bolts, make the arrow fly fast and true. But that's not all the decoration. Before he's finished Lame Elk also will mark the shaft with a series of colored bands so the warriors will be able to identify their own arrows. This is particularly handy during the hunt."

"And the feathers?"

"That's a good question," Legendre said. "Lame Elk believes that turkey buzzard and wild turkey make the best fletching but not every arrow maker agrees with that."

"And the heads?"

"You mean the points. The points are now made mainly of metal that the Brulé get through trade with us, but Legendre says Lame Elk tells him he remembers when he was first learning the trade how he was taught to chip them from stone. Metal, Lame Elk says, is better."

"Fascinating," Dobbs said. "Absolutely intriguing. But tell me, does Lame Elk make bows as well?"

Legendre grinned and nodded enthusiastically, speaking so rapidly that even Benoit at first had trouble understanding him.

"He says," Benoit paraphrased, "that Lame Elk does indeed make bows but there is another man in the village, Eye-that-Looks-Crooked, who is much more adept than he. Bow making, too, is a highly skilled trade and a lot of attention is given to it because the Indians depend so heavily upon their weapons for survival."

While Legendre was returning the shaft to Lame Elk, Dobbs studied a group of women who were walking to the river to fill their water jugs.

"It's strange," he mused, "but I had always thought Indian women were fat and ugly, that they did not take care of themselves, and had nasty tempers. These women do not appear to be that way at all."

"I can answer that without Legendre's help," said Benoit. "That's because most of the Indian women you've seen have been those that hang around the fort or trading post. As a rule, they *are* old, fat, and ugly because they are the ones who have been unable to secure or hold husbands and many of them either have mental problems or are willing to desecrate their bodies by working as prostitutes for the soldiers. The ones here are not like that at all."

"I can see that," Dobbs said, glancing around appreciatively. "But look there," he said, pointing to one figure on the far side of the group. "She's tall and rather huskily built," Dobbs said. "She looks very much out of place among the others."

Legendre, returning from his visit with Lame Elk, arrived in time to see Dobbs's gesture. When he saw where the surgeon was pointing, he began chuckling.

"That is Blue Feather," the trapper explained. "*Un travestie.*"

Benoit's eyes widened in surprise. "I didn't know that!" he exclaimed. "I've been here six weeks and no one told me."

"Told you what, for God's sake?" Dobbs asked. "What is it?"

"That person you were pointing at, the one with the women."

"Yes, what about her?"

"It's not a her. According to Legendre, the 'her' is a 'he.'"

"No joke?" asked Dobbs. "I've read about that. Technically they're called berdaches."

"Ber . . . what?" Benoit asked, raising his eyebrows.

"Berdache," Dobbs repeated slowly. "It means men who assume the identity of women."

"How do you know this stuff?" Benoit asked. "I've never heard of such a thing."

Dobbs shrugged. "I read a lot," he said. "I've read about berdaches but I've never seen one that I know of. Is that, uh, person, really one of them?" he asked Legendre.

"Alas, it is true. Among the Lakotas," he explained, "they are called *winktes*. They are men with the souls of women. They dress and live as women and they do women's tasks, such as tanning and quilling."

"And they are readily accepted?"

Legendre rolled his eyes. "Yes and no. They are *tolerated*. There is no stigma, but most warriors are afraid of them, they think they have some strange power."

"Where do they live? Do they have their own lodges?"

"Of course," said Legendre, "but generally they live on the edge of the village in the area reserved for widows and orphans."

"Are they homosexual as well?" Dobbs asked.

"Yes." Legendre nodded. "Many of them. Some are prostitutes as well, serving the young men of the camp who are not yet married. But men also become winktes because they are unable to compete among the other males. Being an Indian warrior is a very demanding thing. They undergo much hardship. From the time a boy is very young, he is expected to perform tests of bravery and strength, and these tasks only get more difficult the older he gets. Even the games boys play are very violent because they are part of the training for adulthood. For one reason or another, winktes feel they cannot live up to expectations so they retreat to the lodges with the women. Some of them make good shamans and are capable of curing many diseases. They are sought after when parents want their children to have a secret name. I have heard it said that if a child is named by a winkte he will grow up healthy and well."

"So much for today's lesson in the Brulé customs," Benoit said, rising stiffly to his feet. "Come. I think the ear-piercing ceremony is about to begin."

When they returned to Red Horse's lodge, they found that the warrior's wife, Summer Rain, had prepared a bed of sage and had put the baby, Badger, in the center.

"Let me explain," Benoit whispered to Dobbs. "Red Horse is not the baby's father. The child was sired by his older brother, also named Badger, who was murdered by a renegade warrior named Blizzard."

"So Red Horse married his brother's wife!" Dobbs exclaimed. "Very interesting! It's called levirate, the counterpart of Legendre's intention to marry his dead wife's sister."

"Yes." Benoit nodded. "Sounds complicated, doesn't it?"

"Not at all. In fact, it's very practical given the circumstances. But tell me, why hasn't Red Horse been friendlier to me? He's barely acknowledged my presence but I was very good to him and White Crane when they were under my care."

"Oh, he appreciates what you did." Benoit smiled. "Look what he did for me. He saved my life. That's just his way. Don't get your feelings hurt. Oh," he broke off, looking up as a man Dobbs had not seen before slipped into the lodge. "Here's Deer Dreamer."

"Is he the medicine man?"

"Not exactly," said Benoit. "He is what the Brulé call a *wicasa wakan,* a very wise man who they believe has a connection to the gods."

Deer Dreamer walked to where Badger was lying and knelt at his head. Without preamble, he launched into a long series of chants which, although Legendre did not try to translate, Dobbs understood were prayers asking the gods to watch over the child. Reaching into a pouch around his waist, Deer Dreamer produced a small block of wood and a sharpened buffalo bone. Placing the wood under the lobe of the baby's left ear, he pierced it with the bone. Quickly, before the child began thrashing about uncontrollably, he repeated the process on the right ear. Reaching again into the pouch, he produced two short lengths of sinew, which he threaded through the holes to keep them from healing closed. Then he stepped back, his task completed.

"It is the Brulé belief that whoever pierces a child's ears then becomes responsible for making sure that child is brought up knowing the tribe's customs," Legendre explained.

"Ahh," Dobbs grunted in recognition. "Something like the Christian godfather."

After the brief ceremony, Red Horse gave Deer Dreamer an elaborately quilled pouch that had been made by the Cheyenne. "It was my brother's," he explained. "He would want you to have it because of the service you have performed for his son."

As they were eating the chunks of tender elk that Summer Rain had prepared for the occasion, Benoit told Dobbs that Red Horse and White Crane would ride with them when they left the next day.

"Are they returning with us to Fort Laramie?" Dobbs asked in surprise.

"No, they are going only part of the way with us. When we get to the Platte, they will swing northeast, up toward the Black Hills."

"If I'm allowed to ask, where are they going?"

"Remember how I told you earlier how Red Horse had become Summer Rain's husband?"

Dobbs nodded. "Yes. So what?"

"Well, Red Horse heard from a group of Cheyenne that Blizzard was not killed at Blue Water Creek as they believed and is living with a group of outcasts in the northern mountains. He and his best friend, White Crane, are anxious to see if that is true."

"Why would he want to have contact with Blizzard?" Dobbs asked innocently. "That's a long way to travel."

"It isn't so far if you're obsessed with the thought of revenge," Benoit said. "Red Horse and White Crane intend to find the band and, if Blizzard indeed is alive, cut out his heart."

Tired and dusty, the three men rode into Fort Laramie an hour before sunset, heading straight for the stable. As they were unsaddling their horses, Private Len Bianchi came running up.

"Welcome back, lieutenant." He greeted Benoit heartily. "Damn good to see you, sir. But, begging your pardon, you don't look too poorly. I was 'specting they'd be bringing you back on a travois."

"Just call me lucky." Benoit smiled. "It takes more than a little knife wound to keep me down. You seen Miss Schmidt lately?"

Bianchi grinned. "Reckon she's over in the kitchen, sir. It's that time o' day."

"Do me a favor, private?"

"Sure, sir. What's that."

"Take care of my horse for me. I'm going to go see if I can find something to eat that wasn't roaming the plains an hour ago. It's been a long time since I had anything but buffalo, elk, or dog."

"They tell me dog ain't bad, sir."

"Yeah." Benoit chuckled. "Ask Lieutenant Dobbs. I think I'm going to see if I can't find something a little more plebeian, like maybe a nice hunk of ham. And some rice. Damn, I'd kill for some rice."

"I'll get your horse, sir. No problem. I need a few minutes to talk to the doc anyway."

"See you in a few minutes, Jean," Dobbs said to Benoit's back. "What's going on, private?" he asked, turning to Bianchi. "You constipated or something?"

"No, it ain't me, sir," Bianchi replied, his face dropping. "And I think it's a little more serious than constipation."

"Oh?" Dobbs said, loosening the cinch on his saddle.

"Let me help you with that, sir," Bianchi volunteered, grabbing Dobbs's saddle. "Remember them three troopers that deserted awhile back?"

"Yeah," Dobbs said. "Vaguely. Real physical misfits. One of 'em had an abnormal bone growth in the center of his forehead, if I remember right."

"That'd be 'Unicorn,' sir. 'Unicorn' Breedlove. Don't recall what his proper first name was. Jim or John or David or sump'in like that. Never called him anything but 'Unicorn,' though. Right fittin' nickname it was, too."

"And the other," Dobbs said, straining to recall, "had a big chunk missing out of his ear. Left one I think."

"Yes, sir. You got a damn good memory, sir. That's 'Notch' Henderson. Real nasty character. A bully and a braggart. He used to organize scorpion fights behind the barracks. Made quite a few dollars at it, too. You remember the third 'un?"

"No," Dobbs said. "Can't say I do. Except I recall he seemed an unlikely companion for the other two. They were real troublemakers, but the third guy . . . "

"Ryan, sir," Bianchi interjected.

"Ryan! That's right. Tall, blond-haired fellow. Looked about as Irish as you could get. Had a funny first name. A girl's name, seems like."

"That's right, sir," Bianchi confirmed. "His name's Cornelius, but everybody called him 'Connie.' I recollect he had more'n one fight because of his name."

"Okay, now we've got all that straight. What's this about? I've been in the saddle for two days. My bones ache and my mouth's as dry as Big Nancy Creek in August. I'd very much like to get a bath, change into a fresh uniform, and see if I can talk Lieutenant Benoit, if he's not otherwise occupied, that is," he added with a wink, "into making a big pot of coffee."

"Well, sir," Bianchi said, "I'm afeared I got some bad news for you."

Dobbs, who had been brushing his horse, stopped in mid-stroke. "Oh?"

"Yes, sir. You see, Connie's back."

"Ryan? The soldier we were just talking about?"

"Yes, sir."

"What do you mean 'he's back'? You mean he's been captured?"

"Not exactly captured, sir. He came in on his own. Yesterday about this time."

"You mean, he surrendered?"

"Not exactly, sir."

"Goddamn, Bianchi. I'm tried, saddle sore, and hungry. This isn't a game. Tell me what you have to say and quit beating around the bush."

"Y-Y-Yes, sir," Bianchi stuttered. "Connie, Private Ryan, that is . . . "

"I *know* who Connie is by now."

"Yes, sir. Anyways, he came straggling in last night. Went straight to the enlisted men's stable and collapsed."

"You mean he passed out? Had too much to drink, did he?"

"Not exactly, sir. He dropped like he'd been poleaxed.

Just hit the ground like a sack o' shit. But liquor had nothing to do with it."

"What then? Was he wounded? Was he bleeding?"

"Not wounded, sir. Sick. Burning up with fever. Had blisters all over his face and hands. I think it's the pox, sir."

"Pox!" Dobbs almost yelled. "Jesus Christ! Where's he now?"

"In the infirmary, sir. We carried him there straightaway."

"Who carried him?" Dobbs asked urgently. "Who's been in contact with him."

"Just me and Private O'Malley, sir. When I tol' Cap'n Harrigan what had happened, he put a guard outside the door to keep everyone out until you got back. "

"Thank God for that." Dobbs sighed. "Have you ever been inoculated?"

"Matter o' fact, I had the inoculation, sir. Back at Leavenworth a couple years ago. There was a scare and the commander ordered everybody on post to get hisself scratched. See the scar," he said, rolling up his sleeve.

"I don't need to see the scar, Bianchi. I'll take your word for it. How about O'Malley? Has he been inoculated, too?"

"Don't rightly know for certain, sir, but I reckon he has. He served at Leavenworth, too, but he was in a different unit and I didn't know him there."

"Where is he now?"

"Guess he's in the barracks, sir. That's where he'd normally be this time o' day."

"I'm going to the infirmary to check on Ryan," Dobbs said crisply. "You go tell O'Malley to get his ass over there as quick as he can. You still wearing the uniform you had on yesterday?"

"Yes, sir. Laundry day's tomorrow."

"Well, go get a clean uniform and put yours in a pile over there by the hay rack. Then finish taking care of my horse and wait here for me until I come back. Is that clear?"

"Yes, sir," Bianchi said nervously. "You think there's gonna be a problem, sir? Did we do right?"

"You did exactly right, private. I don't know about a problem until I examine Ryan. He might have the chick-enpox or something else entirely. We'll worry about that when we get there. In the meantime, it doesn't hurt to take a few precautions. Now go find O'Malley."

"Yes, sir," Bianchi replied, setting off at a trot.

"Hello, Ryan," Dobbs said softly. "You remember me?"

Ryan's eyelids fluttered open. When he focused his blue eyes on Dobbs, the surgeon noted they shined bright with fever. "Yes, sir. You're Doc Dobbs. You're the man I come to see."

"I understand you're feeling poorly," Dobbs said, laying a hand lightly on Ryan's forehead, which was covered with pustules oozing a foul-smelling pus.

"It's the pox, sir. I know it for certain."

"Oh, you do, eh? Where's your medical degree from?"

"Don't need no medical degree to know that I caught the pox from a blanket intended for the injuns. It was infected with pox. It was meant to spread the disease, 'cept I caught it instead. Me an' Fletch."

Dobbs studied him carefully. "That sounds like a long story, private. And it's certainly one I want to hear. But first I want to examine you. You don't mind if I give an expert opinion, do you?"

"No, sir," Ryan replied weakly. "But you'll see I ain't

making it up, sir. I know I got the pox and I figure I'm a goner."

"Well, let me see," Dobbs said. As he reached out to unbutton Ryan's shirt there was a loud knock on the door. "Goddamnit!" he mumbled. "Just a second," he called loudly. "I'll be right back, Ryan," he said to the man in the bed. "I suspect that's O'Malley."

Striding briskly to the door, Dobbs quickly interrogated the private, learning that he, too, had been inoculated two years previously, before being posted to Fort Laramie. After telling O'Malley to get a clean uniform and go to the stable to wait for him, Dobbs returned to Ryan's cot.

"Okay, private, I'm back. Now let me have a look."

"I'm dying, sir, ain't I?" Ryan asked, his lower lip trembling.

Dobbs studied him. "You want the truth, private?"

"Yes, sir," Ryan said, his voice quivering.

"If you're right and you've got smallpox and not chickenpox, it doesn't look good. From the condition of the pustules, I'd say you've been sick for awhile."

"Week or ten days, sir. When them blisters first popped out, they itched like crazy. Thought I was going to rub myself raw. Then they started runnin' a bit. Looked like water coming out at first. Then they just kinda sunk in, like a hoofprint in mud. That's when the pus started coming out and I come down with the ague."

"Okay, private. I'm going to examine you now. Then I'm going to give you some medicine. It won't help the disease, but it'll make you sleepy."

"I don't want to go to sleep, sir," Ryan said urgently.

"Why not? You must be tired, what with fighting the fever and all. And your joints must ache something fierce."

"That they do, sir. But if I go to sleep, I'm scared I won't wake up."

Dobbs sighed. "I understand, Connie. But if you don't get some sleep there's no chance you're going to get better. If you've got smallpox there's nothing I can do. We'll just have to wait it out and see if you recover on your own. It isn't *always* fatal. I take it you've never been inoculated."

"No, sir."

"Still, there's a chance you have some natural immunity to the disease. A lot of white people do. They don't get as sick as Indians and the disease doesn't always kill them, especially if they're young and healthy when they're exposed."

"It killed Fletch an' he was young and healthy. I know 'cause I watched him die. His body was hot as a campfire and he went screaming. I ain't anxious for that to happen to me, too."

"Neither am I," Dobbs said softly. "Neither am I."

"What a welcome back, huh?" Kemp said, leaning back in his chair. His office was small and windowless, hardly large enough to provide pacing room. His scarred desk stretched almost from one wall to another and took up about a third of the available space. "Tiny, ain't it?" he said with a tight grin. "That's why I conduct most of my business in the dining room. But I figure this is something we perhaps ought to discuss in private and see if we can't nip a potential panic in the bud."

"Good thinking, sir," Dobbs said, his face etched with fatigue.

"Sit down, sit down," Kemp urged, pointing to the single straight-backed chair that rested in front of the desk. "This isn't a formal occasion. Now tell me," he said as Dobbs collapsed wearily, "what do you think?"

"It's smallpox, sir. I'm certain of it."

"Shit!" Kemp exploded. "I was afraid of that."

"*But,*" Dobbs added. "It may not be as bad as it sounds."

"Oh, that's good," Kemp said with a sigh, reaching for a cigar. "Give me some welcome news."

Dobbs watched him curiously. I've never seen Kemp smoke when Harrigan wasn't around to light his cigar, he thought idly. This is going to be interesting.

"You think we may be able to contain it?" the colonel added, producing a match from the matching pocket and striking it on the underside of the desk.

"Harrigan used his head," Dobbs explained. "He sealed the room immediately and that may keep anyone else from being exposed. That was damn quick thinking."

Kemp smiled ironically. "Of course it was. Harrigan ain't dumb. You think I keep him around just to carry my matches?"

"No, sir, that's not what I meant. It's just that not every non-medical officer would act that quickly."

"Well, he did. Now tell me what the situation is," he said brusquely.

"Yes, sir," Dobbs said, throwing back his shoulders. "Ryan is a damn sick man. Personally, I don't think he's going to make it."

Kemp shrugged. "Doesn't make much difference. He's a deserter and even if he lives through the disease he's got a long time in the stockade staring him in the face. At best. If he's been out committing crimes around the countryside he could be hanged."

"That's a pretty cold-hearted way of looking at it."

"I ain't paid to hold the men's hands. He made his bed, now he has to lie in it."

"Yes, sir. As I was saying, I don't think there's any doubt Ryan has smallpox, especially not after what he told me."

Kemp raised his eyebrows. "Oh?" he asked quizzically. "And what's that?"

Dobbs exhaled. "It's kind of complicated, but let me see if I can sum it up."

"Please do, lieutenant. I'd like to get some sleep myself sometime today."

"Okay. Ryan ran off with privates Breedlove and Henderson . . ."

"I *know* that, lieutenant."

"They wandered around the hills for awhile," Dobbs continued, "trying to figure out how to get that strongbox . . ."

"What strongbox?"

"The one that was stolen from the Salt Lake stage. Remember?"

"Oh, yeah. It had about ten thousand dollars in it, didn't it?"

"That's what Ryan says, too."

"Wasn't it taken by the injuns? A group of Brulé, I believe."

"That's right. A group of outcasts led by a warrior named Blizzard."

"Never heard of him."

"Neither had I, sir. Until two days ago. But that's immaterial. The point is, Ryan, Breedlove, and Henderson couldn't figure out how to get that strongbox without getting themselves killed in the process. In Ryan's words, 'There was just too many fucking injuns.'"

Kemp smiled. "I'll just bet there were."

"So they'd just about given up that idea and were planning to head for California when they ran across another group of deserters."

"God*damn*," Kemp swore. "The countryside must be full of 'em. Did he say where they were from?"

Dobbs nodded. "A couple from Fort Kearny and a few from Fort Leavenworth. Their leader was a civilian named Silas Connors."

"Is that name supposed to mean something to me?"

"Not really. But you'll see the connection. His brother was Darcy Connors."

"Now *that* name sounds familiar."

"He was a corporal with H Company, Sixth Infantry. He was killed at Blue Water. Benoit can tell you all about Darcy Connors. You had a chance to talk to him yet? Benoit, I mean."

"I know who you meant. But no, I haven't had a chance yet. Things have been popping pretty good."

"That's for sure," Dobbs agreed. "Anyway, Silas, according to Ryan, went sort of crazy when he learned about his brother's death. Blamed it on the Indians and vowed revenge. Sold the small store he had in Independence and headed west to carry out his own personal vendetta."

"You mean, he intends to kill some injuns."

"Not just *some*," Dobbs said. "He wants to wipe 'em all out. His plan, as improbable as it seems, calls for genocide."

"Oh, sweet Christ. As if we didn't have enough on our hands already."

"What he planned to do," Dobbs said, plunging ahead, "was take some blankets that had been infected with smallpox and trade them to the Indians, making sure he bargained low enough to get rid of the goods. He had just left Independence when he ran into the deserters and he convinced them to join up with him. Promised them they could get all the Indians' gold if they went with him."

Kemp frowned. "Indians don't have any gold. Unless you're talking about the lot in the strongbox."

"I know that. And you know that. But these deserters apparently didn't know that. They agreed to go with him."

"And then the three men from here joined up with them?"

"That's right. They figured if the Indians died of the disease, they could pick up that strongbox without any opposition. But that's when they had a problem."

"How's that?"

"A couple of weeks ago we had a late spring storm move through. You remember?"

"Yeah. Sort of. One storm's just like another in this country. They come through all year, summer, spring, fall—it don't seem to make much difference."

"That's true," Dobbs smiled. "But it got real cold in the camp the deserters had set up in the mountains. According to Ryan, him and a deserter from Kearny named Nathaniel Fletcher had guard duty—old habits die hard. They were about to freeze and they couldn't light a fire 'cause they didn't want the Indians to find 'em."

"Don't tell me! Those dumb shits got into the blankets meant for the Indians?"

"Exactly. They looked alright so they figured it wouldn't hurt to just 'borrow' a couple for the night. In a couple of days, they both started running a fever. Then the pustules appeared."

"So Connelly . . . "

"Connors."

"Sorry. Connors, who probably isn't a genius but may be smarter than Ryan and Fletcher, figured out what happened."

"Right."

"So then what?"

"Connors and the others panicked. They kicked Fletcher and Ryan out of the group and they took off. By then, Ryan had figured out they'd exposed themselves to smallpox, what with showing the first symptoms and all. So he and Fletcher headed here, figuring I was the closest physician and if anybody could help them, I could."

"What happened to the other guy? What was his name? Fletcher?"

"He died two days ago. Ryan left his body for the scavengers and he continued on."

Kemp's shoulders sagged. "What a fucking mess."

"That it is, sir. But that's not all."

"Oh, Jesus," Kemp moaned. "You mean it gets worse?"

"Yes, sir. I'm afraid it does. On their way here, Ryan and Fletcher were approached by three Indians—Cheyenne, Ryan believes—who tried to beg some tobacco from 'em. The Indians got a close look at 'em, saw how sick they looked, and got the hell out of there."

"Phew!"

"But before they fled, one of the Indians stole a pouch from Fletcher."

"So they might be infected, too?"

"It's a long shot, but they could be."

Kemp was silent for several minutes. Putting his feet up on the desk, he puffed at his cigar until it was a stub. Grinding it out on the heel of his boot, he looked up at Dobbs. "Okay," he said, "what do you recommend?"

"That's easy," Dobbs said. "I've already burned Ryan's clothing, his saddle, and the clothing Bianchi and O'Malley were wearing. They're the two troopers who carried Ryan to the infirmary. Later, I'll burn my clothing—don't look panicky, this is a different uniform I'm wearing now—the sheets, towels, mattress: everything he's come in contact with."

"That sounds reasonable."

"Then I want to inoculate everybody at Fort Laramie, soldier and civilian."

"You have enough serum or whatever the hell you call it?"

Dobbs nodded. "I made sure I brought enough to inoculate every human west of the Missouri."

"Some of the troops have already been inoculated."

"Do you know which ones?"

"Unfortunately, no. We'd just have to take their word for it."

"That's too risky. Just to be safe, let's inoculate everybody. It won't hurt if they get it twice."

"Okay, that's easy enough to arrange."

"How about the wagon trains? What's the schedule?"

Kemp slapped his forehead. "Oh, damn! I'd forgotten about them. Anyway, the first train isn't expected for a couple of weeks. Will that be enough time?"

"That should be more than enough. If we don't have any fresh cases by then, we're in the clear. If we do, we'll have to quarantine the post."

"I sure hope we don't have to do that. The emigrants need our facilities."

"I know. I hope we don't have to go that far, too. Let's worry about that later. But there's one other thing. Actually, two others."

"And those are?"

"How about the women at the Hog Ranch? Can you guarantee none of the troopers has been down there since Ryan showed up? Or none of them have been up here?"

"No."

"Then I'd like to inoculate them, too."

"That's no problem."

"And then there's the Indians."

"Ah-hah," Kemp sighed. "That's where things gets tricky. You have any suggestions?"

"Yes, sir. If we don't have any fresh cases in a week, I think we're safe. I'd like to visit the Cheyenne camp, since Ryan believes it was Cheyenne they met on the trail. See if any of them are sick and, while I'm there, inoculate all of them."

"Ummmm," Kemp mumbled thoughtfully. "Actually that's not a bad idea at all. As you probably know I disagreed strongly with Harney's strategy at Blue Water."

"I had that feeling, sir."

"But he's a general. I'm a brevet lieutenant colonel. It isn't as if he asked my advice."

"I understand that, sir."

"On the other hand, I'm the one that has to live with the situation. He's halfway to Fort Pierre by now and his next move will probably be to the War Department, since he's a goddamn hero for killing a lot of women and children. I'd like to cement some kind of relationship with the tribes. Given the belligerency that's flowing out of Washington it won't be long before we're involved in a full-scale war with the Indians. I'd like to prevent that, or at least postpone it."

"Sounds logical to me, sir."

"That's why I think it would be a good idea for you to offer to inoculate as many of them as will agree to have it done. I'm not optimistic. I don't think you're going to be welcomed with open arms. But if we don't try, we'll never know, right?"

"Right, sir."

"Okay, here's what we do. You inoculate the troops

and the women at the Hog Ranch. Then, if it looks as if the disease isn't going to spread here, you make a quick trip to the Cheyenne camp and inoculate as many of them as you can. Am I clear?"

"Perfectly, sir."

"Good. Now let's both of us get some sleep. Oh, by the way, how's Ben-oight? I didn't see him at dinner tonight. Come to think of it, Miss Schmidt wasn't there either. She's probably not feeling well."

Dobbs blushed. "Benoit's fine, sir. Totally recovered from his wound. He's ready for service. He's also putting together a report for you, which I think will help clarify at least one of the incidents at Blue Water. That's probably what he was working on this evening. But . . ." Dobbs said hesitantly.

"Yes, lieutenant, what is it?"

"He prefers to be called 'Ben-wah,' sir."

"Goddamnit, I know that. But I'm the commander and I'll call him Ben-oight if I want. Understood?"

"Yes, sir," replied Dobbs, groaning.

"Besides," Kemp added with a wink. "I like to have him riled up. It keeps him on his toes."

"But there haven't been any troops down here since Saturday night," Ellen O'Reilly protested. "Why do you think we've been exposed?"

"But have any of your, er, girls, been to the fort?"

"Oh, damn! I hadn't thought of that. I was there myself yesterday. We needed some flour. But I didn't go anywhere but the sutler's. I didn't talk to anybody but Mr. Sevier."

"Why take the chance, Ellen? Believe me when I tell you that you don't want to get smallpox. The inoculation is relatively painless."

"Painless my butt. I'll bet it's about as painless as losing my virginity."

Dobbs smiled. "That's what I like about you. You have such a way with words."

"So, I'm forthright. What's wrong with that? And how do you expect the madam of a whorehouse to talk? Like a Sunday school teacher?"

"I'll bet you gave your husband fits."

"That worthless piece of trash. Best thing that ever happened to me was when he got caught, how do you say it? In flagrant . . .

"In flagrante delicto."

"That's it. He got caught with his pants down, is what it was. Deserved exactly what he got. Ol' Miles put a bullet clean through the back of his head."

"You can sound awful cold sometimes."

"Cold, huh? I'll tell you cold. You ever spend a winter in Minnesota without enough money to buy firewood? You ever have to wear patched clothes and be laughed at by all the 'ladies' in town? Well, that's what happened because of the fact Charlie left me broke. Not one damn cent. He spent it all on his whores. That spring is when I decided that I'd had enough. I decided to go west and go into business."

"Speaking for myself," Dobbs said, "I'm glad you did. Come west that is. As far as the business goes, I'll reserve judgment on that."

"Oh, you will, eh?" Ellen said with a smile. "Well until you decide you want to support me I guess you're just going to have to learn to live with it."

"I guess I can do that." Dobbs grinned. Ellen O'Reilly is a damn good-looking woman, he thought, not for the first time. In her late twenties, petite and small-boned, with hair as dark as an Indian's and large eyes the greenest Dobbs had ever seen. The physician figured it would be hard for any man not to find her attractive. Why her husband—make that late husband—had felt it necessary to seek sexual favors elsewhere, Dobbs had never understood. What he really appreciated about her, though, was her mental toughness. For a woman who had more than her share of setbacks, both financial and personal, she had rebounded with astonishing alacrity. While there were some who might look down their noses at a madam, Dobbs was not one of them. In his mind, she had simply proved herself an astute businesswoman, recognizing the need for a specific product, she had done her best to satisfy the demand. Her employees—her girls—were uniformly young, honest, and fairly attractive. If one of them got caught stealing, Ellen shipped her out on the next stage. "See how she likes the Mormons," he remembered her saying after arranging for transportation westward for one girl who tried to lift a soldier's wallet.

"You want to hear something funny?" Ellen asked, tilting her head slightly to one side.

"What's that?" Dobbs replied, staring at the thin band of freckles that ran across Ellen's slightly upturned nose.

"The woman Charlie got caught with—Ida Hanover—I'll never forget that name, Ida. I had a cousin named Ida. I think it's so beautiful. Anyway, Ida had somehow heard I was leaving Minneapolis for Fort Laramie and she asked if she could come along. Said she had all she could stand of *her* husband and wanted to know if she could go to work for me. I should have taken her on. She must have been pretty good in the sack for Charlie to risk getting killed over. And Charlie *knew* good women." She added, laughing, "I mean, look at me."

I agree with that, Dobbs thought.

"Tell me about this inoculation," Ellen continued. "Does it hurt?"

"Not much. It's just a couple of scratches, really. I rub in cowpox material through the scratches. People don't catch cowpox, but this inoculation prevents smallpox, which, if it doesn't kill you, leaves your face all scarred up."

"Is that all?"

"Well," the physician hedged, "sometimes you get a little sick for a couple of days."

"Oh, a little sick, eh?" Ellen frowned. "Like sick enough to keep my girls from working?"

"Maybe for a day. It's normal to get a little fever, and achy joints. But the injection site quickly scabs over."

"Scabs over!" Ellen blurted. "That means there's a scar."

"Well, with men, the inoculation is usually administered on the arm and the scar isn't that big. About like this," he demonstrated, making a coin-sized circle with his thumb and forefinger. "But with women, who sometimes bare their arms, we usually use the hip."

Ellen looked at him, not sure if he was joking. "Have you forgotten who you're talking to?" she asked laughing. "You think a scar on the hip isn't going to be noticeable on a whore?"

Dobbs colored. "By God, I hadn't thought of that. I could use the thigh."

Ellen laughed loudly. "And you think that's going to be better?"

"Well, damn," Dobbs said in frustration, "I can put it wherever you want it. By the way," he said, anxious to change the subject, "you have any more aftereffects of that run-in with the good reverend?"

"No, except for getting mad all over again every time I think about how I was stupid enough to let myself get in a position like that."

"Don't blame yourself," Dobbs said. "You had no way of knowing he might turn violent."

"Look," she said patiently. "In my business I *have* to know how to read men. If I can't tell when a man is so horny he's willing to do anything to get some satisfaction, I'd better go ask for a job selling thread for Mr. Sevier."

"You have a point," Dobbs agreed, wondering if she was having any difficulty reading him and seeing that he was immensely attracted to her.

"I don't want to rush you, but I need to get this done so I can be off north."

"For heaven's sake, what are you going to be doing up there?"

"I need to inoculate as many Cheyenne as I can find. We have reason to suspect they may have been exposed, too."

"Oh, the Cheyenne!" Ellen said brightly. "In that case you may be running into Reverend Longstreet, at least if he's still following his professed belief that God himself is a Cheyenne currently residing somewhere near the Black Hills."

"I might run into him," Dobbs said carefully. "Do you have a message for him?"

"Sure," she said sweetly. "Tell him to come back. Tell him I have a present for him. A shiny new bullet I've been saving particularly for him."

"Now, now," Dobbs chided. "Don't turn homicidal on me. Besides you almost amputated his penis with that riding quirt, if you remember."

"You're right." She grinned. "And I'd like the chance to finish the job."

"Listen," said Dobbs, turning professional. "I really do need to go. Can you call your girls in and I'll get to inoculating?"

"What if they don't want to?"

"Hmmmm, that's true." Dobbs nodded. "I can't force them. But," he said, brightening, "it would help if you'd go first. Serve as a role model, as it were."

Ellen looked up at him and batted her eyes. "I guess I could do that," she said, struggling to smother a smile. "You want to see my hip or my thigh?"

"Why won't you listen to me?" Silas Connors asked shrilly, trying to raise his high voice enough to be heard above the wind shrieking down the canyon. A short, stoop-shouldered man with a tight, almost perfectly round potbelly that protruded abruptly from his mid-section, Connors commanded attention through his pocketbook, not his charisma. "Have I led you wrong, yet? Has anything I told you been incorrect?"

"Goddamnit, Si, that ain't the issue," argued Breedlove, a burly, hairy man in his mid-twenties, some ten years younger than Connors. "You know as well as I do what you're suggesting is just plain, fucking stupid."

"I don't take kindly to being called stupid," Connors said angrily, turning a bright red from his chin to the top of his mostly bald head, his beady brown eyes flashing like pieces of flint struck against metal.

"Take it easy, Si. You, too, Uni," suggested Amos "Notch" Henderson, a tall, gangly man of twenty-eight with heavy eyebrows that met in a thick, almost straight line over the bridge of his somewhat bulbous nose and hair that hung to his shoulders, the better to cover his left ear, which was mangled in a long ago barroom brawl. "There's no sense getting at each other's throats over this," he urged, assuming the role of peacemaker among the band of deserters. "Some of us is spooked, that's all. What you had in mind seemed like a good idea at the time but now we ain't so sure, now that we seen what happened to Connie and Fletch."

"They was plumb crazy," Connors said, his face returning to its normal pasty color but the anger still evident in his voice. "If I told 'em once, I told 'em a hundred times: LEAVE THE FUCKING BLANKETS ALONE!"

"We know you told 'em," Henderson continued smoothly. "It's nobody's fault but theirs. But the men," he said, gesturing toward the others who were slouched around the campfire, leaning close for warmth in the cold night air, "think we probably ought to re'valuate the situation." Even in June, as a result of the Plains' elevation, the temperature dropped into the thirties once the sun went down, and it was colder still when there was a brisk wind out of the north.

"Reevaluate my ass," Connors replied. "You want to take over. You want to burn my blankets."

Instead of answering immediately, Henderson reached for the coffeepot that was sitting on a bed of coals near the edge of the fire. Slowly, he poured himself half a cup, then lifted the container to his mouth. "Ahhhh, that's some strong coffee," he said, blowing on the steaming liquid. "Now what was you saying?"

"You know goddamn good and well what I was saying. I was saying I think you have a mind to divert this mission entirely. To ease me out. And I ain't going to stand for it."

"You see, Si, that's where you're wrong," Henderson said, keeping his voice low. "When me and Uni joined up with you, it sounded like a pretty good idea: 'Let's spread some smallpox among the injuns,' you said, 'then sit back and wait for 'em to die off.' Once they was gone, we could walk in and take whatever we wanted, including that ten thousand dollars they stole from the Salt Lake stage."

"That's still my plan," Connors insisted stubbornly.

"Well," Henderson said, glaring, "then I guess you're going to have to go it alone, 'cause me and the boys just don't feel right having them blankets around. It's like death waiting in the shadows. What's to say they can't infect one of us, like they did Fletch and Connie?"

"Because they wrapped the damn blankets *around* theirselves, that's why," Connors contended. "If you just leave 'em alone, you ain't got nothing to worry about."

"The point is, Si," Henderson said, trying to sound conciliatory, "why fuck with them blankets at all?"

Connors jumped to his feet, balling his fists at his side. "I *told* you why!" he screamed.

"Now listen to me, Si," Henderson said, raising his hands, palms outward in a gesture of peace. "We all know you're upset. There ain't one of us who think them injuns should have killed your kid brother. I flat know how that feels because I lost my own little brother when I was sixteen. We were out hunting rabbits for the pot and he tripped over a rock and blew his head off with his shotgun. He weren't but twelve years old. That's still a baby, practically. I felt right bad about that. Asked myself over and over if I couldn't have done something to keep it from happening. Like maybe told him he was too young to be using a shotgun. Or making sure he had the safety on. I felt so bad I went out and joined the Army. And look where that got me. But 'ventually, I decided it didn't do no good beating up on myself. And that's when I started to realize that there ain't nothing for certain in this world and we either have to learn to live what's handed to us, or we stick a pistol in our mouth and end it all."

"That's quite a goddamn speech," Connors said, pacing angrily in front of the fire. "But I can't see where it applies to me."

"It applies to you," Henderson argued, "because you're letting what happened to your brother run your life. Now me and Uni and them other boys, we joined up with you 'cause you offered us a fairly decent wage if we was to help you—what'd you say, 'Solve your problem.' Well, right now we have come to realize that what you're paying us, plus what we might gain out of actually recovering that strongbox, just ain't worth the risk of getting kilt. If we're gonna die, we figure it ought to be for something a little more valuable."

"I'm sure you have something in mind," Connors said icily. "Otherwise, you wouldn't have brought it up."

"We sure do," Breedlove interjected. "and it makes a lot more sense than what you're planning."

Connors spun on his heels, stomping over to Breedlove. "I don't recollect anyone talking to you, Mr. Smartmouth."

Unicorn flinched involuntarily, certain Connors was going to try to strike him although he was six inches shorter and twenty pounds lighter.

"Damn it all to hell, Uni, what'd you have to go and open your big mouth for?" Henderson grumbled. "Why don't you just sit down and shut the hell up until me and Si can work out a few things."

"I was just trying to help," Breedlove mumbled apologetically.

"Know you were, Uni. Know you were. But just be

patient. Now, Si," Henderson began anew, "tell me again about your store in Independence."

"It was a nice little store," Connors said. "Made a pretty good living selling goods to the emigrants, not to mention my contract with the Army."

"So you was seeing emigrants on a regular basis?"

"Course I was. They come in to stock up before beginning the trek out West."

"And you got to be friends with some of 'em. Not just the emigrants, but the wagonmasters and the men who worked for 'em, even some of the soldiers who usually escorted the train."

"That's true," Connors said. "What you getting at?"

"Well, since you was friends with 'em, they likely told you things they might not of told anyone else."

"Well, yeah. They told me about the injun problems and how they was having to carry more supplies cause it was getting harder to live off the land like they use to done before the trail first started getting busy."

"Sure, sure. I understand that. But you also heard about 'special cargoes' didn't you?"

"What do you mean, 'special cargoes?'"

"Well," Henderson said, trying to keep his voice light, "I recollect what it was like when I was soldiering at Fort Laramie. How them winters was real brutal and what with one blizzard after another, it was months more often than not before we'd get a supply train coming from Fort Leavenworth."

"I don't see what you're getting at," Connors said, frowning.

"Well, them supply trains wouldn't just be bringing flour and sugar and the mail. They also was carrying the fort's payroll."

"Payroll?" Connors asked, brightening.

"Yep. Soldiers is likely to get upset when they have

to go too long without getting paid. I mean thirteen dollars a month ain't much, but when it's all you got it suddenly takes on new meaning."

"Guess I never really stopped to think about it," Connors said, scratching his cheek.

"Well, think about it now. Think real careful. There was times, right, when they had more soldiers than usual riding with the train?"

"That's true. But they never said nothing about a payroll."

"Course they never said anything about it. If they did, they'd just be asking for trouble."

"Guess you're right," Connors conceded. "There was times when the wagonmasters would seem kinda nervous and when there were more troopers than normal out on the streets. I just never stopped to consider it."

"That's okay, Si. It weren't really important. Not until now, that is. Now think back real good. You left Independence about two weeks ago, right?"

"That's right."

"And when you left was there a train forming up? Must of been since the season is about to begin."

"Yep. There was a train s'posed to leave right after I did. Big 'un, too, since it was the first of the year."

"Now when you left do you remember seeing an unusual number of soldiers about? They probably would've been carrying more weapons than normal. Maybe them new rifles."

"By cracky, you're right," Connors said, his dark mood forgotten. "That must mean they've got a payroll on that train."

Henderson nodded slowly, a smile creeping across his craggy face. "Now what if we was to set a little ambush for that train? Maybe relieve them Blue Boys of all that heavy gold?"

Connors looked slightly shocked. "You mean attack the train? Kill them soldiers? And maybe some emigrants, too?"

"Well, Jesus Christ, doesn't get all righteous about it, Si. You was ready to kill all the injuns in the whole fucking West just twenty minutes ago."

"But them's *injuns*," Connors said heatedly. "They ain't people. Besides, they killed my brother."

"Well, look at it another way." Henderson sighed. "You brother wouldn't have been killed if the Army hadn't sent him to Blue Water, would he?"

"You got a point there," Connors said slowly.

"So the Army's as much to blame for your brother's death as them injuns."

"By God, I think you got him," Breedlove whispered, a hint of admiration in his voice.

"Uni, shut *up*!" Henderson commanded sternly. "Ain't I right, Si? Ain't the Army at least partially responsible for Darcy's getting killed?"

"Scalped, too. And mutilated from what I hear. I was told them sonsabitches cut off his jewels. Goddamn heathens."

"I'm sure that's probably true. But he got caught in a bad place because the Army put him there. Now why don't you consider taking some revenge against the Army, too, and not just the injuns? 'Sides, it's the Army that's got all the money."

"How much money you figure's in that train?" Connors asked. "Not that I'm agreeing. I'm just curious."

"Sure you are, Si. That's just natural. Gotta have all the facts on the table to make a decision."

"Well, how much?"

Henderson waved his hand. "Oh, I don't know. Let's see, there's about 150 troopers at the fort and none of 'em been paid in a long, long time. Plus, the commander needs some operating funds. And so does the injun agent, who's always bribing the redskins to do something or other . . . "

"I asked how much!"

"I'm figuring," Henderson said impatiently. "Sums ain't my long suit, but I reckon, oh, maybe thirty thousand dollars. 'Haps a little more."

"Holy Jumping Jesus!" Connors said excitedly. "That's a lot of money."

"It's more'n what we'd ever get from the injuns, that's for fucking sure," Henderson agreed.

"But could we do it? I mean do we have enough men?"

Henderson looked around the fire. "Well, there's me and you and Uni, plus Jeb, Frank, Will, and Oscar. That's seven, with six of us who've been trained in weapons and tactics."

"Oscar ain't nothing but a boy."

"I was a *soldier*, goddamnit," Oscar Anderson said angrily. "I got me an injun scalp and I cut up a man something good in a poker game once. I may be young but I can fight like a man."

"Okay, Oscar, take it easy," Henderson said. "Si wasn't questioning your ability to do a man's job. But when you get his age you tend to think of nineteen as being a kid."

"I ain't a fucking kid," Anderson said stubbornly.

"Course you ain't, Oscar, and I'm sorry if I hurt your feelings," Connors said. "You been right good on this trip. Always ready to take on your share."

"Anyway," Henderson interrupted, "that should be more'n enough if we plan it well. Get in, get the money, and get the hell out before most of the people in the train knows what's hit 'em. They'll think it's an injun raid and they'll try to get them wagons into defensive positions to fight a battle. By the time the confusion dies down, we'll be halfway to the Black Hills and they'll never find us." Leaning toward Connors, Henderson dropped his voice. "Now what do you say we do that and forget about all this smallpox shit? Let's just burn them blankets before any more of us get sick and concentrate on stealing that government money."

"What if we get away clean with the payroll?" Connors persisted. "Then would you help me get them injuns?"

"Let's take it one step at a time," Henderson said, shaking his head. "Money first, then the injuns."

"Let me sleep on it," Connors said hesitantly. "Although I got to admit it sounds pretty reasonable."

"Course it does, Si," Henderson said, winking at Breedlove. "Now let's see if we can get some rest without this storm keeping us up all night, then we can talk about it some more in the morning. Oscar," he said, turning to the younger man, "you and Jeb take first watch."

"Aw, shit," Anderson grumbled. "I figured when I ran away from Fort Kearny there wasn't going to be no more watches."

"There will be as long as we're in the middle of injun country," Henderson argued. "Just think of your share of thirty thousand dollars. That ought to be worth a few hours lost sleep."

Long Leg looked around the lodge uncomfortably, panic building in his eyes.

"Don't worry," said Crooked Nose, sensing the other man's discomfort. "There are no Pawnee hiding in the shadows."

"I know that," Long Leg said, embarrassed. "It's just

after months of being in the hills I feel uneasy when I come into the village. Especially into a lodge. I feel as if I'm going to smother."

"What made you decide to become a Coyote Man?" Cut Neck asked, unable to suppress his curiosity.

Long Leg looked at him as if he had just uttered a curse. "You're just a boy," he said levelly. "How would you be expected to know about the feelings of a man?"

"I won't always be the youngest warrior in the village," Cut Neck replied indignantly. "Besides, how am I ever going to learn anything if I don't ask questions? I meant no disrespect."

Long Leg shifted restlessly, rearranging his white buffalo robe and feeling for his war club, which lay reassuringly at his side. The white paint that covered his body seemed to glow in the flickering firelight, giving him an eerie, ghostlike appearance. "I feel it is my duty as a *Kananacich* warrior," he said impatiently. "When you get older and learn more about the ways of the Arapaho, it will become clear to you that warriorhood brings certain responsibilities. Although I do not feel it necessary to explain my motives to you, I answer your question out of respect for Frozen Eye, who has offered me his hospitality."

"Long Leg is right," Frozen Eye said solemnly. "He has taken it upon himself to live with the other Coyote Men in the hills, giving up shelter and companionship and forsaking relations with women simply because he understands what a valuable service he performs. Because of Long Leg and the others we are made aware when any outsider passes through the territory of Our People. If danger is approaching, it does not escape detection by the Coyote Men."

"But," Cut Neck persisted, "don't you feel . . . "

"Enough!" Frozen Eye said sharply. "One of the first

things you must learn as a young warrior is when to keep your mouth closed. And now is the time for you to listen and not to talk. If you prove your mettle, Long Leg may consider you as a successor when he feels it is time to rejoin the village. And then you can ask him any questions you want. Right now, we have business to discuss."

"Yes," Cut Neck said humbly. "You are right. I apologize."

Frozen Eye nodded curtly. "Long Leg," he said courteously, "please excuse the boy's impetuosity. Tell us again, if you will, about the men you have been watching."

Long Leg sighed. "One more time. Then I would like to return to the hills. Being around so many people, even if they are *my* people, makes me nervous."

"I understand," Frozen Eye said with a smile. "I sometimes feel the same way. Once more, then you may go. There are seven white men, is that right?"

"That's correct." Long Leg nodded. "They arrived from the north three days ago and they are camped in a canyon near the place where the two rivers meet."

"Does it appear as if they are waiting for someone?"

"No. Although they post lookouts at night I think it is for the same reason I am in the hills: to watch in case anyone approaches. I don't get the impression that they are expecting someone."

"Or that they plan to do us harm?" Crooked Nose interjected.

"There has been no indication they are planning an attack," Long Leg conceded.

"And they are not soldiers?" asked Bear Claw, a warrior nearing middle age who had been sitting silently on the edge of the group crouched around the fire.

Long Leg paused. "That is not an easy question to answer. They are not wearing uniforms, but they carry themselves like soldiers. Their horses carry the soldiers' marks and the way they do things—setting up their shelter, for example, posting lookouts—is done in the way of the soldier. But I do not think they are, indeed, soldiers. The one who appears to be the leader is older, almost as old as you, Bear Claw," he said with a smile, "but he does not have the appearance of a soldier. He looks more like an emigrant."

"And they have done nothing the whole time they have been there?" asked Frozen Eye.

Long Leg shook his head. "They talk. From morning to well after dark, they do nothing but talk. Sometimes they yell at each other and look as if they want to fight. But one of the younger men, the one with the missing ear, acts as the peacemaker."

"Are they well armed?"

"That is a good question, Crooked Nose," Long Leg replied. "No, they are not. They each have a pistol and a rifle, but the rifles are the older kind, not like the ones the white soldiers used at Blue Water when they attacked the Brulé and the Miniconjou."

"It sounds as if these men once were soldiers, but are not any longer," Frozen Eye mused.

"But why are they in our territory?" asked Bear Claw. "They do not seem to be looking for our village since they are not sending out scouts. They are not hunting. They don't seem to be waiting for others to join them. It is very curious."

"Have I explained the situation satisfactorily?" Long Leg asked, nervously fingering his club.

"Yes!" Frozen Eye replied. "You have done very well. I know you are anxious to leave. Please keep a watch on the men and let us know immediately if the situation changes. In the meantime, we will discuss what, if any, action we should take."

"Of course I will do that," Long Leg said, rising. "And you," he said, turning to Cut Neck, "You must learn what it means to be an Arapaho warrior. Prove yourself able and maybe we will talk again."

"Yes, Long Leg," the boy replied meekly. "Thank you for suffering my questions."

"Do you think these men pose a threat to us?" Elk Ear asked when Long Leg had gone.

"No," Frozen Eye replied slowly. "I don't pretend to know why they have chosen to camp in our territory but I do not think they mean us any immediate harm. If they did, they would have come more stealthily and they would have acted by now. If they were Pawnee, the situation would be different."

"Then I think," Bear Claw said sagely, "that it is best if we do nothing until we know more about their intentions."

"I think that is wise," said Frozen Eye. "Long Leg is a very dedicated Coyote Man; he will let us know if the white men present a threat. Do you all agree?" he asked, looking from man to man. "Then that is what we will do," he added when no one dissented.

"I wish everyone would quit treating me as if I were a child," Cut Neck complained.

"Then you have to quit acting like one," Yellow Wolf replied. "I think if you were not my brother I would be very impatient with your endless stream of questions myself. I know you and I know your curiosity has no limits, but you must understand the limits of other people."

"Did you *really* insist on questioning Long Leg?" Snowy Mountain asked, impressed. "He's a *very* respected warrior and one of the best of the Coyote Men. But he's so, what shall I say, *frightening*. Painted white. Wearing a white robe. He comes and goes like a spirit. And his way of life? How can anyone *do* that? Living alone in the hills all the time, not even building a shelter. And no *woman*. I don't see how he stands it. I don't see how you could fail to be intimidated."

"Please, don't you begin as well," Cut Neck replied sullenly. "It's bad enough I have to listen to criticism from my brother without hearing it from my sister-in-law as well."

"It's only because you deserve it sometimes," Snowy Mountain said. "I've never known anyone who asks as many questions as you. Don't you realize that some people don't like to be questioned? Sometimes you are very impertinent. If Little Antelope proves to be as inquisitive as you, I think I'll sew his lips shut."

"You hear that, little one?" Cut Neck sighed, anxious to change the subject. Scooping up the boy, he held him high above his head, grinning broadly when the toddler's face clouded in fright. "You had better be careful," he said affectionately, lowering the boy to his lap. "Your fate could be sealed if you try to increase your knowledge," he said gravely. "There are some," he said, glancing at Snowy Mountain, "I'm not saying who, mind you, but there are *some* who would do you great harm simply because you want to increase your knowledge."

"Increasing your knowledge is one thing; being a pest is quite another," Yellow Wolf said. "And being discourteous is the worst of all."

"I wasn't being discourteous," Cut Neck said, groaning. "At least I didn't mean to be."

"You had better hope Long Leg didn't think so either," Yellow Wolf said. "I would hate to have him as an enemy."

"Come Little Antelope," Snowy Mountain said, reaching for her son. "It's time for your dinner."

Cut Neck peered curiously into the bowl Snowy Mountain had prepared for the boy. "Uggghhh," he said, making a face. "What is that you are feeding him? It looks like bird eggs."

"That's exactly what it is," Snowy Mountain replied defensively. "Meadowlark eggs."

"Oh no!" Cut Neck cried. "Don't tell me you really believe that old saying."

"Of *course*, I do. It is a well-known fact that the meadowlark can speak our language and if we feed its meat and eggs to our young, they will learn to talk sooner. Why do you have to question *everything*?"

Cut Neck turned to his brother, who rolled his eyes and shrugged. "Don't you see how contradictory your attitude is?" Cut Neck said to Snowy Mountain. "You're trying to help your son talk early, but you don't want him to use that newfound ability to ask questions."

Snow Mountain reddened. "Sometimes you are impossible, Cut Neck. If you ever find a wife, I'll be very surprised."

Yellow Wolf guffawed. "Respond to that, younger brother, if you can" he said, clutching his sides. "One of the first things you have to learn as a man is that you will never understand a woman."

"I agree with that," Cut Neck said, rising and walking toward the entrance. "And people say Long Leg and the other Coyote Men are depriving themselves by not having wives. The more I see of marital relationships, the more I think it's a wonderful idea."

"Do you think your brother will ever make a good warrior?" Snowy Mountain asked after Cut Neck was gone.

"I don't know," Yellow Wolf replied, shaking his

head. "He is brave. I know that. But he has to learn to be more respectful of his elders. That could cause him many problems in the future."

"How do you know he's brave? He's barely sixteen. That's still a boy."

"It doesn't matter how old he is. I know for a fact that he is courageous. Much braver than I, for example."

"You are talking foolishly," Snowy Mountain said. "He has never been on a raid. He has never really faced danger."

"Oh, yes, he has."

"How?" Snowy Mountain asked skeptically. "What has he ever done besides ask endless questions?"

"You have to trust me," Yellow Wolf said. "I can't tell you why I am so sure of his valor."

"Certainly you can tell me," Snowy Mountain said authoritatively. "I'm your wife. Why shouldn't you tell me?"

"Because it is something between me and Cut Neck," Yellow Wolf replied ambivalently. "Besides," he added hesitantly, "it was a long time ago."

"That doesn't matter," Snow Mountain said firmly. "Tell me about it. Was it something that happened?"

Yellow Wolf looked down at his feet. "Cut Neck saved my life," he whispered.

"What do you mean he saved your life?" Snowy Mountain asked, puzzled.

"It's embarrassing," Yellow Wolf stammered.

"Well, tell me now," Snowy Mountain insisted. "There are to be no secrets between husband and wife."

"It isn't a *secret,*" Yellow Wolf said stubbornly. "It is just something that I don't talk about very much."

"Well, talk about it now. Tell me about it."

"Cut Neck," he said in a rush, "was about twelve and I was sixteen. We had been hunting rabbits and were returning to the camp. I remember it was late afternoon and the weather was still cool, even though it was almost time for the summer buffalo hunt. Just like now."

"You're being evasive," Snowy Mountain said sternly.

"We were hurrying because we wanted to get back to the village before dark," he said, ignoring his wife's aside. "And we got careless. We were joking and playing like children, not paying attention to where we were. There was a grizzly sow feeding on the berries and we walked upon her totally unawares, putting ourselves between her and her cubs."

"Oh, how dreadful," Snowy Mountain gasped. "Even I know better than that."

"It isn't that we didn't *know* better," Yellow Wolf said tersely. "It's just that we were not paying attention."

"And you paid the price," Snow Mountain said softly.

"Yes." Yellow Wolf sighed. "Since I was closer, the sow attacked me first. It still gives me nightmares. When she raised up on her back legs, she looked as tall as a pine tree. Her eyes were as red as the setting sun and saliva was flying out of her mouth. And the roar! I'll never forget that as long as I live. When she bellowed I urinated all over myself. I couldn't help it."

"I would have done the same," Snowy Mountain said emphathetically. "It is a natural reaction."

"Not for a young warrior-to-be who was preparing to go on his first raid against the Pawnee. I was petrified. Paralyzed. I could not move. All I could do was stare up at that bear; I couldn't take my eyes off her mouth, which was big enough to engulf my entire head, and her teeth. I was too frightened even to scream."

"What about your bow? Couldn't you have fired?"

"A lot of good that would have done," Yellow Wolf replied scornfully. "We were carrying arrows meant for rabbits, not maddened grizzly sows."

"Well, what happened?" Snowy Mountain asked impatiently. "Obviously the story has a happy ending or you wouldn't be here."

"The fact that the incident ended as it did was not because of what *I* did," Yellow Wolf said. "It was because of Cut Neck's bravery. He jumped on the bear's back and plunged his knife into the animal's eye. It was a *very* lucky blow. If he had stabbed her anywhere else, it would simply have made her madder. But the blade penetrated straight to her brain. She fell as if she had been struck by lightning."

"So it was luck, pure and simple?"

"No," Yellow Wolf said harshly. "It was *not* luck. The wound was lucky, but Cut Neck's bravery was not. I, the one who was soon to become a warrior, was powerless. But my younger brother, this *boy*, had the presence of mind and the heart to act. I asked him later if he intended to stab the bear in the eye."

"And what did he say?"

"He said no. He told me he was just trying to stab and he did not consciously guide his knife."

"Didn't that make you feel better?"

"No! I was still terribly shamed because my younger brother had the courage to act while I could do nothing."

"Why haven't you ever told me about this?" Snowy Mountain asked.

"Because I have never told anyone. I swore Cut Neck to silence. I told him that if he told the villagers what had happened I would not be allowed to go with the raiders and my career as a warrior would be ruined. I would have to go live with the women and learn to weave baskets."

"But you have since proved your bravery several times. You have two Pawnee scalps and you have been chosen to carry the notched wooden club of the *Betahanan*, the most respected of our military societies."

"That is because no one knows what happened that day on the trail when Cut Neck and I encountered the bear. It could still bring me much shame if the incident were to become known."

"Don't worry," Snowy Mountain said, smiling. "The secret is safe with me even though I think you exaggerate its importance. Now that you have become a man, you have more than shown your worth as a warrior."

"Nevertheless, it continues to shame me. The memory burns at my soul."

Snowy Mountain was silent for several minutes, lost in thought. "I have an idea," she said, with a smile. "Listen to me carefully."

"What is it?" Yellow Wolf asked grumpily.

"I think the way to relieve your guilt is to realize that what happens in childhood is not always indicative of what will happen as an adult. To help you understand this, I propose a game."

"A *game*?" Yellow Wolf asked, surprised. "What kind of game."

"I will be a she bear." Snowy Mountain grinned. "And as such, I may pounce upon you at any time."

"I don't understand," Yellow Wolf said uncertainly. "What am I supposed to do?"

"You will stab me."

"Stab you? You must be joking."

"Not with a knife, of course. My vagina will be my eye and your penis will be your knife. Your duty will be to plunge your knife into my eye and keep stabbing me until I no longer move."

Yellow Wolf grinned. "What a good idea!" He laughed. "I think I will like that game."

"That's good. Because I warn you this time. I'm preparing to pounce."

"We been making good time," Jim Ashby allowed, stroking the neck of his piebald pony, a deceptively emaciated-looking, slightly swaybacked animal that troopers at the fort teased him wasn't fit for a meal for a starving wolf. "I reckon we'll be there 'bout supper time."

"You think they'll be expecting us?" Dobbs asked.

Ashby smiled crookedly, exposing twin rows of badly neglected teeth. "The way we travel we sure'n hell ain't gonna surprise no Cheyenne," Ashby replied, laughing. "Anyways, they knowed we comin' since yestidy."

"How do you know that?" Dobbs asked, surprised.

"We found their tracks," Erich Schmidt answered. "Last evening, when me and Jim were making our check around the camp."

"You mean they brought their horses that close to our camp and we didn't know about it?" asked Benoit, who had ridden up to join the threesome.

"*You* might not a knowed it." Ashby smiled. "But me an' the boy did. Fact, it were him who found the tracks. The boy's gettin' pretty good, for a sprout that is."

"Gee, thanks, Jim," Erich said excitedly. "Coming from you that's high praise indeed."

"Don't let it go to your head, boy," Ashby replied, leaning to the side to spit a stream of tobacco juice into the dust. "You still got one hell of a long way to go."

Erich slumped. "Damn it all, Jim. Just when I thought you were fixing to say something nice about me."

"You two are a barrel of laughs." Dobbs chuckled. "You maybe ought to put together an act to entertain the men next winter, when everybody's sick of the barracks and they're all at each other's throats."

"You're even starting to looking something alike," added Benoit, pointing at the tight-fitting, slightly worn buckskin pants Erich had taken in trade from a Minniconjou for two threadbare wool shirts and a jackknife. Erich, Benoit noticed, also had discarded the heavy, ankle-high leather boots he had worn all the way from Independence and replaced them with a comfortable-looking pair of Arapaho moccasins.

A stocky, solid-looking youth of sixteen, Erich had his mother's blue eyes and firm jaw and a direct, determined mien inherited from his father. If he successfully escaped his mother's scissors, Erich wore his blond hair tumbling to his collar. But more likely than not, following a brief visit to the post between hunting trips and scouting expeditions, he left Fort Laramie with his locks cropped straight across the back at ear level, prompting Ashby to begin ribbing him about his "squarehead" heritage. From the day he met Ashby soon after the wagon train started westward, Erich hero-worshipped the scout, dogging his footsteps and imitating his mannerisms.

Far from being repulsed by the boy's adulation, Ashby seemed to bask in the attention, taking Erich under his care and treating him like a younger brother.

It was a somewhat strange relationship, Dobbs and Benoit agreed, because it would be hard to find two more disparate individuals. In contrast to Erich's blond-haired, blue-eyed, undeniably Teutonic appearance, Ashby was dark and grizzled, with black eyes and long, dark hair that he wore braided into a single pigtail.

Aged somewhere between thirty and fifty, Ashby was angular and wiry, an easy twenty pounds lighter than Erich. At 5-foot–7 he was rib-counting thin and, although he looked as if he would blow away in the first wind that came howling down across the Plains from Canada, in reality he was as tough as a horse-flank steak and, if the occasion demanded, as ferocious as a treed cougar.

The epitome of the Plains-toughened frontiersman, Ashby clad himself winter and summer in a stained, much-patched, elk-skin shirt and dirty buffalo-hide trousers. Not given much to small talk and the concept of camaraderie, Ashby preferred solitude to sociability. Still, when the scout walked into a group of troopers they normally took one look at his cracked, wrinkled face and the long knife scar that cut diagonally across his left cheek, a souvenir of a fight with a late Crow warrior named One Antler, and lapsed into deferential silence.

One dark February afternoon, when the cold made it impossible to venture out of Old Bedlam and the snow was blowing in drifts higher than a horse's head, Dobbs and Benoit, over a fresh pot of Benoit's potent Cajun coffee, had turned to Ashby as a topic of discussion, pooling their combined intelligence about the scout to see if they could get a clearer fix on the man both of them liked and admired.

"He told me once that he came West when he was only twelve," Benoit had proffered. "Claimed he ran away from an abusive father. Simply walked off their Illinois farm and never looked back."

"I believe it," Dobbs had added. "He has the look of a man who's been among the Indians for quite a while. Did you ever see the tattoos on his chest?"

"No, but I saw his bare feet once. Two toes missing on the right foot and one on the left. Frostbite, he said. Like it happens all the time to everybody."

"I guess it does if you're wintering with the Indians," Dobbs replied dryly.

"Did you know he was married once?" Benoit asked.

"At least once," Dobbs replied. "To an Arapaho. That's when he got the tattoos."

"Know what happened to her?"

"Died of cholera, I understand."

"He's probably been married more than once. How else could he become so fluent in Cheyenne and Siouan?"

"I think that's a distinct possibility," Dobbs agreed.

Both men grew quiet, their knowledge of Ashby exhausted.

"In the long run," Dobbs had finally said, "I guess we don't know much."

"Damn!" Benoit exclaimed as he laughed. "There go my plans to write his biography."

In an effort to further emulate his idol, Erich had begun collecting an assortment of weapons—Ashby called them "tools"—that contributed to longevity in a tough, dangerous occupation. He not only dressed like an Indian, he armed himself like one as well.

Around his waist was a rawhide strap from which dangled a ten-inch-long, bone-handled Lakota skinning knife encased in a beaded sheath of sufficient size to completely envelop the weapon. The seemingly oversized case, Erich patiently explained, served two purposes. One, it protected the knife from moisture and everyday knocks, and two, it made it less likely that it would fall out and be lost along the trial. The knife hung on Erich's left side with its butt pointing forward to make it more accessible, the same way, Benoit noted, a cavalryman wore his sabre.

Ashby, Benoit observed, carried a similar knife, plus a tomahawk cast in the Spanish style with a blade resembling a miniature broadax. "Used to have me a pretty li'l war club with a egg-shaped, four-pound rock for a head," Ashby said proudly, noticing Benoit's attention to the tomahawk. "The shaft was painted red and black and there was a horsehair tail adangling down. Took it offen a Blackfoot during a li'l spat up on the Yellowstone when I was trappin' up that way. It had a scalplock on it when I collected it, but I tossed that in the fire. Really loved that ol' club but I ended up tradin' it to a 'Ho for this here hatchet. The club were great for crushing skulls but it weren't much good for splitting kindling."

"See you got yourself a rifle, too," Benoit said to Erich, remembering how he had taught the youth how to shoot with his own heavy Sharps during the westward journey from Missouri.

"Ain't she a beaut?" Erich beamed, passing the firearm to Benoit for his examination. "I'm buying it from Mr. Sevier. He's letting me pay for it a little at a time."

"A Hawken, eh?" Benoit mumbled in appreciation. "You think," he added, trying to be facetious, "that's going to give you enough stopping power?"

"Oh, hell, yes," Erich said, grinning. "I don't want to mess around. If I shoot something, I want it to stay shot. The Hawk's .50 caliber ball'll drop a bull dead in his tracks at 350 yards."

"As if the boy could *hit* a buffler at 350 yards," Ashby

teased. "It's a fair to middlin' rifle but it can't hol' a candle to my ol' Hall," he said, rubbing his weapon affectionately, the same way, Dobbs perceived, a man might stroke his wife's back. "This sweet li'l thang'll fire twice as fast as anythang the injuns have."

Dobbs shook his head in mock disgust. "I've seen platoons with fewer weapons than you two have," he commented sardonically.

"You'll change your mind about that pretty quick the first time you meet up with a Crow war party alookin' for your scalp," Ashby replied.

"Scalp!" Benoit roared, pointing to Dobbs's retreating hairline. "The last thing Jace has to worry about is losing his hair to an Indian."

"What kind of reception you figure we're going to get from the Cheyenne?" Dobbs asked, unamused. "You think they'll be receptive to letting me inoculate them?"

Ashby shook his head slowly. "I wouldn't reckon they're goin' to be linin' up for the privilege."

"Do they distrust us that much?"

"Sure do," Ashby replied, nodding. "I doubt that what happened at Blue Water changed their opinion much neither. They got it in their heads that we're trouble. Harney attacks for no reason, killin' a bunch of women and chillin in the process. Them we don' kill outright with guns and swords, are wiped out with disease."

"I read that the cholera epidemic of '49 hit the Cheyenne harder than any of the tribes," Dobbs said.

"Tha's right," Ashby agreed. "Kilt almost half of 'em."

"Half of the entire tribe?" Benoit asked, amazed. "That's hard to believe."

"You'd better believe it," Ashby said. "I seen it firs' hand."

"That must have been a bad time indeed," Dobbs said soberly.

"Sure was," Benoit agreed.

"Yep." Ashby nodded. "It came down like a lightnin' bolt. A group of Cheyenne was havin' theirselves a Medicine Lodge . . . "

"A what?" asked Dobbs.

"A Sun Dance," Ashby explained. "A real big ceremony. One of the warriors was dancing and he just keeled over dead. While they was all tryin' to figure out what had kilt him, another one rolled over. That sent 'em into a panic. The chief, an ol' man named Bull Weasel, ordered 'em to run for it, which o' course, they did. They travelled all night and set up camp along the Cimarron River. They no sooner had their lodges up, then others started dyin.'"

"Were you there?" Benoit asked sympathetically.

"Not at that camp. Me and my wife was with another group camped in the Black Hills."

"I thought your wife was Arapaho," Benoit interjected.

"She was. But them and the Cheyennes are friendly. I was trappin' up in Cheyenne country so she was with me. The choler struck us a little later. The firs' ones to get sick couldn't figure out what was happenin'. One o' the camp's best warriors, Little Old Man, put on his war dress, mounted his war horse, and rode through the camp with his lance challenging the invisible killer to come out and face him like a man. He was still lookin' for it when the cramps struck him and he fell off his horse. By the time his wife got there, he was dyin.' That scared the people so bad, they took off runnin' again. Some o' 'em made it to our camp, which is how we got it."

Not sure what to say, Benoit and Dobbs remained

silent. Ashby shivered as if struck by a sudden chill. "Anyways," he said, shaking himself like a wet dog, "they somehow become convinced the white man gave 'em the sickness on purpose. Not that I could blame 'em, you un'nerstan.' We seem to be doin' our damnedest to kill 'em off. We run off the buffalo and cut down all the trees for fuel 'n such. From their point o' view, we're trying to 'radicate 'em every way we can. We're gonna have to do a lot of right smart talking," he said, turning to look at Dobbs gravely, "to convince 'em your medicine ain't meant to kill 'em."

"It's kind of hard to argue a case for inoculation, considering what you say about their experience with cholera and what we heard about that gang of deserters who're trying to give 'em smallpox," Dobbs conceded.

"My point 'actly." Ashby spit. "Although I don' think that happens very often."

"You're right about that," Dobbs said, nodding. "We don't have to go out of our way to try to give them our diseases. They're exposed just by being around us. They haven't built up any immunity to the illnesses we take for granted and when one of them gets a foothold among the tribes, inevitably it's going to be devastating."

"Yep," Ashby nodded. "I seen what choller can do in the lodges. Flux, too."

"I've seen dysentery work its way through a regiment, and it isn't a pretty sight," Dobbs agreed. "I can imagine what it would do in a village of hypo-immune individuals. I think we were pretty lucky back at the post with the smallpox scare. Ryan apparently didn't infect anyone else. Too bad I couldn't save him, but he was too far gone. But other than him, there's not been another case, neither on the post nor at the Hog Ranch. I don't know if we're going to be so fortunate once we get to the Cheyenne camp.

Especially if Ryan and Fletcher infected those braves they met on the trail."

"I sure hope we ain't arriving to a camp full o' poxed Cheyenne," Ashby said. "If we are and they know how they got it, they might not be in the best frame o' min' toward white visitors."

"Let's look on the bright side," said Dobbs. "We're not sure those Indians were infected. Maybe they weren't even from this village. Hell, we're not even sure they were Cheyenne. Ryan wasn't seeing things too clearly by the time their paths crossed and he probably wasn't an expert anyway."

"You're right," Ashby acknowledged. "We'll just play the hand we're dealt."

"What about the kids?" Benoit asked. The problem of what to do about the two kidnapped German boys, Wilhelm and Werner, had been nagging at him for days, ever since Frau Schmidt had pulled him aside and begged him not to come back to Fort Laramie without the children. Unwilling to make any promises he might not be able to keep, Benoit had refrained from committing. "Are they going to let us take them back? Provided they're still here, of course."

"Tha's a mite touchy subject," Ashby said thoughtfully. "I'd reckon you had a better chance of convincing 'em to take the pox medicine."

"Remember what the colonel said, Jean," Dobbs warned. "Don't go trying to push the 'White Soldier' role. We have to remember we're there as their guests. We're not in any position to start making demands."

"Don't worry, Jace. I'm not going to do that. My short time with the Brulé taught me *something* about Indians. Besides, I agree with Kemp. He wants to minimize the potential for violence. When he says to negotiate first, I think he's right."

"Sounds smart to me." Ashby added, "Have to admit, I didn't give the colonel that much credit when I first met him but I'm thinkin' otherwise now."

"Yeah, he's surprised me, too," Dobbs confessed. "I think we're lucky Teasley wasn't there. He sure as hell wouldn't want to negotiate."

"I find that a right strange attitude," Ashby said. "For an injun agent, that is."

"Teasley has a government title but he's more a soldier than a bureaucrat," Benoit pointed out. "He's cut from the same cloth as Harney."

"Don't you think you're being a tad harsh, Jean? Sounds to me like you're just jealous because Teasley made a play for Inge."

"Yeah," Benoit said, snorting. "And you see where it got him, too! In any case, I don't think I'm being harsh at all. You weren't at Blue Water. I was. What I'm saying is, if the Indians consider Teasley a friend, they sure as hell don't need any enemies."

"Ya'll can jabber politics all you want," Ashby said. "Me 'n Erich gotta get to work. We gonna ride up ahead a piece. See if we can see how close we are to the village. I know we ain't fer."

"You think we need to check our weapons?" Dobbs asked somewhat nervously. "Make sure they're loaded and ready to fire?"

"Naw." Ashby smiled. "If the Cheyenne is watchin', which they pr'lly are, it might make 'em 'spicious. If they're plannin' an unfrien'ly reception, it won' do you no good nohow."

Dobbs looked at Benoit. "Now that's what I call encouraging words."

"Cheer up," Benoit replied, laughing. "Maybe they're going to welcome us with a dog feast. Don't ever tell Holz, but I've kind of developed a liking for it."

"We'll be back in an hour or so," Ashby said, digging his heels into his horse's side. As he and Erich rode off, Benoit marvelled at how much they looked alike. They were about the same height and they were dressed almost identically. The main difference was Erich's black slouch hat, an article he started wearing after Ashby warned him how his blond hair stood out among the muted colors of the high desert and marked him as a highly visible target.

"Erich's transformation has been amazing, hasn't it?" Dobbs remarked, apparently reading Benoit's thoughts.

"His father would never recognize him," Benoit agreed. "It might be wrong to say this, but I think Erich's a lot better off here than he ever would have been in Oregon."

"And what about his sister?" Dobbs asked. "When are you going to do the right thing and ask the woman to marry you?"

"Jesus, Jace, how many times do we have to go over this? She's not a woman, she's just a girl."

"A girl, huh? Apparently she wasn't too young to attract Teasley's attention."

"He's an evil-minded man," Benoit said angrily. "His . . ."

Benoit stopped in mid-sentence, looking up to see Ashby galloping back in their direction.

"Is something wrong?" he asked anxiously as they reined to a stop. "Where's Erich?"

"He's up ahead a piece," Ashby said, "waitin' for us. Nothin' wrong. I just came back to tell ya that we ain't fer at all from the camp. It's just a couple miles ahead."

"Is everything all right?" Dobbs asked. "Do they appear hostile?"

"Not very goddamned likely." Ashby laughed.

"We're in for a real treat. They're having a Council of Chiefs, the whole damn tribe is here."

"Is that unusual?" Dobbs asked.

"You bet," Ashby replied. "Somethin' special must be going on. This ain't the year for electing chiefs."

"What do you mean, 'the year?'"

"You gotta know a li'l bit about the Cheyenne," Ashby explained. "The tribe's made up of ten bands and each band has four chiefs."

"So they have forty chiefs," Dobbs said. "I had no idea there were that many."

"Actually, forty-four 'cause there are four head chiefs, too."

"And they're all here, now?"

"Looks that way from the way the camp's set up. You'll see what I mean when we get there."

"You still didn't explain what you meant about the year," Dobbs reminded him.

"Oh, yeah. Well, each chief is elected for a term of ten years. I recollect that the last election was five years ago, the year before White Deer died."

"Who's White Deer?" Benoit asked, puzzled.

"My wife," Ashby said softly.

"So they had an election in 1850," Dobbs said. "That means another isn't scheduled until 1860. Why would they be meeting now?

Ashby shrugged. "Could be any number of reasons. Maybe one of the head chiefs died and they need to 'lect another one. Maybe they ain't found many buffler this year and they need to make a decision about moving to new territory. Or maybe they got some issue they want to discuss that has to do with the whole tribe."

"Like what to do in the wake of the incident at Blue Water?" Benoit asked.

"Could be," Ashby said, nodding. "Whatever it is, this is good for you," he said, looking at Dobbs.

"How's that?"

"Two reasons. One is they wouldn't all be together like this if they had a major sickness, they'd be all scattered around the mountains. The second is, you got all the leaders in one spot and you can ask 'em about that pox thang. It'd be a lot easier for you if the council was to give its approval. There's a whole bunch more injuns here than you thought there'd be. I hope you brung enough pox juice."

"I've got enough to inoculate every Indian between here and the Yukon," Dobbs said eagerly.

"Just be patient," Ashby cautioned. "This may take us a few days but there's no way to hurry the Cheyenne through their ceremonies. My advice is just relax and enjoy it. By an' by we'll get to talkin' 'bout the pox."

"Would you look at that?" Benoit exclaimed.

Dobbs sucked in his breath. "It's spectacular all right. I've certainly never seen anything like it."

Their route to the camp had taken them up what appeared to be a hillock. But once they got to the top, the ground dropped away precipitously, leaving them on an overlook high enough to get a view of the entire camp as it stretched for more than a mile along the shore of a pristine mountain lake, a body of water Ashby told them was named after the beaver that populated the shores. The lodges were arranged in a huge C with the open end of the compound facing the east. In the large open space in the center there were three lodges, a smaller one on the south and another on the north. In the exact center of what would be a circle if the eastern end were closed was a single lodge several times larger than any of the others.

"How many lodges you figure are there?" Benoit asked, spellbound by the sight.

"You can count 'em if you've a min'," Ashby said. "I reckon about three hun'erd.

"What are those lodges in the middle?" Dobbs asked, pointing. "The ones about fifty yards from the others."

"The li'l one on the east, the top from where we're standin', is the *Mahut* lodge. *Mahut* means 'medicine arrow.' The Cheyenne have four arrows they believe were given to them a long, long time ago by one of their main heroes, *Mutsiluiv,* which means Sweet Medicine. He got 'em from a supernatural being."

"Just plain old arrows?" asked Benoit.

"Oh, no. These is special. Beautiful workmanship. Shafts on two 'em are painted red and those are calt the buffler arrows. They believe they repr'sent prosperity. The shafts on the other two are painted black and they're calt the man arrows. They're s'posed to lead the Cheyenne to victory over their enemies."

"And they're in that lodge right there?" Benoit asked, gesturing.

"Well," Ashby drawled. "Three of 'em is. Three of the 'riginals, that is. All four o' 'em was captured by the Pawnee in a fight more'n twenty years ago. But the Lakota took three o' 'em back from the Pawnee about ten years after that and returned 'em to the Cheyenne. That's why the Cheyenne and the Lakota 're so friendly. Never found out what happen' to the fourth one, but the Cheyenne made a replacement."

"And the other small lodge?" asked Dobbs. "The one just below the medicine arrow tipi?"

"Tha's where they have their other big medicine."

"More arrows?" asked Benoit.

"Nope." Ashby smiled. "A hat."

"A *hat*!" Dobbs exclaimed. "What kind of *hat*?"

"The Cheyenne call it *Issiwun*," Ashby said. "Means 'buffalo hat' 'cause that's exactly what it is, a hat made out o' buffler hide. So that's the Issiwun lodge."

"Did it also come from Mut . . . Mutsi . . . ?

"Sweet Medicine? Nope. Ya see, a long time ago the Cheyenne was two tribes. One was the *Tsis-tsis-tas* and the other was the *Suh-tai*. Each had it's own traditions and beliefs. Sweet Medicine was the Tsis-tsis-tas' hero. The Suh-tai's was named Erect Horns or Standing on the Ground, depending on who's doin' the translatin.' He give 'em the buffalo hat so they'd always have plenty to eat."

"What's it look like? Dobbs asked curiously. "I can't imagine an Indian hat."

"I ain't never seen it myself, but I heard it described. It ain't really a hat, that's just what the white folks call it 'cause it's worn on the head. It's more of a bonnet actually. It's made from the skin of a buffalo cow. There's a horn on each side, just like a real buffler."

"I've never heard of the *Suh-tai*," Dobbs commented.

"Tha's 'cause they're most all gone now. They been ass . . . assim . . . how do you say it?

"Assimilated."

"Yep. They been *assim'lated* into the Tsis-tsis-tas. There's still a band o' 'em, as you'll see when we get into the camp. They're different from the other Cheyenne."

"Do you know where we're supposed to go?" Dobbs asked. "When we get into the camp, I mean."

"Ya see," Ashby said, pointing to the right side of the camp circle, "there's a lot of order down there although it ain't readily recognizable from here, specially to you since you don' know what to look for. The Cheyennes is right rigid. Eve'ythang they do has a reason an' a tradition behin' it. Whenever they meet in a council like this or for a Medicine Lodge—"

"A what?" asked Dobbs. "I don't think I've ever heard that term."

"White folks call it a Sun Dance. But whenever the bands come together, each one of 'em has its own spot to camp and tha's where they go time after time. We're gonna stay with an ol' friend of mine named Short Hair. He's a Scabby—"

"A what?" Benoit asked in surprise. "Did you say 'scabby'?"

"Yep," Ashby said with a grin. "If you wan' to be particular about it, he's a *Oivimanah*. That means 'Scabby Band.' "

"Where in hell did they get a name like 'Scabby'?"

"Long time ago, way I un'nerstan' it, this band had a bunch of horses that was infected with these little sores that scabbed over—"

"Mange," interrupted Dobbs.

"Right," Ashby said, nodding. "Tha's why they're calt Scabbies. But, as I was sayin', he's a Scabby but he's married to a *Iviststsinihpah*—"

"By God, that's a mouthful." Benoit laughed.

"Means 'aorta.'"

"Aorta?" Dobbs asked, raising his eyebrows. "As in 'heart'?"

"Yep. 'Cept it's buffler heart, not human heart."

"How'd they ever get a name like that?"

"Legend is, a war party from the band set off for a raid but they forgot their war pipe. Rather'n goin' back to get it, they made one out of a buffler aorta."

"Damn, they're inventive little cusses ain't they?" Benoit mumbled.

"As I was sayin,'" Ashby continued. "Under

Cheyenne custom, after a man gets married he goes to live with his wife's people. That's how come his lodge is with the Aortas. An' the Aortas always camp on the right han' side where the circle opens."

"Well, let's go on down," Benoit said, spurring his horse, a large bay gelding.

"Slow down a li'l," Ashby said. "There's a few thangs I need to 'xplain to you 'fore we get there. Some rules of Cheyenne etiquette."

"Like what?" Dobbs asked.

"Oh, simple thangs. Like when you go into a Cheyenne lodge turn to the right, never to the left."

"Why's that?"

"'Cause the left is reserved for the family what lives there. It's considered impolite to go into that area."

"Okay. Right, not left. What else?"

"When you pass the pipe always pass it to your left, never to the right."

"Jesus," Benoit said, shaking his head. "First it was right not left, now it's left not right. How in hell are we supposed to keep that straight?"

"Just keep your eyes open and don' do anything too quickly. Imitate what I do. There must be a million thangs you can and can't do in a Cheyenne camp and nobody remembers 'em all, not even the Cheyenne. Besides, you're a *Notaxe-vehoe*, a white soljer, so you ain't 'xpected to know. They'll figure you're ignoran' from the get-go."

Dobbs laughed. "Well, I guess we *are*. Ignorant, that is. At least as far as the Cheyenne are concerned."

"There's one other good thang about arriving in the middle of a council," Ashby added.

"What's that?" asked Dobbs.

"The food'll be good. There's be a lot o' feasts."

"Dog?" Benoit asked brightly.

"Yep. Tha's for sure. Since they pr'lly just got through with a hunt we'll have lots of good buffler."

"Roasts? Ribs?"

"Oh yeh. But a lot of stuff you pr'lly never tasted, 'fore too."

"Such as?"

"Buffler tongue," Ashby said, licking his lips. "Nose . . . "

"Nose?" Dobbs asked incredulously. "They eat the *nose*?"

"Damn good, too. Maybe some roasted lung. A little raw liver seasoned with gall if the hunt was recent. They also take buffler blood and cook it in the renne'—"

"The *what*?" asked Benoit.

"One of the buffalo stomachs," Dobbs said. "They have four, you know, since they're ruminants."

"God," Benoit grumbled. "A lesson in buffalo anatomy yet. I thought you were a medical doctor, not a veterinarian."

"They cook the blood in it," Ashby continued, ignoring Benoit, "until it gets like a jelly. Right tasty."

"Is there *any* part of the buffalo they don't eat?" Dobbs asked, screwing up his face.

Ashby thought for a minute. "Never heard of anythang being done with the hooves. Bones neither, 'cept they do eat the marrow."

"I knew it," Dobbs mumbled. "We should of brought Holz. She could learn a few new culinary tricks, then we could have buffalo blood whenever we wanted it. Make it a regular Monday night dinner."

"Don't pay any attention to him," Benoit whispered to Ashby. "He's from New England. All they eat up there is beans and boiled potatoes. By the time he leaves Fort Laramie he may even be looking forward to a meal of buffalo chips."

"Now tha's a new one on me!" Ashby laughed. "I

seen the Cheyenne use some chip shavin's to light their pipes 'cause it helps get the tabaccy goin', but I ain't never heard of nobody *eatin'* 'em. But then you're soljers and I always reckoned soljers was kinda crazy anyway."

If it had not been for the boy's blond hair and blue eyes, Dobbs would never have known that Werner was not just another five-year-old Indian child. His skin was tanned a deep berry-brown and his only item of clothing consisted of a miniature version of the traditional breechclout. Although it had been only eleven months since he and his brother were kidnapped in a raid on the emigrant train, his English had deteriorated almost to the point of nonexistence.

"Do you remember me?" Dobbs asked, speaking slowly and distinctly.

Werner, who had been renamed Puma by Short Hair and his wife, Red Berry Woman, looked solemnly from the physician to Benoit. "*You* . . . ," he said haltingly, pointing at Benoit, "I . . . re . . . re . . . remember. Inge's . . . *Freund. Wo ist Inge*?"

"She's at Fort Laramie," Benoit replied. "She and her mother would very much like to see you again. Do you remember Frau Schmidt?"

"*Ja, Ja,*" Puma replied enthusiastically. "She . . . good . . . *kochen.* Almost like *Mutter.*" At the mention of his mother, his face darkened and Benoit was afraid he was going to start crying. "This . . . new *Mutter,*" he said proudly, pointing at Red Berry Woman. "And . . . here . . . ," he said, walking over to Short Hair, "is *Vater.*"

Abandoning his attempts to communicate in fractured German and English, Werner reverted to Cheyenne, speaking in long bursts that left Dobbs and Benoit staring at each other in incomprehension.

"He says," Ashby translated, "that he loves Short Hair and Red Berry Woman, that his real mother and father are now dim in his memory. He says he wants to be a good son to his Cheyenne parents, that he wants to be a good warrior so he can take care of them. He is sorry about his sister, Beaver Woman, and he misses her very much."

"What happened to this girl?" Dobbs asked. "What was her name, Beaver Woman?"

"She was kilt by the Pawnee two months ago," the scout explained after a brief conversation with Short Hair. "They grabbed her durin' a raid and later sacrificed her to Morning Star. Tha's one of their chief gods," he added. "I'm right s'prised 'cause I ain't heard of a sacrifice for several years now."

"What . . ." Dobbs started to ask. Although he was deeply curious about the Pawnee sacrifice, he decided to hold his questions until later.

"I wish Erich were here to try to talk to the boy in German," Benoit said in frustration. "When do you think he'll be back?" he asked Ashby.

The scout shrugged. "I tol' him to go get some deer so we would have something to contribute to Short Hair and Red Berry Woman's larder in return for their hospitality. He could be back this evening, but it may be a couple of days. What with all the Cheyenne here now I imagine the immediate area is pretty well hunted out."

"How about the boy's brother?" Dobbs asked. "Wilhelm."

"He's called Magpie by the Cheyenne." Ashby chuckled. "I un'nerstan' he never stops chatterin'. He's living with Large-Footed Bull and Lightning Woman. But when they heard we were coming, they took the boy and went into the hills. They were afeared we'd try to take him back by force."

"Damn!" Benoit cursed softly. "I was hoping we could at least see him."

"They may come back 'fore we go," Ashby said encouragingly. "Once they realize we don' plan to snatch Puma here they may figure it's alright."

Benoit opened his mouth to reply, but was cut off by Short Hair, who launched into a conversation with Ashby.

"What was that all about?" Dobbs asked when the two men fell silent.

"Short Hair was tellin' me about a big fight they had with the Pawnee along the South Loup River a couple of months ago. He says him and Red Berry Woman stood side by side against the Wolf People—tha's what they call the Pawnee—and they counted a lot o' coup. Says Red Berry Woman even came back with a scalp."

"That's very interesting," Dobbs said. "Isn't it unusual for a woman to be involved in a fight?"

"You bet," drawled Ashby. "Short Hair says she was so angry about them Pawnee grabbin' Beaver Woman that she insisted she be allowed to go along with the war party. She done good, he says, and she made him very proud."

"A real live heroine," Dobbs exclaimed. "I'm impressed. Tell Short Hair that I'm in awe of his and Red Berry Woman's courage and I'd like to hear more details about the fight with the Pawnee at the appropriate time."

Short Hair grinned broadly when Ashby translated Dobbs's words of praise.

"He says to tell you that he would like to recount the battle for you and he 'preciates your interest. He says you ain't at all like tha' other white man."

"How's that?" Dobbs asked, surprised. "What other white man?"

"They call him Thunder Tongue," Ashby related after questioning Short Hair. "From what he says I reckon they're talkin' about that preacher who took off after he raped that woman from the Hog Ranch."

"Longstreet!" Dobbs exploded, slapping his forehead. "The Reverend W. Cleveland Longstreet. That self-righteous, satirical son of a bitch. Is he here? In the camp?"

Ashby turned to Short Hair and began questioning him in Cheyenne.

"Isn't it strange that he would turn up here, too?" Dobbs whispered to Benoit. "Ellen asked me to keep an eye out for him."

"Come to think of it, I'm not surprised," Benoit replied. "Remember when he left the post he said he was going to live with the Cheyenne. In his jumbled mind he believed God was a Cheyenne warrior."

"Short Hair says he's down with the *Issiometaniu*, the Hill People Band," said Ashby. "They're camped over in the northwest quadrant. He says they call him Thunder Tongue 'cause he's prone to makin' loud speeches. 'Course nobody can un'nerstan' him but they still like to lissen to him even if they don' know what he's talkin' about. But they don' like him too much 'cause o' the way he treats Cheyenne women."

"Maybe we ought to bring *him* back," Dobbs said bitterly. "Have him tried for attempted rape and let Kemp hang him, even though I have to admit I think hanging's too good for him."

"Short Hair wants to know if you'd like to visit his lodge," Ashby said. "He says it might not be a bad idee 'cause Thunder Tongue is powerful sick. In fac' the Cheyenne doctor don' expect him to live much longer."

"Sick?" Dobbs asked, suddenly interested. "What is it? I hope to Christ it's not smallpox."

"No, it ain't the pox," Ashby said after a brief conversation with Short Hair. "This is somethin' 'tirely different. It's somethin' he brung on hisself."

"What do you mean?"

"Well," Ashby said slowly, "firs' you gotta un'nerstan' that the Cheyenne is very puritanical people, not like them infernal Crow, who ev'rybody knows mates like dogs, right out in front of the whole village. The only injuns I know of with looser women and more perverts is the Arikaras. The Cheyenne, though, put a lot of emphasis on chastity and keepin' their women pure, specially the young'uns. They believe that women shouldn't give themselves to men until they're married."

"Sounds reasonable to me," Dobbs mumbled. "They say the same thing in New England."

"Just to make sure their daughters stay chaste, they have a rope device they use."

"A chastity belt!" Benoit said excitedly. "By God, I don't believe it."

"It's true enough," Ashby replied, nodding soberly. "They wrap a rope aroun' a young woman's waist, then through the legs an' down the thighs almost to the knees."

"If Longstreet is in trouble, I should have known it had to have something to do with a woman."

"A girl," Ashby corrected him. "Named Antelope Woman. 'Bout seventeen. Daughter of Big Bear and Pine Woman of the Hill People Band. 'Cording to Short Hair, the preacher waylaid her down by the creek. Knocked her to the groun' and tried to untie her chastity rope. Antelope Woman had been working on some fresh hides all morning and she decided, since it was a hot, dry day, to go for a quick swim. She still had her awl with her, the one she'd been using to work hides, so she stabbed Thunder Tongue with it. She took advantage of the opportunity to run away. 'Course some Cheyenne warriors went lookin' for him, but he was hidin' somewhere until a few days ago when he wandered back into camp lookin' for help. Short Hair says the doctors ain't been able to do much for him, although they been prayin' over him a lot and performin' their usual mumbo-jumbo."

"There's a man with a true appreciation of medical science," Benoit quipped, looking sideways at Dobbs.

"Goddamnit, Jean, the man may be seriously ill. And you needn't go poking fun at Indian healers."

"I wasn't poking fun at *Indian* healers," Benoit grinned.

"I'm quite in awe of some of the results I've seen on people they've treated," Dobbs went on, ignoring Benoit. "They work wonders with broken limbs, for example."

"This ain't no broken arm," Ashby interjected.

"We should just leave Longstreet to the witch doctors, then," Benoit said. "Why do we want to mess with him at all? He made his bed, now he has to sleep in it."

"I can't do that, Jean," said Dobbs. "I'm a medical doctor. If I think a man needs help, especially a white man isolated here among the Indians, I can't just ignore the fact. I'm sworn to help him. Besides, I'm curious. I don't like the sound of his condition. I'm going to have to see for myself."

The lodge was dark and the air redolent with the smell of incense. An old man named Brown Eye was hovering over the fireplace where the wood had burned down to coals. As Dobbs and Benoit watched, he worked a large coal out of the pile and moved it off to the side. After blowing on it until it glowed, he sprinkled it with a large pinch of brown powder. Immediately, the scent of sweet pine rose upward and filled the lodge. Brown Eye thrust his hands into the smoke, as if warming them. Then turning swiftly, he crossed the small space to where Longstreet lay under a buffalo robe. Pulling back the robe with the tips of his thumb and index finger, he placed his hands palms down on Longstreet's shoulder.

"What the hell's he doing?" Benoit whispered to Ashby.

"Transferring the power o' the smoke to the site of the wound," Ashby replied. "I seen it done afore. They reckon it helps the healing process."

Since they had entered the lodge quietly and had been standing off to the side, out of Longstreet's line of sight, the preacher was unaware of their presence. Dobbs used the occasion to study the man he had not seen for several months, not since he attacked Ellen O'Reilly in the Hog Ranch stable.

Dobbs remembered him as a short but powerful-looking man with a thick chest and a large head as round as a full moon. The man that Dobbs saw huddled under the buffalo robe was altogether unrecognizable as the preacher that Dobbs knew. All the color had drained from his once florid face and his heavy jowls sagged downward onto his chest, reminding Dobbs of a mound of half-melted candle wax. The preacher's dark eyes were bright with fright, and his forehead glistened with a fever-induced sweat.

"Hello, Longstreet," Dobbs said softly, moving into the preacher's line of vision.

At first, there was no indication that Longstreet understood, then his face lit up in recognition. "God has answered my prayers!" he called loudly. "This ain't a fever vision. I asked Him to deliver me from the clutches of these bungling medicine men and what does He do? He sends me the good doctor from Fort Laramie."

"How are you doing?" Dobbs asked solicitously. "Are you in pain?"

Before Longstreet could answer, Ashby reached forward and gently tugged Dobbs back a few steps.

"You can jaw with 'im in a minute. He ain't goin' nowhere. But first, let Brown Eye do his work."

The Indian, who looked to be well in his sixties, produced a rattle from a parfleche—a medicine man's medical kit—sitting by the fire, and began shaking it over Longstreet. Dobbs smiled to himself.

"Oh God, oh God, oh God," Longstreet began to wail in a high, wavering voice, the thunderous tones he once used to entertain the Cheyenne a thing of the past. "If you're really a Cheyenne help this man cure what has infected my body," he pleaded, his cry sounding so pathetic that Benoit had to turn his head in disgust.

As if inspired by Longstreet's entreaty, Brown Eye began chanting, pausing occasionally to mumble a few words that not even Ashby could understand.

"What's he doing?" Dobbs whispered, fascinated.

"The rattle is s'posed to expel the evil spirits," Ashby said, "an' the chant is a sort of prayer."

Three times Brown Eye returned to the fire, sprinkled more powder on the coal, washed his hands in the smoke, then returned to Longstreet's side to rub his shoulder anew.

"Why does he keep putting his hands *there*?" Benoit asked.

"Tha's where Antelope Woman stabbed him, an' tha's where Brown Eye figures the poison is."

Brown Eye began chanting louder, then he leaned over Longstreet and began probing his shoulder. With a shout of exultation, he leaped back, holding his hand up in the air. Turning to the white visitors, he proudly opened his fist. On his palm was a small, green chameleon, frozen in panic.

Grinning toothlessly, Brown Eye jabbered at Ashby.

"He says he got to the root o' the problem," the scout translated, struggling to keep up with the outburst. "Now that he's removed the blamed thang, Thunder Tongue will get better."

Quickly repacking his parfleche, Brown Eye made a hasty exit.

"Do *you* think that's what was causing your problem?" Dobbs asked Longstreet, moving close to the couch.

"Lord a'mighty, no," Longstreet grunted.

Dobbs frowned, staring at the preacher's face which seemed frozen in a grotesque grin, exposing small, pointed teeth coated with green.

"Yesterday it was a hunk of buffalo hair, and the day before that it was a half-dozen black pebbles. Don't know where he's getting all that stuff, but I guarantee you it isn't out of my shoulder. I fear he's never going to be able to cure me." Staring straight into Dobbs's eyes, he whispered: "Can you?"

"I don't know," Dobbs replied. "Tell me what happened."

"Well, I was having a conversation with this girl—"

"I've already heard about Antelope Woman," Dobbs

interrupted. "Tell me what happened after she stabbed you."

"Nothing happened," Longstreet said. "I knew I was in trouble so I went off in the hills to hide for a few days to let the situation calm down. That awl didn't go in real deep and I'd just about forgotten about the wound.

"A little less than a week, just when I was wondering if it was safe to go back into camp, I was pulling on my boots when my shoulder started trembling a little, twitching like."

"After that, did you find you couldn't move it normally?" Dobbs asked.

"Sure did," Longstreet said, looking surprised. "That worried me a little bit, but not too much. Figured I'd just slept on it wrong. I was getting my equipment together and all of a sudden I realized I was cold, but the sun was shining bright. A few minutes earlier, I'd been right warm. Figured it must've been a fever, like I was coming down with the ague."

"Did you have any trouble maneuvering? Were your muscles stiff and sore?"

"How'd you know that?"

"Go ahead," Dobbs said earnestly. "What happened next?"

"Well, I wasn't very hungry, which is unusual for me. And I was feeling more and more poorly. I decided to lie down for a while and that's when my jaw started twitching. Felt like there was a whole nest of mice under the skin. Then I started having trouble swallowing and I bit my tongue something fierce. Couldn't stop myself. That's when I really got scared and decided to come into the camp and take my chances. I've seen these medicine men do some good healing and I reckoned I didn't have much to lose."

"Did you have trouble walking?"

"Yep, my neck and back were so stiff I could hardly move."

"Did you think this might have some connection with that stab wound in your shoulder?"

"What? That little bitty thing? I could hardly even see where the awl had gone in! Why should that make me feel stiff and feverish?"

"Is that it?"

"Just about. Except I ain't getting any better. My face and neck hurt something terrible. I reckon I'm pretty sick, ain't I?"

"I'll be honest with you, Longstreet," Dobbs said in measured tones. "Yes. You're in pretty sad shape."

"It's that bad, huh?" he asked in a quavering voice.

"I'm afraid so. If you have what I think you do, there's nothing I can do for you."

"Oh, Jesus," Longstreet sobbed. "I was afraid of that. I know I ain't never been this sick before, but I thought it might get better."

"I don't want to raise any false hopes," Dobbs said solemnly. "You aren't going to get any better."

"What is it, doc? What's going to finally lay me low?"

"From what you've told me and from what I can see, I think you're in the later stages of tetanus."

"Oh, Jesus God," Longstreet cried, sucking in his breath. "Lockjaw!"

"That's the popular phrase," Dobbs confirmed.

"I had a cousin once who had lockjaw." Longstreet sighed. "I was just a kid, but I'll never forget. He died a terrible death. I couldn't sleep for weeks afterwards. I kept having nightmares about watching him thrash about gasping for breath."

"Is there anything you want us to do?" Dobbs asked gently. "Any unfinished business you want us to take care of?"

Longstreet shook his head slowly. "Nope. I've no family to speak of. Just a wife who left me a long time ago. Even if you could find her I don't want to give her the pleasure of knowing my fate."

"What about your possessions? How do you want them distributed?"

"There ain't enough to talk about," Longstreet mumbled. "Give 'em to the Cheyenne if they want them. They've treated me decently. You've been right kind to me, too," the preacher said, locking his eyes on Dobbs. "Considering what I done to that woman and all. She hold any grudge against me?"

"No," Dobbs replied, shaking his head. "She wrote it off as an occupational hazard."

"'Occupational hazard,'" Longstreet wheezed, trying to laugh. "That's pretty good. You might tell her though she scarred me pretty good. That riding whip left a good mark right across my tallywacker."

"I'm sure she will be happy to know that," Dobbs said dryly.

"How long have I got?" Longstreet asked, his voice pregnant with fear.

"It's hard to tell," Dobbs said. "From your symptoms I'd guess not too long."

"By God, you're brutally honest."

"Like I said, I don't want to raise any false hopes."

Longstreet rolled his eyes upward and stared at the smoke hole. "Can you do something about that light? It's giving me a ferocious headache."

"I'll talk to the Indians about it," Dobbs promised.

Longstreet tried to nod but his neck was too stiff. "Why don't y'all go away now," he said feebly. "Let me make my peace with God. I feel right weary."

"If that's what you want," Dobbs said somewhat dubiously.

"It's what I want," Longstreet replied firmly. "I reckon I've done enough wrong things in my life that I need to talk to God about privately."

"Is it as bad as it sounded?" Benoit asked as he and Dobbs strolled along the creek. After leaving Longstreet's lodge they decided to take the long way back to Short Hair's lodge, walking along the stream. "You think for sure he's a goner?"

"Barring a miracle, yes," Dobbs replied. "I saw more than a few cases of tetanus during the war and from what I've read and what I've heard from other doctors, once it sets in there's nothing that can be done."

"He seems to know what's coming," Benoit said, kicking at a small cottonwood limb that had fallen across the narrow path.

"I doubt if he realizes the full implications."

"What do you mean?"

"Tetanus is very unpleasant," Dobbs said in a detached voice that Benoit perceived as the tone of a medical school lecturer. "The name comes from the Greek word *tetanos,* which means muscle spasms. They seize the neck and the jaw. *Trismos,* the Greeks called it. In the texts it's described as 'Tonic contraction of the muscles of mastication.' The jaw clamps closed tighter than a vise. You wouldn't even be able to pry it open."

"How does that kill you?"

"It doesn't directly," Dobbs said, sounding tired. "Usually the victim strangles or asphyxiates. Sometimes they starve to death."

"Starve? My God, how long does it take?"

"Who knows? It progresses at different rates. I've seen it last anywhere from several days to several weeks."

"It doesn't sound very pretty," Benoit said softly.

"You're absolutely right about that," Dobbs agreed. "*Pretty* it is not."

For several moments neither man spoke, each lost in his own thoughts.

"You know, Jean," Dobbs said at length, "sometimes I get very disgusted with myself."

"Why's that?" Benoit asked, glancing keenly at his friend. "Because of Longstreet?"

"Yes. That primarily. I've been thinking for weeks how much I hate that man . . . "

"Because of what happened with Ellen?"

Dobbs nodded.

"You're pretty fond of her, aren't you?"

Again Dobbs nodded. "That's strange, isn't it? Me, a very proper Bostonian. I think I'm in love with a whore."

"She's not a *whore*!" Benoit said staunchly.

"You're right," Dobbs said, smiling without humor. "She's only a madam. She simply *employs* whores."

"Look, Jace," Benoit began, fumbling for words. "She's running a business . . . "

"The business of harlotry."

"It's a *business*, Jace. It's how she puts food on the table. Would you rather she starved to death?"

"Can't you just imagine what my children would think? If they knew their father was in love with a pros—excuse me, a *madam*?"

"They need never know that, Jace. Just stop for a moment and think about it. Say this uh, *relationship*, is carried out to the end . . . "

"You mean marrying her."

"Yes! Okay! Marrying her. Say you two got married and you went back East. There's no reason for *anyone* to ever know what Ellen was doing out here. Least of all your children."

"You're being very naive, Jean."

"What do you mean?"

"This is the *Army*, for Christ's sake. How many soldiers do you think have or will pass through Fort Laramie? However many it is, I'd be willing to bet you that every damn last one of them has been or will be a customer at the Hog Ranch. You think they won't remember Ellen O'Reilly, no matter what her name is? The Army is a very small world, really a sort of brotherhood. Do you honestly think Ellen's past could be kept a secret?"

Benoit was silent for a long time. "No, Jace," he said finally. "I guess it couldn't. In the long run I reckon it just depends on how strongly you feel about her and how much criticism you have the courage to face."

"It would mean the end of my career as an Army surgeon."

Again Benoit was silent. "Yes, I guess it would mean that," he reluctantly agreed. "But that doesn't mean you couldn't continue to practice medicine."

"I'm an *Army* surgeon, Jean. I've spent my whole professional life in the military. The military is my home. I can't conceive of life as a civilian."

"That does create quite a problem, doesn't it? What does Ellen say about it?"

"I don't know," Dobbs said softly. "I haven't mentioned it to her."

Benoit's head jerked up. Stopping, he grabbed Dobbs's arm and spun him about. "What do you mean you haven't mentioned it to her? Are you telling me you've been agonizing about this for God knows how long and you don't even know that you have anything to agonize *about*? I mean, for God's sake, what if she doesn't feel the same way about you that you do about her?"

"Oh, she does," Dobbs said quietly, walking ahead.

"Oh, she does, does she?" Benoit blurted, hurrying to catch up. "My God, man, I never knew you were that conceited."

"Conceit has nothing to do with it," Dobbs replied tersely. "I am sufficiently experienced with women to know when there is a mutual attraction."

"*Merde alors,*" Benoit swore. "This is a side of you I've never seen. Jason Caldwell Casanova. Lover *extraordinaire*. Philanderer *par excellence . . .* "

"Don't get insolent."

"I'm not getting insolent, I'm just trying to understand the situation."

"It isn't very difficult. Even you should be able to figure it out."

"Now who's getting insolent?"

"You're right." Dobbs smiled. "My apologies. It's my problem, not yours."

"No, that's another thing you're wrong about," Benoit said. "I'm your friend, and that's what friends are for. It's *our* problem."

"Well," Dobbs said brightly, "what do you say we put it aside for awhile. There's plenty of time to discuss this. Right now we have some more urgent issues."

"We *do*?" Benoit asked in surprise. "Like what?"

"Like Puma and Magpie."

"You mean Werner and Wilhelm?"

"No, I mean Puma and Magpie! Judging from Puma's situation I'd say right now he's definitely more Cheyenne than German. And I would assume that Magpie's degree of assimilation is even greater, considering he's younger and more susceptible, less likely to remember what life was like before he came to the Cheyenne."

"Well, what do *you* think about that? I don't see it

where we have very much option. As much as I'd like to, I don't think we'd be able to kidnap them. At least not get away with it. I doubt if we'd get a mile."

"I think you're absolutely right about that," Dobbs agreed. "So if we ever have any hope of getting them back to Fort Laramie, we're going to have to negotiate."

"Which is what Kemp figured from the beginning."

"Basically, yes. I'm impressed with his foresight."

"Guess that's why he's a colonel and I don't even have my second lieutenant's bar."

"There's some truth to that, too," Dobbs said with a grin.

"Goddamnit, Jace. You're trying my patience."

"Take it easy, Jean. I'm just pulling your leg. But let's look at this thing rationally. We've been very lucky so far."

"How do you figure that?"

"Well, there's no sign of smallpox in the camp, for one thing. You don't know how *that* was bothering me. You have no idea how vicious that disease can be. If you think what you witnessed at Blue Water was a tragedy, it's only because you've never seen variola on the rampage."

"Is that what you call it, variola?"

"It's one of the names. Not only do we escape that situation, but we're fortunate enough to arrive in the midst of a Council of Chiefs."

"A meeting called to elect a new head chief. They need to replace the one who was trampled to death by a buffalo in the spring."

"That's true, but that doesn't mean that's all they can discuss."

"Oh, I see," Benoit said cheerfully. "You want to see if we can get them to make a decision on the inoculation."

"That's one thing."

"The boys! Of course. You want them to agree to return the boys."

"Exactly," Dobbs said. "Can you think of a better venue than the Council of Chiefs? I mean, if the chiefs say the boys are to be returned, there's not a Cheyenne anywhere who will argue too hard against it."

"By God, that's a brilliant idea. I'm sure glad I thought of it."

"It doesn't matter who thought of it," Dobbs said, laughing. "The question is, can we get the matter on the table for discussion."

"Good point," said Benoit. "We need to talk to Ashby about this. There must be some sort of procedure for introducing issues."

"Yes," Dobbs agreed, bobbing his head. "There must be. I'm certainly glad you came up with the idea."

"Jace," Benoit said carefully.

"Yes?"

"What if the council says no? Then we'd *never* get them back."

"I thought of that, too. It's a calculated risk. Are you willing to gamble? Can you approach this like a very high stakes game of *bourré*? You've taken enough of my money with that damnable Cajun diversion. You think you're up to some real gambling?"

"Jace, it's not just us taking the risks. We can't gamble with the boys' lives."

"Sure we can," said Dobbs. "I gamble with lives all the time. It goes with being a surgeon. I have to make judgments like that every day. Do I do what I think is right even if it might prove fatal? Only in this case, it isn't really a question of living or dying. Besides, what do we have to lose? If the council says yes, take the boys, than we're way ahead. If they say no, then we're in no worse position than we are already."

"I need to think about it. Don't you want to consider it some more, too?"

"I've *been* thinking about it," Dobbs replied. "I've given it a lot of thought. And I think that's what we should do."

"Still . . ." Benoit began.

"Lieutenant Dobbs! Lieutenant Benoit!" Ashby called, racing forward in his peculiar crablike fashion, the result of his missing toes.

"It's Longstreet, isn't it?" Dobbs asked, feeling his stomach tighten.

"Yep." Ashby nodded. "He ain't feeling too good. He's asking for you to come."

"I was dreading this," Dobbs said, sighing. "You lead the way."

It took several seconds for their eyes to adjust to the gloom of the tent. While they stood in the dark trying to regain their breath, they could hear Longstreet from his pallet, gasping for breath and muttering incoherent pleas to God in a high-pitched voice.

"God, he sounds terrible," Benoit muttered.

"It's the ailment," Dobbs explained. "It's begun to effect his esophageal muscles. Where's Brown Eye?" the surgeon asked, looking around.

"I don't think he's going to be back," Ashby said. "He don't want to be a'sociated with a failure."

Dobbs grunted, then quickly crossed the open space to where Longstreet was stretched rigidly along the pallet, his back arched, his arms and legs sticking straight out from his body, which was as stiff as if already in rigor mortis. His teeth were clenched firmly together and his lips were drawn back in a grotesque grin. "Jesus . . . Jesus . . . Jesus . . . ," he mumbled half incoherently.

"Sumbitch," Ashby said, leaning forward for a closer look. "I ain't never seen nothin' like tha' afore."

The movement caused Longstreet to open his eyes wide, as if in intense pain. "Uh . . . uh . . . uh . . . ," he hissed, rolling his eyes in panic, like a coyote in a trap.

"Move back, Jim," Dobbs said brusquely, pushing the scout on the shoulders. "Either get out of my way or go outside."

"Sorry," Ashby mumbled, retreating several feet.

"Listen to me, Longstreet," Dobbs said calmly, looking directly into the preacher's eyes, which had stretched open as wide as they would go. Tears were flowing copiously out the corners.

"Hurts," he mumbled. "Goddamn . . . " He paused, then broke into a terror-stricken laugh that sent shivers up Benoit's spine.

"I'm sure it does," Dobbs said soothingly.

"Doc?" Ashby said, leaning closer.

"Yes!" Dobbs replied, sharper than he intended.

"They shoot horses what breaks their legs," he said steadily.

"I can't do that, man. I'm a doctor. It's against my oath."

"It ain't agin mine."

"Kill . . . me," Longstreet muttered. "End . . . suffering. See . . . God."

"I can't let you do that," Dobbs said abruptly.

"You don' have to do nothin', doc. Just go outside and get yerself a breath o' air."

"No!"

"Had a frien' oncet was gored by a buffler. He was dyin' and both of us knew it. He was in a lot o' pain and begged me to help him . . . "

"Goddamnit, I said no!"

"A'right," Ashby said softly, retreating. "Just wanted

to offer my services." Turning to Benoit, he whispered, "If you ever see me like tha' and you don' put a bullet through my head, I swear I'll come back and haunt you."

"Maybe we ought to wait outside," Benoit said kindly, taking Ashby's arm and maneuvering him into the sunshine.

Longstreet tried to talk but his words ended in a gurgle. It took two more days for him to die.

Abruptly, Red Berry Woman put down the bowl into which she had been ladling chunks of venison cut from the haunch of the deer Erich had brought in the previous day. Wiping her hands, she turned and slipped out of the lodge.

"What's wrong?" Benoit asked. "Did we offend her?"

"No." Ashby smiled. "She's just going outside where she can hear the crier better."

It was only then that Benoit became fully conscious of the monotonous, sing-song voice calling weakly from the distance. The daily appearance of the crier, the old warrior designated to spread the latest information to all sections of the camp, had become such a part of the routine that he barely noticed it. Each morning, as the women were preparing breakfast and the camp was slowly awakening, the crier made his rounds. Beginning at the opening of the "C," the eastern open side, and working his way clockwise around the compound, he called out announcements that the Cheyenne needed to know to bring the day into focus.

"What is it today?" Ashby asked a few minutes later when Red Berry Woman returned.

"The important thing is that the Council of Chiefs has ended its meeting and the camp is to begin breaking up tomorrow," she replied.

Two days previously the council had elected a middle-aged man from the *Ohktounna* Band to fill the vacant spot created by the death of Crooked Horn. Once that item had been taken care of, the agenda was opened for discussions about a myriad of other issues members of the various bands wanted to bring before the chiefs.

In short order, the forty-four-man council had disposed of the suggestion that Dobbs be allowed to inoculate all the Cheyenne gathered at the campground. While the council ruling did not preclude individual inoculation of any Cheyenne who might request it, the council emphatically declined to recommend it for the tribe as a whole.

"They're still too s'picious of the white man's medicine," Ashby had explained after listening to a long-winded accounting of the council's action from Short Hair, who had sat patiently through the entire session so he could report the results to his guests.

Since the lodge in which the council met was too small to accommodate all the members who wanted to keep abreast of the group's discussions, even though it was by far the largest in the compound, it was common practice to roll up the buffalo skin side walls so anyone who desired could come and sit on the ground outside and listen to the proceedings.

"I guess it didn't help any when I proved powerless to save Longstreet," Dobbs said sourly.

"Short Hair's too polite to mention that, but I reckon thar's some truth to what you're saying," Ashby replied. "If you could've pulled him through after Brown Eye gave up, it would've shown that you had some mighty powerful medicine. An' I guess that would've been in your favor."

"The good reverend never stopped being a problem even when he was dying," Benoit interjected. "If he had come down with something simple like a case of flux, he might've done us some good."

"In that case," Ashby said with a smile, "ol' Brown Eye probably would've been able to cure him hisself. You'd be right surprised at what these injun healers can do."

"No sense crying over split milk," Dobbs said philosophically. "Given the history of what our diseases have done to the tribes, I'm not a bit surprised the council voted the way it did. I was a lot more disappointed over the vote on the boys."

"Don't beat yourself to death on that one neither," Ashby cautioned. "It were an uphill battle all the way. The injuns feel captives rightfully belong to them an' they ain't anxious to give 'em up."

"I thought Jace's idea to offer them money for the boys was a stroke of genius," Benoit said. "I'm a little shocked they didn't take it."

"Goes to show that thangs are more important to the injuns than money," Ashby said. "It don't mean much to them. On the other han', they see those kids every day and figure that's a big investment in the future. I weren't surprised when they refused to return 'em outright. I thought the fac' that they said Short Hair could bring 'em to the fort when he returns Legendre's son at the end of the summer was a mighty big step. I reckon it helped when Lieutenant Dobbs promised that nobody would try to keep the boys thar if they didn't want to stay."

"But what if *they* decide they'd rather stay there than come back and live with Short Hair and Red Berry Woman?"

"That's a chance the Cheyenne's willin' to take," said Ashby. "I reckon they feel pretty confident it ain't gonna happen."

"What do you think, Erich?" Benoit asked suddenly. "You had better luck communicating with them in German than we had in English."

Unaccustomed to being consulted on matters of such importance, the youth began to stammer. "G-G-Gee," he stuttered, "I can't say. All I can tell you is their German isn't very good. They've forgotten a lot of words and their grammar is rotten. Both of 'em said they were happy here and their memory of living as white folks is disappearing fast. Based on what they told me, I'd say if they have a choice they'll stay with the Cheyenne."

"We could just scoop 'em up and . . ." Benoit began.

"No!" Dobbs cut him off. "We've had that discussion before. That's not an option."

"It would be easy enough . . . "

"Listen to me, Jean. That's something we're not going to even talk about. Kemp made it abundantly clear before we left Fort Laramie that he didn't want to do that. He said if the Indians wanted to release the boys, fine. Bring them back. If not, don't force the issue. You remember him saying that, don't you?"

"Yes, but . . . "

"No buts. As reluctant as I would be to pull rank on you don't think for a second that I wouldn't."

"Holz's heart will be broken."

"She'll just have to get used to the idea. Kemp is looking at the big picture. He wants to avert a war with the Indians."

"I don't think taking two white boys would touch off a war."

"Maybe not that in itself but it would be one more

thing they could use against us later. Now let's talk about something else."

"Why don' you let me take you 'round the camp," said Ashby, who had been uncomfortably following the exchange between the two soldiers. "You may not ever get to see another Cheyenne council gathering."

"Sounds good to me," Dobbs said, rising stiffly. "What with the Longstreet incident I've hardly seen anything at all of Cheyenne life."

"I'd like that, too," echoed Benoit. Turning to Dobbs, he added: "Jace, don't hold it against me because of the way I feel about getting the boys back."

"On a personal level, I agree with you to a certain extent," Dobbs conceded. "But this goes beyond any feelings you or I might have. We still have to follow orders."

"We can discuss it with Kemp again when we get back, can't we?"

Dobbs sighed. "I swear, Jean, you're probably the most mule-headed man I've ever known. Yes, goddamnit, you can discuss it with Kemp when we get back but I doubt if it will do any good."

"What the hell," Benoit said, laughing, "we've got another six to eight weeks to work on him. It'll be that long before Short Hair comes back with David."

"Where do you get this 'we' crap, Jean? As far as I'm concerned, you're all by yourself on this one."

"Fair enough. As long as we know where we stand."

"Do you mind if I disappear?" Erich asked. "Jim tells me Short Hair wants to go out looking for elk. If he'll take me with him, I'd like to go along. See how a real injun hunts. No offense, Jim," he added hurriedly. "I reckon you can hunt as good as any Cheyenne, but I might pick up some ideas we can use later."

"Don't be gone more than a day," Dobbs said. "When the big camp breaks up we're going to be going too."

"Right," Erich said cheerfully. "You know," he added somewhat dreamily, "in a way I envy Wilhelm and Werner. I'd give anything to be able to live up here for a year."

When Ashby, Benoit, and Dobbs exited Short Hair's lodge they emerged into a world teeming with activity. Men were gathering their horses, preparing, like Short Hair, to ride into the hills to search for game. Because of the social obligations demanded of them as a result of the large meeting, what with feasts once or twice a day to celebrate old friendships or cement new ones, the supply of fresh meat in virtually every lodge was running low. Once the camp broke up individual bands would scatter and each would hold its own buffalo hunt. In the meantime, though, the larder had to be replenished.

The Cheyenne, like other Plains tribes, kept their horses pastured some distance from the camp. The longer they stayed in one place, the farther outward the pastures moved as the animals depleted the nearby grass. For the most part, boys too young to join the raiding parties but too old to engage in the children's games were entrusted with watching and collecting the herd. Every day, as soon as the sun peaked over the horizon, they gobbled down their boiled meat and raced to the pasture to gather the horses and bring them back to camp. The warriors then moved among the animals, selecting the ones they felt they would need for whatever activities they had planned for the day. Once they picked their horses and tethered them outside their lodges, the boys took the others back to pasture.

As the men went out to hunt or scrutinize the council's actions, the women busied themselves with tasks that needed to be performed to keep the camp operating smoothly. If their husbands had recently returned with game, they prepared the meat and dressed the skins. If there was no butchering to be done, they set to work repairing lodges so they would be in good shape when autumn arrived, or they began their food preparation, taking advantage of the long summer days and the availability of fresh fruits and vegetables.

Considering the aridity and the harshness of the winters, the Plains was a remarkably bountiful supplier of food. In addition to the buffalo, there was deer, elk, mountain sheep, and antelope. The lakes that dotted the mountain valleys provided fish and a variety of fowl such as geese, ducks, and cranes. The high-altitude forests were also home to bears and a variety of small game, such as rabbits and raccoons. In the fall, the Cheyenne held communal skunk hunts in which an entire village would converge on an area in which the animals were abundant and track them down as enthusiastically as they hunted buffalo. At the end of the day, all the skunks that had been killed were brought into camp and parcelled out to individual families, who utilized both the meat and the hides. Vegetables and fruits, such as cherries and berries, were available for the picking, as were bird and duck eggs.

Originally an agrarian people from the western end of the Great Lakes, the Cheyenne spoke a dialect of the Algonquian language and lived in large earth lodges like the Pawnee, growing corn and other vegetables while depending heavily on fish and small game. Moving westward in response to population pressures after the arrival of the white man, they acquired the horse and drifted to the Plains, where they learned to adapt to an entirely new lifestyle.

Although game and fish supplemented their diet,

nothing could supplant the buffalo, which provided not only food but the raw materials for an amazing variety of items invaluable to the tribe. Tanned buffalo hide was used for lodge coverings, robes, and practically every item of clothing a Cheyenne might own, from belts and caps to dresses and leggins. Rawhide was fashioned into moccasin soles, shields, drums, saddles, and other tack. The horns were carved into utensils used for cooking and eating; the bones provided material for knives, arrowheads, and tools. Buffalo hair was woven into rope. The buffalo's internal organs—the bladder, paunch, and stomach—were used as cooking pots or water jugs, while sinew served as thread and bowstrings. Buffalo brains were used to tan the hides, and the chips were used as fuel. One would be hard put indeed, Ashby explained to Benoit and Dobbs, to find a part of the buffalo that was not utilized by the Cheyenne and the other Plains tribes in some form or fashion.

When the Cheyenne warriors went off to hunt and the women busied themselves with duties necessary to keep the camp functioning, the children turned to play.

"One thang you'll notice about injun children is that they're hardly ever disciplined," Ashby pointed out. "They don't whup their kids like white folks do, figurin' it makes more sense to talk to 'em than to whack 'em. 'Cept for cryin,' that is. Since a cryin' child could give away a hidin' place, they begin teachin' 'em real early that silence is golden."

"How do they do that if they don't spank them?" Dobbs asked.

"They hold their nostrils shut or pour water in their noses until they get the idea. It don' take long."

"Doesn't the lack of physical discipline make the children harder to control?" Dobbs asked.

"Naw," said Ashby. "Le's stop here for a minute and watch. Firs' you gotta un'nerstan' that the Cheyenne, like the others, believe that all chillin are under special protection from the Creator. While they don't whack 'em they're also careful not to love 'em too much because they believe that might send 'em back to the Creator."

"In other words, they believe it's possible to kill 'em with love?"

Ashby nodded. "Tha's right. At the same time, they don' want to make 'em too unhappy either because tha' might rile the Creator."

"So they spare the rod?"

"It ain't really a question of sparin' it; the idee that they could use a rod in the firs' place never enters their minds. All in all the system works right good 'cause the chillin's are continually gettin' lectures about their responsibilities to the tribe. Pretty soon they begin to realize that they should do what's right not 'cause they're gonna get walloped iffen they don', but 'cause it's their duty. But I ain't never seen a society in which the young'uns can have more fun than among the injuns. See them kids over thar? They ain't old enough yet to participate in the serious games so they can do prac'cally anythang they want."

Dobbs and Benoit looked to where Ashby was pointing. A group of children roughly between four and eight were splashing in the creek or chasing each other around a large cottonwood. Another group sat along the creek bank, molding figures out of mud.

"There goes David," Benoit said, laughing as Legendre's son raced by astride a stick meant to serve as a horse, dragging another stick—his war horse—behind him.

"And there's Puma." Dobbs pointed. The boy, easily

recognizable because of his almost-white hair, wrestled with an older boy, the two of them tumbling down a creek bank and into the water. Both came up laughing and shaking themselves like wet dogs.

"When they git a li'l older, about like that group over thar," Ashby said, gesturing, "they begin to play games associa'ed with the roles they're gonna have to perform later. See them girls? They're playing with dolls, treatin' 'em just like they was real babies. But the boys over thar—" he pointed in the opposite direction "—are learnin' about huntin' by playin' with li'l bows their fathers whittled for 'em. Them over thar are playin' a game calt *ehyoanisko*. It means 'arrow mark.' They use special arrows which is about twice as long as a re'glar arrow. It's also heavier on the pointy end. The object is to heave one arrow about fifty yards away to use as a mark. Then the others try to toss their arrows as close to that first 'un as possible. They git right damn good at it, too. I seen contests where there may be thirty or more arrows within a four-foot circle, so close to the mark they have to use a piece of sinew to decide who's closest."

"Those boys over there are using a moving target," Benoit said excitedly.

"Tha's one of the wheel games they play," Ashby said. "They make a wheel about a foot in diameter by bending a willow branch and then addin' rawhide webbing. One boy rolls the wheel and others try to spear it with their throwing sticks."

While Benoit, Ashby, and Dobbs watched the stick throwers, a group of older boys divided themselves into two factions, then went at each other with all the enthusiasm of Cheyenne and Pawnee trying to kill each other in a skirmish. The action, however, stopped short of serious physical harm.

"These games can get kinda rough," Ashby explained. "Sometimes they act like they're raiding a village an' have at each other pretty good. They fight with lances made outta willow branches an' li'l shields, or with tiny bows an' arrows tipped with prickly pear thorns. The objec' is to grab specially prepared hunks of buffalo hair danglin' from poles, which repr'sent scalps. Sometimes the gals get involved, too, treatin' the wounded an' all. Afterwards, they even blacken their faces, just like members o' a successful war party would do, and perform a scalp dance."

"The boys and girls separate pretty quickly, don't they?" Dobbs asked, pointing at a group of older girls in a circle off to the side. One of the girls was balancing in the instep of her foot a ball about eight inches in diameter.

"The ball's made o' buffalo skin stuffed with antelope hair," Ashby explained. "They try to see how many times the girl with the ball can kick it up without lettin' it touch the ground. Generally," he continued, "once the chillin' get to be about eight or nine they go their separate ways. After tha', there ain't much contact between the sexes 'cept for courtin'."

"How *do* they conduct a courtship?" Benoit asked, "considering what you said earlier about the emphasis on chastity."

"It's a real interestin' thang to observe." Ashby chuckled. "Kinda like animals tryin' to get together. A boy might sit by the trail waitin' for a special girl to pass, then try to get her atten'n by tuggin' at her robe. Or he might carve hisself a flute and try to influence her with his playin.' Occasionally, a couple will sneak off into the bushes together but it's pretty rare. Iffen a girl gets carried away and beds with a boy and the others find out about it, her life is just about ruint. Nobody else'll marry her. As an example of how seriously they take it, it's agin the custom for a boy, once he gets to warrior age, even to *talk* to his older sister."

"Do they have much say-so in who they want to marry?" Dobbs asked.

"Naw, not a lot. Occasionally you hear of a couple elopin' but usually the girl marries who her family wants her to."

"Does a man take just one wife?"

"Usually depends on how well he's been doin'. A man with a lot of horses may take a second wife. More offen than not, she's a younger sister of his first wife. I knowed one man what had five wives, all of 'em sisters. The Cheyenne believe if the wives aren't related, that makes for trouble in the tipi."

"What happens if a man and woman don't get along?" Benoit asked, caught up in the spirit of the discussion.

"Oh, they git divorced," Ashby said matter-of-factly. "Just like white folks 'cept it ain't nearly as formal. What usually happens is a man who's unhappy with his wife goes to a meetin' of his military society and takes along a stick. Oncet all the members get there, he starts singin' a special divorce song and beatin' on a drum with the stick. Then he throws the stick in the air and says tha's his wife and anybody who wants her can have her. I heard one o' 'em oncet say he'd toss in a horse to boot to the man what picked up the stick. One warrior picked up the stick quick enough and claimed the horse, but said he didn't want the woman."

"Sounds to me like it's very handy to be a male in the Cheyenne society," Benoit joked. "Seems as if the women don't have much authority."

"Oh, no, tha's where you're wrong, lieutenant. Don' git fooled by 'pearances. It's the women who actually run the camp. They may look like they're just slaves to the men, but once they get in their lodges they can say whatever they want to their husbands and give 'em hell. There ain't nothing to stop 'em from gettin' into politics, neither. I heard about several women chiefs. Sometimes, the women even go on to war, like Red Berry Woman did after the Pawnee took her daughter. She stood right up thar with Short Hair and fought them Pawnee just as viciously as any warrior in the group. If I remember correctly, she kilt two of 'em all on her lonesome."

"What's that lodge over there," Dobbs asked, pointing to a tipi that stood alone on the very edge of the encampment, well away from any of the other lodges. "I've never seen one painted red before."

"I was wonderin' if you'd notice tha'," Ashby said with a smile. "Tha's whar Big Nose lives."

"Am I supposed to know who Big Nose is?"

"Naw, I reckon not. You ain't been out here long enuf yet. Big Nose is a famous Cheyenne warrior, one hell of a good fighter with a whole bunch of honors to his credit."

"Is that why his lodge is painted?"

"Nope, that has nothin' to do with it. Big Nose's lodge is red 'cause he's a *hohnuhke*."

Dobbs and Benoit looked at each other. "Is that one of the bands?" Benoit asked.

"Does it mean he has a special job, like a shaman?" Dobbs echoed.

The scout grinned. He was enjoying himself tremendously. Being a guide and instructor for two Army officers was not an opportunity that presented itself every day. Ignoring their questions, he started walking toward Big Nose's lodge. "Let's go say hidy," he said.

Big Nose, as long and lanky as Dobbs, was sitting in the sun, resting his back against a cottonwood trunk. On his head was a hat made from some sort of feathers,

Benoit noticed. The Indian's hair, visible beneath the cap, was divided into braids, which were wrapped with hide. Around his neck was a piece of wood about as thick as Benoit's index finger. Looking closely, Benoit could see that it was a whistle.

Big Nose's torso was crisscrossed with old battle wounds, including one long, raised scar that ran over his shoulder and down his chest, almost to his sternum. "I'd say that was a whip scar," Dobbs said, studying the old wound with a professional eye. "At one time somebody really laid into him."

"When you said his name was Big Nose," Dobbs added, turning to Ashby, "I was expecting to find a man with a large proboscis. But his isn't extraordinarily outsized."

"The name came from the trappers," Ashby explained. "When he was a young'un he used to sidle up to every white man he ran acrost and badger him with questions. They took to calling him 'nosy,' which got translated to Big Nose."

Seeing them approach, Big Nose sat upright. Yelling loudly, he gestured to them, signalling they should not come any closer.

"What was that he hollered?" Dobbs asked, stopping in his tracks.

"He tole us to go away," Ashby said, chuckling.

"What's so funny about that?" Dobbs asked, irritated. "If he doesn't want our company we should let him be."

"Wha' I ain't tole you yet is that hohnuhke means 'contrary.'"

"Contrary to what?" Dobbs asked, frowning. "What's he opposed to? Is he some sort of troublemaker?"

Ashby bent over laughing. "'scuse me," he gasped. "Can't help myself."

"I wish I knew what was so damn funny," Dobbs grumbled.

"I wish I knew why we're still going to the lodge when that injun told us to get lost," added Benoit.

"Lemme explain to you," Ashby said, gulping for air. "Contraries is injuns who do things backwards. When they say, 'go away,' they really mean 'come on over and set.' If they say 'no,' they mean 'yes.' If they tell their woman they have plenty of water, she knows she'd better hurry on down to the stream. If Big Nose says he ain't hungry, what he means is he could eat a whole damn buffalo all by hisself."

"Are you serious about this?" Dobbs asked, astonished. "This isn't some kind of joke?"

"I'm as serious as mortal sin." Ashby laughed. "Contraries is part of the injun culture. Every Plains tribe I ever heared about has 'em. Las' I heard, the Cheyenne had about three of 'em, Big Nose here and two o' 'em with the *Hofnowas* Band. They live in a lodge painted 'actly like this 'un and they live by the same rules."

"If every tribe has these contraries, how come I never heard of them when I was with the Wazhazhas?" Benoit asked, sounding doubtful.

"Don' know," Ashby replied, shrugging. "Maybe there ain't one in that band. Or maybe you just never noticed 'cause they always live off by theirselves and never in the main camp."

"I guess that's possible," Benoit said grudgingly. "That they might be there and I never saw them, that is."

"What function do they perform?" Dobbs asked. "What sets them on this curious path?"

The way I un'nerstan' it a man becomes a contrary because he's petrified of the thunder."

"Thunder?" Dobbs asked incredulously. "You mean like with the rain? Boom!"

"Yep." Ashby nodded. "But really it's the lightnin' they afeared of. They got a special device they carry called a 'thunder bow' an' they believe they're safe as long as they have that. The thunder bow keeps 'em from being hit by a lightnin' bolt. Le's go see if Big Nose'll shown you his 'un."

When they approached, Big Nose stared at them in apparent anger and turned the corners of his mouth down in an exaggerated demonstration of distaste.

"See how glad he is to see you?" Ashby roared. "He's damn near droolin' with delight."

While Big Nose and Ashby jabbered in Cheyenne, Benoit looked at Dobbs and rolled his eyes. "Do you believe this?" Benoit whispered. "I'm thinking it's some sort of elaborate prank designed to make us look silly."

"Big Nose wants me to tell you that you are not welcome in his lodge," Ashby translated. "That means he wants us to come inside."

At first glance, the interior seemed to Dobbs to be no different from the inside of the lodge in which they had been staying as guests of Short Hair and Red Berry Woman. In the center was a fireplace with coals glowing redly. Big Nose went directly there and began preparing a meal of boiled meat to honor his guests.

"Look," Benoit said, nodding with his head. "There's no bed at the back of the lodge, which is the favorite spot in other Cheyenne tipis."

"Big Nose don' have a bed," Ashby said. "It's agin the custom. He has to sleep on the groun'. Can't even *sit* on a bed. The place at the back o' the fire, the spot of honor, is reserved for the thunder bow. If there's a storm, Big Nose brings it in and puts it thar. If you ever see one inside a lodge, remember never to try to pass between it and the fire. Tha's one of the taboos."

"Where is it now?" Dobbs asked, gesturing to the empty spot.

"If it ain't rainin' or snowing, it's kept hangin' on a pole out back."

While waiting for the water to boil, Big Nose went outside. When he returned he was carrying an object about five feet long wrapped in tanned hide. Lashed to the bundle was a short forked stick, painted red, and sharpened at one end.

"Big Nose must like you to fetch his thunder bow," Ashby said. "But don't try to handle it," he cautioned. "If anybody but Big Nose touches it, that person has to be purified by being wiped down with white sage. A contrary's wife ain't even allowed to pick it up. The only time someone else might touch it is when Big Nose asks a young warrior to hol' it for him if he's tryin' to do somethin' else. But after he gits it back, he has to rub the man down with white sage."

"What's the penalty for violating the prohibition?" Dobbs asked.

"The Cheyenne believe you'll be struck by lightnin'."

Seeing the twin looks of disbelief, Ashby shrugged. "Tha's what they believe. I ain't swearing it's true."

Frowning mightily, Big Nose peeled off the hide cover and exposed the thunder bow. Pushing the forked stick into the ground, he reverently laid the instrument down with its end resting in the Y of the sharpened branch. Benoit and Dobbs leaned close to examine it, careful to keep their hands on the ground at their sides.

"They call it a *hohnukawo*, which means 'contrary bow,'" Ashby said.

"It has two strings," Benoit pointed out.

"And a lance head on one end," added Dobbs, indicating the pointed end that rested in the forked stick.

"What's that?" he asked, pointing with his chin, at what appeared to be a small collection of feathers.

"Tha's the skin of a tanager," said Ashby. "See the bird's red head? Whenever Big Nose goes on a raidin' party or the camp moves, he paints hisself red, s'posedly because of the red in the bird. The Cheyenne believe the bird represents the man's body."

"What are all those carvings?" asked Dobbs.

"Dun' know," Ashby replied. "They have meaning only to Big Nose."

"And those other feathers?"

"Them is owl, same as the ones his hat is made of. Contraries got a partic'lar fascination with owls but I ain't sure what it means."

"He actually *fights* with that?" Benoit asked in awe.

"Well, sorta. You can bet your ass he fights. When he goes into a tussle he can fight just like anyone else, that is he can move forward or back'ard depending on conditions, as long as he's holdin' the thunder bow in his left han'. Howsomever, if he transfers it to his *right han'*, blows his whistle, an' makes a call like a burrowin' owl, tha' means he can't retreat under no circumstances. He has to keep chargin' the enemy 'til he wins, they run, or he gets kilt. While he has the thunder bow with 'im he don't use it as a weapon. It's only for countin' coup."

"Fascinating," Dobbs whispered. "Absolutely fascinating."

"I only tol' you a li'l bit about a contrary," Ashby said. "There's all kinds of customs and taboos, a lot of which I don't know myself. I know when one o' them's on the march he has to go off by hisself and walk on the side 'cause the Cheyenne believe if anyone steps in his tracks they'll go lame. Whenever they fin' enemy tracks, they call the contrary over and let him stomp on the footprints hopin' it'll cripple the enemy or they'll get exhausted and the Cheyenne can catch up with 'em. If he sees horse tracks made by an enemy, he jabs 'em with the point o' his thunder bow for the same reason. There's a whole other set o' rules about what applies in camp. I know he can't go into a crowd, for example, such as a group at a dance, an' he can't enjoy hisself like the others 'cause he's forbidden from jokin' aroun'."

"Why in hell would anyone want to be a contrary then?" Benoit asked. "It doesn't seem like a very attractive way to live."

"They don't have no choice," Ashby said gravely. "They usually have a vision in which they're *ordered* to become contraries. The injuns is plumb big believers in visions."

Big Nose interrupted with a burst of Cheyenne.

"He says we should go now," Ashby said. "Tha' means it's time to eat."

Apparently without giving it a second thought, Big Nose plunged his bare hands into the water in which the meat was boiling, submerging them up to his elbow.

"Good God!" Dobbs gasped, making a move to rescue the man.

"Just sit!" Ashby said sternly, grabbing Dobbs's shoulder and pulling him down. "Big Nose knows what he's doin'."

Nonchalantly, Big Nose kept plunging into the container until he fished out all the meat, which he then put in bowls and handed around, keeping one for himself.

"Jesus Christ. I don't believe what I just saw," Dobbs exclaimed breathlessly. "Jean, tell me I wasn't hallucinating. I *did* see him repeatedly stick his hand in boiling water, didn't I? And he gave no outward indication of trauma."

"I saw it, Jace," Benoit whispered. "But I don't know what it means."

"Is it some kind of trick he's performing for our benefit?" Dobbs asked Ashby.

"I seen it any number of times at ceremonies," Ashby replied, grinning. "They want you to believe it's some kind o' magic but I 'spect it ain't no real mystery. A Cheyenne friend of mine oncet showed me a plant he said was calt *onuhkiseeyo*, which means 'contrary medicine.' The contraries dry the leaves, then grind them to powder which they rub on their arms to get protection from the heat. Big Nose musta rubbed some on when he went to get the thunder bow."

"Well, thank God there's some sort of rational explanation for it." Dobbs sighed in relief. "But I'd sure like to see some of that plant."

"It ain't found 'round here," Ashby said, "but next time I'm in an area where it grows, I'll bring you a few twigs."

Big Nose gobbled his meat and carefully put his bowl on the ground, next to a carved horn he'd been using as a water goblet.

"What curious artwork," Dobbs said, reaching for the horn.

"Don' touch that!" Ashby said loudly, reaching out to grab the physician's hand.

"Wh-Wh-what did I do?" Dobbs asked, pulling his hand back as if it had been jabbed.

"Didn't mean to scare you," Ashby said, "but that's a taboo. Contraries have special utensils only them can touch."

Frowning, Big Nose removed a handful of white sage from a container he wore around his waist, and delicately wiped his plate before setting it aside.

"I think it's time we got goin'," Ashby said. "We don't wan' to wear out our welcome."

Thanking Big Nose profusely for his hospitality, the

three men backed out of the lodge. Just as they lowered the flap, Big Nose called out in Cheyenne.

Ashby looked at Dobbs and Benoit, trying to smother a grin. "He says not to hurry back."

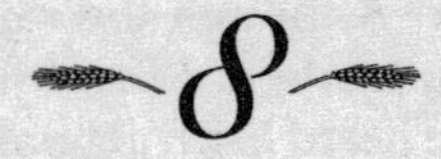

There was a flash of lighting that lit the midnight darkness brighter than noon. Milliseconds later, a peal of thunder rolled and reverberated across the valley like the sound of a hundred siege cannons. Then, with a powerful gust that whistled and shrieked through the cottonwoods, the storm was upon them, catching the three men and teenage boy before they could stumble out of their bedrolls. Pelted by fist-sized hailstones and raindrops so large a single one would half-fill a shot glass, they dashed about in mad confusion, staggering like drunks. "God*damn*it!" Dobbs screamed when he stepped on one of the hot coals scattered around the campsite by the same sudden, violent gust that uprooted a fifty-year-old tree twenty yards up the creek and sent it crashing to the ground. "My boots!" he howled, hopping on one leg like a crippled kangaroo. "I can't find my fucking boots!" Abandoning the search, he hopped across the clearing on one leg, grimacing and cursing when his burned foot happened to touch the rough ground. "Get the horses," he bellowed. "Goddamn these rocks! Don't let the horses get away."

"Putain de merde," Benoit cursed as he tripped over a

half-buried boulder and pitched headfirst into the stream, which already was beginning to rise as a result of the downpour. Although the rain was pounding down so loudly it made it difficult to hear distinctly, Dobbs was sure he heard Erich giggling.

After gathering the horses, they decided to pack up and move on since everything they carried was soaked. "There's no sense trying to go back to sleep," Dobbs explained. "We may as well get an early start."

Three hours later the thunder and lightning had abated somewhat, but the rain continued to fall as heavily as before.

"Back in New Orleans, I've seen storms that made kindling out of mansions," Benoit commented philosophically as the waterlogged party slogged down the muddy trail, "and rain comes two or three times a week as regular as clockwork. But I've *never* seen a storm that sprung up as rapidly and hit as hard as this one."

"We're lucky we got the horses 'fore they could scatter," said Ashby. "Otherwise, we'd still be searchin' for 'em. They plumb don't like that crackin' 'n flashin'."

"Just goes to show they aren't so stupid after all," agreed Benoit.

"That was the hardest I've laughed in a long time," Erich said, grinning brightly through the water that poured off his hat brim and down the back of his neck like water rushing off a pitched roof.

"I'm glad you can see the humor in it," Dobbs grumbled, trembling from the sudden chill that shook his body from his water-filled boots to his dripping nose. "How much longer you think it's going to go on?" he asked wearily, turning to Ashby. "We need to get in some dry clothes pretty soon or we're all going to come down with pneumonia."

"Hard to tell," the scout replied, unable to see more

than a few feet through the rain and clouds. "I've seen 'em like this that go on a coupla days."

"Now *that*'s encouraging."

"Guess we should have stayed at the camp one more day." Dobbs groaned. "A nice dry tipi would have been preferable."

"Doan reckon we're goin' to find many tracks after this gully washer. You wanna keep on lookin' for them injuns?" Ashby asked Dobbs.

"I think we should," the surgeon replied grimly. "If those infected braves never made it to the council meeting they may have gotten sick along the way."

"Maybe they wasn't even Cheyenne," Ashby pointed out. "They coulda been 'hoes or Pawnee. I mean, they might not been headin' north atall, as Ryan thought. They coulda been going northeast or even south."

"I realize it's a long shot, but I don't want to give up so soon. If there's any chance we can avert a smallpox outbreak, we need to keep trying to find them."

"I say we give it two or three more days and if we don't have any luck we head on back to Fort Laramie," Benoit suggested. "We've been gone almost two weeks."

"That's reasonable," agreed Dobbs. "Let's do this. We'll keep heading south until we reach the Platte. If there's no sign of them by then, we'll turn west and head back to the post."

"Sounds good to me," Ashby concurred. "Me 'n Erich gotta start thinkin' about stockin' up on some buffler. The summer ain't gettin' any longer."

"Did you hear that?" Ashby asked, jerking his pony to a halt.

"Hear what?" asked Benoit, who was slumped in his saddle convinced he was as tired, cold, and wet as he had ever been. "The only thing I hear is the squishing sound we make with every step."

"I thought I heard gunfire," the scout replied, cocking his head.

"Must have been the thunder," Dobbs said, his pale lips trembling from another chill. "I don't hear anything."

"There it is again," Ashby insisted. "By God, I think that's rifle fire."

"You're hearing things," Benoit mumbled. "Your ears are full of water."

"No he isn't," Erich said excitedly. "I hear it too. Up ahead, over the hill. Sounds like several rifles. Hunters?" he asked, turning to Ashby. "Injuns after bufflers?"

"Doan think so," Ashby replied, straining. "Hesh for a second."

Dobbs and Benoit looked at each other, then at Ashby, who was leaning forward in his saddle as if six extra inches would give him an advantage.

"Tha's gunfire all right. Rifles and pistols, too, I reckon. Tha' means it ain't no hunters. Must be a fight o' some kind."

"Then lets' go see what it is," Benoit urged, preparing to dig his spurs into his horse's flanks.

"Hang on," Ashby said, grabbing the reins to Benoit's horse. "It doan pay to go runnin' into somethin' we doan know what it is. Lemme ride ahead 'n take a look-see. No sense jest walkin' into trouble. Fer all we know it could be a trap o' some sort."

"Go ahead," Dobbs said, momentarily forgetting his discomfort. "But don't be gone too long. If you aren't back in twenty minutes, we're going to come looking for you."

"Make it thirty," Ashby said, riding off. "It mite be further'n it sounds. C'mon, Erich, you come with me."

"What do you think it is?" Benoit asked anxiously. "Could be those deserters fighting with some Indians."

"Maybe some Indians fighting among themselves?"

"With pistols? I've never heard of them using side arms."

"Me either," Dobbs said. "Must be the fever making me talk nonsense. Anyway, no sense trying to strain our brains working out possibilities. I figure we'll know soon enough. Your ammunition dry?"

"Good point," Benoit said. "Wouldn't hurt to reload, would it?"

"It's a wagon train," Ashby barked, galloping back to join Benoit and Dobbs fifteen minutes later.

"Indian attack?" Benoit asked excitedly.

"No, doan think so," Ashby replied, puzzled. "I topped the rise jest in time to see a group riding off to the west and they didn' look like no injuns to me."

"Must be those goddamn deserters," Benoit swore. "Why in hell are they raiding a wagon train?"

"Payroll, I'll bet," Dobbs said somberly. "They must be after the money. Let's go see what damage they did. Was anybody riding after them?"

"Not yet," said Ashby, "but I reckon there will be soon. I imagine there's a lot of 'fusion down thar right about now."

"Just who in hell you think you're giving orders to?" an angry Alf Stuart demanded of Dobbs. "This is *my* train and you ain't got no say in what we're gonna do." A gray-haired, middle-aged man with a huge belly and a bellowing, whisky-deepened voice, Stuart was a minor legend on the Plains, a former trapper turned emigrant guide infamous from the Missouri River to the Pacific Coast for his fierce temper and bullying ways.

"I see he hasn't changed at all, has he?" Benoit whispered to Ashby. "Still the same lovable old son of a bitch he was last year."

"I heard that, you goddamn pup," Stuart said, spinning angrily to face Benoit. "Guess a year's experience in the West ain't taught you nothing atall. But then you never were too bright to begin with."

"Goddamnit, Stuart . . ." Benoit said, rising out of his saddle.

"Hold on, Jean," Dobbs said, grabbing his friend's arm. "He's right. He's in charge of the train and what he says goes. We're just here to offer assistance if he wants it."

"And I don't." Stuart spat. "Not from you or any other soljer. We take care of our own troubles."

"How many were there?" Dobbs asked.

"I counted seven, including the two we dropped."

"You killed two of them?"

"I didn't say killed. I don't know if they're dead or not. I know they're on the ground and they ain't moving much."

"How about the emigrants? Are there any wounded?" he asked, pointing toward the train a mile away. The group from Fort Laramie had been riding toward the group when they met Stuart and a dozen of his men heading out, following the fleeing raiders.

"Yep," Stuart replied. "There's some hurt."

"But the rest of the attackers got away?"

"Yep. Along with the Army's money an' a mucketymuck civilian."

"A civilian?" Dobbs asked, his eyebrows arching in surprise. "Why would they take a prisoner?"

"Ain't got time to chat," Stuart replied brusquely. "Not iffen we got any hope o' catching those bastards."

"I'll go see what I can do for the wounded," Dobbs said. "Jean, you and Jim and the boy go with Stuart. Give him a hand."

"I don't recall asking for any help from you or your kind," Stuart growled. "Howsomever, I guess I kaint refuse any able bodies. Nothin' else, I can use 'em for bait. 'Specially that Cajun dandy."

"Stuart," Benoit began, his face as red as a desert sunset, "it'll be a cold day in hell . . . "

"That's enough, Jean," Dobbs said sternly. "Remember your duty. Kemp'll flat eat you alive, you cause any problems."

"Okay, Jace," Benoit mumbled sullenly. "I'll go but I don't much like taking orders from this Yahoo."

"What's this Yahoo crap?" Stuart said menacingly. "You calling me a bad name?"

"Not at all," Benoit replied, grinning. "The Yahoos are a famous people in a novel by an Englishman named Jonathan Swift."

"Famous, huh?" Stuart asked, eyeing Benoit suspiciously.

"Known throughout the English-speaking world," Benoit said, struggling to keep from laughing.

"Okay," Stuart said, mollified. "'Bout time you showed some respect. Let's go get them sons o' bitches."

Dobbs, bloody to his elbows, contemplated the pulsing wound in the side of his moaning patient, a lean, tow-haired youth who appeared to be still in his teens.

"Goddamn, doc," the youth said, staring at Dobbs through eyes opened wide in pain, "can't you go a little easier?"

"What makes you think I'm a doctor?" Dobbs asked distractedly, probing into the tear made by the bullet below the man's rib cage. "I never introduced myself as a physician."

"Saw your epaulets 'fore you took off your blouse."

"You a soldier, son?"

"Used to be. Private Oscar Anderson, Sixth Infantry. Fort Kearny. Besides, I remember you from last year. When you and that other soldier killed the trooper who didn't take kindly to being branded."

"You got a good memory, son. Was that man a friend of yours?"

"Not exactly. We were in the same company, that's all."

"You a deserter, too?"

The youth eyed Dobbs warily. "I don't think I ought to answer that, lieutenant."

"You don't have to." Dobbs smiled. "You've already told me. Besides, how long you think it would take to learn that once you're at Fort Laramie?"

"Is that where we're going? Provided I live that long, that is."

"Oh, you'll live to make it. Your wound may be painful, but it isn't mortal. You took a big slug, but near as I can tell it missed your vital organs, particularly the liver."

"How can you tell that?"

"Give me some credit, private. I've seen enough wounds to know if the liver's been damaged. The blood is a different color. If your liver had been damaged it would be dark, not bright red like it is now."

"I don't know if that's good news or bad, sir," Anderson said quietly. "If I don't die now they'll surely hang me at Fort Laramie."

Dobbs studied the youth, not sure how to answer. "I have to admit," he said at length, opting to respond honestly, "the chances of you getting the death sentence are pretty good. The Army doesn't look with favor on its men who run off and then commit murder."

"I didn't murder nobody!" Anderson said shrilly. "My job was to take care of the horses."

"That may be," Dobbs said, wrapping a length of cotton cloth around the youth's wound, "but if I were you I'd start practicing right now on what you're going to say at the court-martial. Even if you were just holding the horses, ten emigrants are already dead as a result of the incident you and your associates initiated and two more probably aren't going to make it. I don't know if the board is going to appreciate the fact that you claim your role was a minor one."

"The attack wasn't my idea," Anderson said stubbornly. "They would have killed me if I hadn't gone along."

"Whose idea was it then?"

"Henderson's. He's a private that ran off from Fort Laramie."

"I know who Henderson is. Who's the dead man?"

"A merchant from Independence named Si Connors. His brother was a soldier that was killed by the injuns at Blue Water."

"I've heard a lot about Mr. Connors," Dobbs said gravely.

"You have?" Anderson asked in surprise, his eyes widening. "From who?"

"Whom. From another deserter named Connie Ryan."

"Ryan! I'll be dipped in horseshit. So he made it alive to the post?"

"Barely. But he died a couple of days later. What about the blankets infected with smallpox? Did you give them to the Indians?"

"Naw," Anderson said, shaking his head. "Not after we seen how easy Ryan and Fletch caught the disease. That's Nate Fletcher . . . "

"I know."

Anderson shrugged. "After they got sick we decided

we didn't want to have nothing to do with them blankets. So we sort of convinced Si to burn 'em . . . "

"They've been destroyed?"

Anderson nodded. "Every goddamn one of 'em. And good riddance, too."

"What made Connors agree to that?"

"Well—" Anderson tried to laugh. "Oh God, it hurts when I do that," he said, grimacing and grasping his side.

"Then don't do it," Dobbs said dryly. "About Connors?"

"Oh yeah. He didn't *want* to destroy them blankets but Henderson and another guy named Breedlove . . . "

"I know who Breedlove is, too."

"They sort of convinced Si it weren't such a good idea."

"Convinced him how?"

"I think they just plumb scared the shit out of 'im, if you'll pardon my language. Henderson and Breedlove is right mean bastards. Si weren't stupid. I think he got the idea pretty quick that if he didn't go along he might be in more trouble than he bargained for."

"I see," Dobbs said, nodding. "And what's this about a prisoner?"

Anderson looked shocked. "Prisoner? I don't know nothing about no prisoner."

"I think I can answer that, lieutenant," said a female voice from behind Dobbs.

"Who are you?" Dobbs asked, swivelling. Standing over his shoulder was a slim, very pretty blonde whose cornflower-blue eyes displayed the slightest hint of a smile, as if she were thinking of something humorous but didn't want to share it.

"My name," she said, "is Marie Fontenot . . . "

"Oh, no!" Dobbs said, astonished. "So *you're* Marie! Jean's Marie!"

"And what exactly is that supposed to mean, lieutenant?" the woman asked icily, the look of secret humor disappearing like a wisp of smoke. "I don't think we've been introduced."

Dobbs blushed. "Nothing. I mean, it's not supposed to mean anything. Pardon my manners. My name is Jason Dobbs. I'm a friend of Jean Benoit's . . ."

"Oh?" Marie said frostily. "You must be a very good friend indeed if Je . . . Lieutenant Benoit . . . has been spreading my name around."

"Oh, no. It's nothing like that," Dobbs stammered, glancing angrily at Anderson who was beaming. "He just told me that you and your father, Senator Emile Fontenot isn't it?"

Marie nodded.

". . . Were going to be making an inspection trip of the Western Army posts. That is," he stammered, "your father was going to be making an inspection tour and you were going to be coming along . . ."

"How long ago did he tell you this?" Marie said, her face as rigid and as pale as if it had been carved in marble.

"Oh, it was months ago," Dobbs said, recovering slightly. "But he only told me about that one letter you wrote him saying you were coming. He never mentioned that you were actually enroute."

"That's because he didn't know. Where is Jean? I'm very anxious to see him. I need his help."

"He was with me until two hours ago. We were on a mission—it's a long and complicated story," he said when he noticed her eyebrows shoot up.

"Please go on."

"We heard shots and we rode to see what was the matter. Before we could get here, we met Alf Stuart, who was riding with a group of men to try to track down the attackers. Jean went with Stuart and I came on here to see if I could help the wounded. Why do you need his help? Are you injured?"

"Just my pride," Marie replied. "When the shooting started, I fear I wasn't much help. I jumped in a wagon and hid under a blanket."

"Very wise if you ask me."

"Not really," she said, giving him a grateful look. "But it is very chivalrous of you to say so. Some of the other women in the train were not so easily intimidated."

"That's beside the point," Dobbs said. "If you haven't been trained in the use of a firearm it is better for yourself and those around you if you do not try to use one. You'd only add to the danger."

"My, my," Marie said, smiling for the first time. "You *are* quite a gentleman. It is definitely refreshing after a month with Mr. Stuart and his uncouth crew. Truly, they give a new meaning to the term Yahoo."

Dobbs burst out laughing.

"What is so funny about that, may I ask?"

"Another long story," Dobbs said with a chuckle. "But you digressed. You said you needed Jean's help."

"Oh, it's not for me so much as it's for Clement," she replied, giving the name its French pronunciation, Clay-manh.

"And who in blazes is Clement?"

"Clement Couvillion," Marie said, enunciating it as three syllables, Coo-vee-yawn, swallowing the final "n." Noticing his blank look she added, "He's my fiancé."

Again Dobbs was shocked. "Fiancé? Jean didn't say anything about you being engaged to be married."

"That's because he didn't know, silly," Marie said coquettishly. "I was keeping it for a surprise."

"I'm sure it will be that," Dobbs said, straight-faced. "But what about Clay-manh Coo . . . coo . . . coo?"

"Couvillion," Marie repeated slowly. "It really isn't difficult to pronounce."

Oh, boy, Dobbs thought. Kemp is going to have a great time with this name.

"What *about* him?" Dobbs asked again.

"He's missing," Marie continued. "When the raid started, poor Clement—he is *such* a sycophant—went running to see if he could help Daddy and left me to fend for myself. The bastard."

Dobbs ignored the reference to the man's paternity. "And then?"

"He never got there. Daddy was travelling with a group of emigrants from Ohio that he had made friends with earlier; the man, I believe, is a school teacher or something mundane like that. In any case, he was several wagons away when the raid started and Clement went dashing to his rescue. Except he never got there. Since we didn't find his body, we have to assume that he was taken off by the bandits, but for what reason God only knows."

"But your father's all right?" Dobbs asked anxiously. "Does he need medical aid?"

"Daddy's fine. Madder than hell, but not hurt. Poor Clement seems to be our only personal casualty."

"Very curious," Dobbs said, rubbing his chin. "Why would they want to take a prisoner."

"He's rich," Marie offered softly. "Very rich."

"But how would they know that?"

Marie shrugged. "His face is very famous. He's a new Congressman from Louisiana . . . "

"Oh, *him*!" Dobbs slapped his forehead. "That Clement Couvillion!"

"I wasn't aware there was more than one," Marie said, a twinkle returning to her eyes.

Dobbs reddened. "You'll have to excuse me," he said. "We got soaked in a storm yesterday and I still haven't dried out. I have a fever and it must be affecting my brain."

"Well, goodness me." Marie smiled. "It wouldn't do at all for the only doctor in the group to become ill. May I fix you a pot of tea? Something to drink while we're waiting for Mr. Stuart and his muscle men to return?"

"I think that's a wonderful idea, Miss Fontenot . . . "

"Please call me Marie."

"Marie it is. Now that I get to know you a little I can see why Jean is so captivated . . . "

"Oh, Dr. Dobbs," she said daintily, "you are *so* gallant."

"Well," Benoit asked eagerly once they had laid their still soggy bedrolls beside the fire. "What did you think of Marie?"

"She's, uh, a very intelligent young woman," Dobbs replied carefully. "I predict she's going to make quite an impression at Fort Laramie."

Benoit roared. "That's wonderful!" he said. "'Quite an impression.' She's a goddamn siren is what she is. Every man at the post is going to be hobbling around with a permanent erection. I feel almost sorry for Ellen O'Reilly and her girls. They're going to be so busy they won't have a moment's peace. Even the sheep had better head for the hills."

"I admit she's, ah, somewhat attractive. In the purely corporeal sense that is."

"Oh, come on, Jace. Be honest. Doesn't she just make your member throb?"

"Jesus, you're a crude son of a bitch," Dobbs muttered, feigning offense.

"That's me all right," Benoit replied with a laugh. "The Crass Cajun. The Boor of the Bayous."

"You're really enjoying this, aren't you?" Dobbs said angrily. "All you can think about is sex, even at a time like this. Just a few hours ago there was a bloody fight right here where we're bedded down. A dozen people were killed or mortally wounded, a man was taken away as a prisoner—your friend's fiancé, for God's sake—and all you want to talk about is sex."

"Go easy, Jace," Benoit said uneasily. "You've got a point. But there's nothing we can do about the people who were killed. We tried to track down the ones who did it, but they were so good at covering their trail that even Ashby had to give up the search. As for Couvillion, I'm not going to waste a lot of sympathy on that ass-kisser."

"You know him?"

"Not Clement. I went to school with his younger brother, Bertrand. He was a real little muttonhead and I have no reason to believe it doesn't run in the family."

"At the very least, you should have some empathy for Marie. It must be hard on her."

Benoit paused before answering. "Don't misunderstand what I'm going to say, Jace. I'm very fond of Marie. I have a lot of very good memories about the times we spent together in Washington and New Orleans. Besides, she's my sister's best friend. But I don't have any illusions. Marie will bounce back no matter what happens. And she will never—never, ever—suffer from any lack of male companionship. I don't know what prompted her to agree to marry Couvillion but I can just about guarantee you it was as much a matter of convenience as anything else."

"That's the way the world runs, Jean. You don't think all those princes and princesses in Europe marry for love, do you?"

"No, I'm not that naive. But I don't personally know any of them. I do know Marie."

"Well," Dobbs said, coughing, "it's going to be very interesting to see what happens when she storms Fort Laramie."

"'Storms' is exactly the right word." Benoit chuckled. "I give it a week before Teasley starts sniffing around like a dog in heat."

"Is this a private party?" Ashby interrupted "Or can anybody pull up a chair?"

"Hey, Jim," Benoit said enthusiastically, "Set. Want some coffee? It isn't my usual but it's better than that boiled stuff you usually find around a campfire."

"Doan mind if I do," the scout said, collapsing comfortably to the ground and folding his legs Indian style.

"Amazes me how you do that," said Dobbs. "My legs go numb in less than ten minutes."

"All a matter of training," Ashby said, grinning crookedly. "You jest gotta tell yourself the pain doan matter. And pret' soon, it doan."

"What do you think about these guys?" Dobbs asked abruptly.

"They're awful goddamn slick. Gotta hand 'em that. But they got lucky, too, cause o' the rain. If the cricks hadn't been so full they wouldn't been able to use 'em so well, ridin' up one, down another until we plumb lost 'em."

"You figure they're halfway to California by now?" Benoit asked. "I sure as hell would be if I had twenty-eight thousand dollars in gold in my saddlebags."

"Tha's a right tricky question," Ashby replied, blowing on his coffee. "Iffen it weren't for tha' guy Coo-vill-ion . . . "

"Coo-vee-yawn," Benoit corrected.

"Okay, Coo-vee-yawn," Ashby said, exaggerating the final syllable. "This Frenchie what's a prominent . . . Did I say that right?" he asked, looking at Benoit. "Prom-e-nint?"

"That's right." Benoit nodded. "You're doing good."

"This prominent political figger from Warshington," Ashby continued. "He's the part tha's got me puzzled."

"Us, too," admitted Dobbs.

"I mean, thar's no way they coulda known who he was, yet they picked him outta all the men in the train to take with 'em."

"Accident?" Benoit suggested

"Maybe."

"Someone must have recognized him," Dobbs said. "It's the only thing that makes sense. They recognized him and decided to take him along for some future use."

"Ransom?"

"That's a possibility. Also, maybe as leverage to keep us from following them too closely."

"I hadn't thought of that," Benoit admitted.

"Whatever the reason I reckon we'll find out soon enough," Ashby said. "I know I ain't gonna miss no more sleep on it. G'nite," he said, putting down his cup. "Where do we go from here? I figger if I got some more time and daylight I can cut that trail and we can pick 'em up tomorrow."

"No," Dobbs said. "I think our best bet right now is to head back to Fort Laramie with the wagon train. Then we'll let Kemp decide what our next move is going to be. From what Stuart said, there's five of them still left and only four of us. Stuart has to stick with the train. We'd be better off going back to the post and letting Kemp decide what the next move will be."

"What about the infected Indians?" Benoit asked.

"Oh, God," Dobbs said, embarrassed. "With all that's been going on I forgot to tell you. According to that kid, Anderson, the gang got worried about those Indians revealing their position so they followed them to their campsite and killed them."

"All of them?" Benoit asked, feeling his stomach tighten. "Just like that? In cold blood?"

"That's what Anderson says. I'm somewhat relieved to the extent that I'm not worried about the pox now. With the only possible carriers dead and the blankets burned, I have to admit I'll sleep a little better tonight," Dobbs said.

"That gives me the shivers," Benoit said.

"Me, too," Dobbs admitted. "But it shows the caliber of people we're dealing with. Knowing what I know now, there's nothing I wouldn't put past them."

"That's for fucking sure," Ashby added. "I ain't goin' to feel bad about killin' 'em myself iffen I ever get the chance."

Dobbs's eyelids flickered rapidly, then snapped open as if they were on springs.

"What's happening?" he half whispered, his mouth feeling as if it had been packed with talc.

"You're a bit under the weather," a man's voice replied.

"Is that you, Jean?" Dobbs croaked, trying to focus.

"None other," Benoit replied, leaning forward until his face was directly over Dobbs's. "How you feeling?"

"Like I've been et by a hog and passed through his digestive tract," the surgeon said, trying to smile. "Have I been sleeping a lot?"

"You could say that. Do you remember getting back to Fort Laramie at all?"

"No," Dobbs said, weakly shaking his head. "I remember having a god-awful headache and lying down to rest in one of the wagons. I vaguely recall Marie piling quilts on top of me because I was shaking with the ague until I thought my bones were going to break."

"That was about a week ago. Right after we started back."

"Jesus. It's really been a week?"

"Seven days tomorrow. You've been pretty sick. We've been afraid you weren't going to make it."

"Me? Not make it? Don't be a fool. Of course I'm going to make it. Just a little fever, that's all. Have you been taking care of me all that time?"

"Me and Inge and Ellen O'Reilly."

"Ellen too?"

"Ellen more than me and Inge. Soon's she heard you were sick she moved a cot into the corner over there and has hardly left."

Dobbs lifted his head and tried to raise himself on his elbow. He got about halfway into a sitting position before falling back, exhausted. "Where is she?"

"She went over to the sutler's a few minutes ago. Said she needed some more tea. Try to stay awake until she gets back. She'll be delighted to see you with your eyes open."

"Bring me up to date," Dobbs said softly. "What's Kemp doing about the gang that attacked the wagon train?"

"A detachment is leaving in the morning to try to track 'em down. Seventeen men under Harrigan. Me, fifteen enlisted men, and Ashby."

"You think eighteen's enough? Those thugs are all deserters; they'll know how to defend themselves."

"Eighteen is all Kemp figures he can spare. He didn't want Ashby to go; said he should be out hunting since we need fresh meat pretty bad. He finally compromised by sending Erich and three privates out to get some buffalo. They left two days ago."

"If you can wait a couple more days, I'll go with you."

Benoit smiled. "Don't think that's very likely. Although," he added hastily, "I appreciate the offer."

"You don't think I can do it?" Dobbs replied, sounding offended. "All I need to do is get myself moving and get a little strength back." Tossing the blanket aside, he turned abruptly and forced himself into a sitting position, his legs dangling off the edge of the bed.

"I wouldn't try that just yet," Benoit warned.

"All it takes is willpower," Dobbs said, gritting his teeth. With tremendous effort he struggled to his feet while Benoit half rose out of the straight-backed chair he had been sitting in.

"Jace . . ." he said in alarm.

"Don't treat me like an infant," Dobbs barked, waving him back. "I can do this. I just have to stand here for a second until the vertigo goes away."

As he stood wavering like a willow in a windstorm, the door opened and Ellen O'Reilly breezed in, stopping abruptly when she saw Dobbs standing beside the bed.

"Jason Dobbs," she said irritably. "Just what the hell do you think you're doing?"

"Hi, Ellen," Dobbs replied as cheerfully as he could. "It's good to see you."

"Well, it's not so good to see you taking leave of your senses," she said in exasperation, putting down the parcel she was carrying and hurriedly crossing the room.

"I'm a physician; I know what I'm doing. And right now I'm going to walk over to that table and pour myself a drink of water from that pitcher."

Ellen glanced worriedly at Benoit. "Jace, I don't think you ought to try to rush things," she said, her voice dripping with concern. "I'll get you a drink. Some soup, too, if you're hungry. You need some food in you before you start trying to exert yourself."

"Who's rushing things?" Dobbs replied. "I'm just testing my sea legs. Figure it's time to start doing for myself again. The soup sounds good, though."

"Then get back in bed and I'll get it for you," Ellen said, watching him carefully.

"Just a minute," he said impatiently. "Just a minute." Shakily, he extended his right leg as if to take a step. Instead, he tottered briefly and fell forward, hitting the floor face first, too weak even to lift his arms to try to stop his fall. "Arrrgggh!" he screamed as his face smacked the floor.

"Goddamnit, Jace," Benoit cursed, rushing forward. "Why don't you ever listen to anybody?" Turning his friend over, he was not surprised to see blood gushing from his nose.

"Oh no," Ellen moaned, looking desperately around for a towel.

"It wasn't bad enough you had be down with a fever," Benoit said angrily. "Now's you've busted your nose, too."

"You think it will make me better looking?" Dobbs whispered.

"I think it makes you crazier than a bedbug," Ellen said harshly. "Help me get him back in the bed," she added, turning to Benoit.

"I'm sure glad I'm getting out of here tomorrow," Benoit grunted, throwing Dobbs over his shoulder. "Watching over this man while he was unconscious was easy enough. Now that he's starting to come around, he's going to be a real handful."

"Not for me," Ellen said firmly. "I'm used to handling drunks and this isn't going to be that much different. You go ahead; I'll take care of him."

"God, it got cold all of a sudden," Dobbs said, trembling. "Could you get me another blanket?"

"Ellen . . ." Benoit began.

"Go on," she said in mock anger. "Get out of here. I can handle things now. There are things you have to do before you leave and you and Inge probably want a little time together."

"Are you sure?"

"Of course I'm sure. Go on. Leave."

"Okay. I'll stop back before we ride out."

"Oh, sure you will. At four o'clock in the morning? Waking everybody up. You go do what you have to do. Jace is going to be all right."

"I'm freezing," Dobbs said, shaking violently.

"Here's another blanket," Ellen said, spreading a quilt on top of the three covers that already were heaped on the bed.

"I'll see you when I get back," Benoit said, leaning over Dobbs.

"G-G-G-Good luck," Dobbs said through clenched teeth. "B-B-B-Be careful. Do you have another blanket?" he said, turning to Ellen.

"That's all I have handy right now. If I put any more on you, you won't be able to breathe."

"I can't stop shivering."

"Well, I guess there's only one thing left," Ellen said. Crossing the room, she turned the key and tested the door to make sure it was locked. "I swear, Jason Dobbs, the things I don't do for you," she said, walking back to Dobbs's side. Turning her back she began to unbutton her dress.

"You don't have to do that," Dobbs argued feebly.

"I know I don't *have* to," Ellen smiled, slipping under the blankets. "But maybe I *want* to."

"Oh, God," Marie panted. "I just love it when you do that."

"Do you really?" George Teasley replied, lifting his head. "Then how about this?"

"Oh, Jesus! Oh, my God! Oh, my God! Where oh where did you learn that?"

"Don't make me stop to talk."

"No! For God's sake don't talk. Just keep doing that. Oh, God, you're going to drive me crazy."

"I can't do that. You're already crazy. If you weren't you wouldn't be here with me."

"My turn," Marie said eagerly, pushing Teasley onto his back. "What's the fun of receiving if you can't give, too?"

"That's the kind of attitude I appreciate," Teasley said, surrendering without resistance. "Don't go too far, though. Not yet."

"Believe me," Marie said, smiling beatifically. "I know just how far to go."

"You don't know how good it is to get away," Marie said a half hour later after both had washed themselves in the nearby creek and gathered their clothing, which had been spread like confetti around the small clearing. "For the last six weeks I've been living like a nun with Father looking over one shoulder and Cle over the other."

"Speaking of Clement Couvillion," Teasley said, "you don't seem too worried about him."

"Of course I'm worried about him," Marie said rather sharply, glancing up from the basket of food she was unpacking. "But just because he was stupid enough to have himself taken captive doesn't mean my life has to end."

"You make it sound like you believe he did it on purpose."

"Oh I *know* he didn't do it on purpose. He's doesn't have the courage to deliberately put himself in that much physical danger. Cle just let his ambition override his common sense. He thought he could make points with Father by rushing to his aid like that. Except he miscalculated."

"What about that note that Arapaho delivered yesterday? Do you intend to pay the twenty-thousand-dollar ransom?"

Marie looked at him as if he were a nine-year-old being exposed for the first time to the multiplication tables. "Don't be absurd! Where would I get twenty thousand dollars? And why would I pay it even if I had it? As far as I'm concerned, Cle got himself into this situation and he can damn well get himself out. You want some cold beef?"

"It isn't beef, it's buffalo."

"It's meat, isn't it? It tastes like beef. Sort of. Do you want some or not?"

"You don't have to get testy."

"I'm sorry." Marie blushed. "I guess I'm more upset about the situation than I thought."

"What does the senator say about the ransom demand? I trust he's more worried about Couvillion than his daughter."

"Oh, Father can be very objective about things like money. He doesn't want to dig into his pocket either. Besides, Cle's family has oodles of money; they're one of the richest families in New Orleans."

"A condition, no doubt, that influenced your decision to accept his proposal."

Marie shot him a piercing glance. "Just because we made love doesn't give you the right to judge me," she said angrily. "The situation that exists between me and Cle has nothing to do with you. To put it bluntly, it's none of your damn business."

"You're right." Teasley smiled, looking abashed. "I

had no business saying that. I think I will have some roast, if you please, and a thick slice of Frau Schmidt's dark bread."

"You know Colonel Kemp much better than either Father or I," Marie said, cutting into the loaf and handing Teasley a large chunk, along with a knife and a pot of butter. "Do you think he's serious about trying to rescue Cle?"

"Oh, definitely," Teasley replied, smearing the bread with butter. "He's not without ambition himself . . . "

"Is that the pot calling the kettle black?" Marie asked, softening the barb with an angelic smile.

"We're *all* ambitious in our own way," Teasley said, apparently taking no offense. "But Kemp feels responsible for what happened. He wants very badly to have this crisis end favorably. That means rescuing Couvillion, recovering the stolen payroll, and bringing those brigands to justice."

"Funny you mentioned 'justice.' Wasn't that just terrible? The hanging, I mean. I felt so sorry for that poor boy."

"Western justice is swift justice," Teasley said. "What was his name? Anderson? Anyway, he got a fair trial. The military, especially the military on the frontier, acts quickly. He was a deserter and he should have known what he was doing when he decided to leave his post. The fact that he joined up with a group of outlaws just sealed his fate."

"But he wasn't even recovered from his wounds."

"You think it would have been kinder to nurse him fully back to health and then hang him?"

"That isn't what I meant," Marie said crossly.

"I know what you meant," said Teasley. "But you have to understand that we do things differently out here. We don't have time for a lot of niceties. Out here you have to be decisive and you have to have the guts to carry through on your decisions."

"Then why has it taken Colonel Kemp so long to put together a group of men . . . "

"A patrol."

". . . to go after those murderers?"

"There's a difference between being decisive and going off half-cocked. Kemp wanted to gather enough intelligence to find out where the raiders might be camped before sending men out without direction. You've seen some of this country, enough to see how vast it is and how a patrol could spend weeks just wandering around if they didn't have some idea where to begin."

"And you think they have that now?"

"From what Legendre and Ashby have discovered by talking to the Indians they think they have the area pretty well narrowed down. They think the gang is camped along the Niobrara River, up in Cheyenne territory."

"Is that far?"

Teasley shrugged. "A three- or four-day ride. If they travel hard."

"Do you think there's much of a chance of success?"

"I think," Teasley said slowly, "that Kemp feels he *has* to be successful. Too much is at stake. The fact that your father, a very influential Senator, is watching his every move at close hand doesn't ease the pressure either. He already feels uneasy. He hasn't said anything to me, but I would guess he's afraid your father is going to accuse him of being negligent by failing to send an escort to accompany the train from Missouri."

"Oh, General Jennings at Fort Leavenworth offered to do that. But Father and Mr. Stuart agreed that would just call attention to the party and might encourage an attack. Besides, they felt after that drubbing the Indians took at Ash Hollow . . . "

"Blue Water Creek, actually."

"Well, it was *near* Ash Hollow, wasn't it?"

"Yes, but . . . "

"They felt," Marie continued, "that the savages had been suitably chastised; that they wouldn't be anxious to start more trouble with the Army."

"Their ignorance never ceases to amaze me," Teasley said, shaking his head.

"What do you mean?"

"It was the Brulé Sioux and a few Minniconjou that General Harney's men massacred at Blue Water. What happened to them has no affect on the actions of the other tribes."

"You mean they aren't all connected?" Marie said, honest puzzlement showing on her face.

"Not hardly," Teasley replied, smothering the temptation to laugh. "And that's one of the first lessons your father needs to learn if he's going to go back to Washington and try to speak knowledgeably about the situation in the West and whether there is a policy change necessary."

"Politics, politics." Marie sighed. "I swear, that's all men ever think about."

"No," Teasley said, grinning. "It isn't *all* . . . "

Marie beamed. "Well," she said, lifting her skirt, "we have to hurry. Daddy wasn't very happy about just the two of us going on a picnic in the first place."

Inge ran her hand through Benoit's thick, dark hair, stuck her index finger in his right ear and playfully wiggled it.

"Don't do that," Benoit said irritably.

"There's no need to pout, Jean," Inge said softly. "I'm just trying to cheer you up."

"You *know* how to cheer me up," he said sulkily.

"Not until after we're married, Jean. We've been through this before and the answer is going to stay the same."

"Don't you think you're being a bit hardheaded?"

"No, I'm being me. I'm not like your former girlfriend, that *Schlampe*. I don't give my body—or my heart—easily. When I do, I want it to be to someone who will appreciate it."

Benoit looked at her curiously. "That what?"

"*Schlampe*."

"What's a slampe?"

"Not 'slampe,' *Schlampe*. It's s-c-h . . . *Schlampe* . . . not s-l. It means schlut."

"Not 'schlut,'" Benoit said with a giggle, "slut. S-l, not s-c-h."

"English is so confusing sometimes." Inge shrugged. "So when are we going to do it?"

"Do what?"

"What we were just talking about," Marie replied, sighing. "Get married."

"Oh, that," Benoit mumbled. "It isn't as though we can just stroll down to the local justice of the peace and get hitched. I'm in the *Army*, for Christ's sake. I have to get the colonel's permission to do anything except breathe."

"Have you asked him?"

"Well," he said hesitantly, "not exactly."

"That means 'no.'"

"I guess it does."

Inge stood, brushing the stray bits of hay from her dress. In the far stall, Benoit's big gelding stamped impatiently, as if anticipating the journey that would begin long before sunrise the next morning. "Why not?" she asked. It was a simple question, not an accusation.

"I don't know," Benoit said sheepishly. "It isn't that I don't want to marry you . . . "

"You mean make love to me."

"That, too, naturally. But that isn't all. Marriage is a big step."

"No less for me than for you."

"These are unsettled times," Benoit began nervously. "The country is on the brink of a divisive civil war. We're at a very crucial junction in our affiliation with the Indians. What happens in the next few years, even months, could make a difference in . . . "

"Oh, *mein Gott,*" Inge interrupted in exasperation. "Spare me the political lecture. I don't think you're serious about what happens to us. I don't think you want to marry me at all. I think you would rather resume your relationship—your 'fucking' to use a good English word—with that blonde whore."

"That isn't fair," Benoit said, flushing. "I haven't had anything to do with Marie at all since I left Washington."

"I don't see why not. *Sie bumst mit jedem.*"

"Now what does *that* mean?"

"She's sleeping with everybody else."

"Not everybody. Just George Teasley."

"Jean, don't you hear what you're saying? She is engaged to be *married*. Married to a man who's being held for ransom by a group of bloodthirsty murderers. But is she worried? Not in the least. Instead, she's conducting a shameless liaison with a married man . . . "

"How do you know Teasley's married? I don't know that."

"Of course he's married," Inge said, as if explaining why the sun rises in the east. "I've heard him talk about his wife at dinner. How she absolutely refused to come back to the West after three years out here with George when he was in the Army . . ."

"He wasn't here. He was at Fort Leavenworth."

"It's still the frontier, Jean. She's staying with her parents in Baltimore. With their two children!" she added for emphasis. "Did you hear me? Two," she said, holding up her thumb and index finger in the German manner. "Two girls. Not much younger than me, for God's sake."

"I didn't know all that," Benoit said, amazed. "How do you learn all these things?"

"It's a woman's way." Inge smiled. "Besides, you men don't pay any attention to Mutter and me. We're as invisible as spirits. But we hear everything. And we remember."

"That's a very unsettling thought," Benoit said.

Inge laughed. "Of course it is. It's meant to be. Just remember that next time you're lounging over dessert and you let your mouth run away with you. But that's not what we were talking about. We were talking about getting married."

"No," Benoit said, "*you* were talking about getting married."

"Are you trying to get me angry, Jean?" she said, her color rising. "If you are, you're succeeding."

"No," Benoit said placatingly. "That's not what I mean at all. I'm just trying to say that marriage is a big step. It's something we ought to consider carefully."

"And just how long do you plan to *consider* it?" Inge asked frostily. "Until your hair turns gray? Until you are so old you will no longer be able to perform your physical functions? Or simply until I get discouraged and give up on you?"

"Your mother might not approve," Benoit said, grasping at straws.

"Don't be ridiculous. For some reason I'm not sure I understand, Mutter thinks you're *wunderbar*. As far as she's concerned, you could dangle the moon . . . no, that's not right. Oh what *is* that expression?"

"Hang the moon."

"*Ja*, that's it. Hang the moon. She thinks you can do anything."

"But how about you? What if you don't like my family?"

"What's to like?" Inge said with a shrug. "It's you I'm marrying, not your family. Besides, it's not very likely that we'll be spending a lot of time around them. Not as long as you're in the Army at any rate."

"That's another point. What if I never get beyond being a brevet second lieutenant? I don't know how to do anything else; I'm not trained for anything but soldiering."

"Oh, you're going to get promoted all right. You're bright and ambitious and you know your job."

"Unless I mess up. Which is something I have a disposition to do."

"I agree with you there," Inge said after a pause. "You *do* have a tendency to do the wrong thing at the wrong time."

"See! And if we were married, you'd be stuck with me."

"Well!" Inge said, stamping her foot. "Part of the tendency you have to do the wrong thing includes not recognizing what a good wife I would make for you!" Turning abruptly, she marched out of the stable.

"Inge," Benoit said, realizing he was talking to her back as she crossed the parade ground, headed toward Old Bedlam.

"Tell me, Senator Fontenot," Kemp said amiably, "what's the latest in Washington on this States Rights issue?"

"That's a very complicated question, colonel," Fontenot replied. "I'm not sure I can answer it in a succinct fashion."

"Well, senator," Kemp said, proffering one of his cigars, "is it all going to blow over anytime soon?"

"Oh, no," Fontenot said and laughed harshly, accepting the smoke. "Don't make the mistake of thinking this is just another 'Washington crisis.' It's something that permeates to the very grassroots of this country; everyone has an opinion about it."

"Can you give me an example?" Kemp asked, leaning forward to take his customary light from Harrigan. "Captain," he asked jokingly, "what am I going to do for a match while you're on patrol?"

"Oh, don't worry about that, colonel," Harrigan said with a grin. "I've been teaching Harry the tricks of the trade. Right, Grant?"

"Absolutely, sir," First Lieutenant Harry Grant said enthusiastically, happy to be included in the conversation.

"You see, colonel," Fontenot said, pausing to puff off Harrigan's match, "everything has sprouted out of proportion. What started as an economic debate has grown into a many-faceted monster. For generations, Southerners have been making their living off the land, primarily supplying cotton to a fabric-hungry world. The crop is such that it demands a tremendous amount of labor. Traditionally, that work has been performed by slaves imported from Africa."

"Do you agree with that practice?"

"Whether I agree or not is immaterial. There are a number of plantation owners among my constituency. I myself own a small amount of acreage devoted to cotton, but my niggers are, in a sense, free. That is, although I technically own them, I pay them a regular wage in addition to the other benefits expected from an owner. That is housing, food, medical care, and clothing."

"You make it sound very, what shall I say? Inviting?"

Oh, no. It is not inviting. My niggers work hard but I treat them fairly. I'm aware that not all owners follow those same principles, but I'm not in a position to be judgmental. I have to look at it from a broader viewpoint."

"Which is?"

"The South needs slaves to maintain its economic base. To continue to produce cotton, which is the lifeblood of our economy, the practice must be continued. Barring, of course, the emergence of an alternative source of labor. And that doesn't seem very likely."

"It sounds to me—begging your pardon, I don't want to sound argumentative—that you're trying to justify slavery."

"Not at all, colonel. Personally, I abhor the institution. But, as I said earlier, this is where it gets complicated. Some forces in the North—the so-called abolitionists—want to bring an abrupt end to the practice. And it isn't just the South. Look at what's happening right now in Kansas and Missouri territories. It wasn't four months ago we had the incident with the Border Ruffians, those pro-slavery Missourians who crossed into Kansas and cast ballots in the legislative elections. Pro-slavery ballots, naturally. Whether it was because of them or not, Kansas now has a pro-slavery ruling body."

"That's true enough," Kemp agreed. "The election was even embraced by the territorial governor."

"But," Fontenot continued, "when the abolitionists

talk about eradicating slavery they are proposing, in effect, taking food out of every Southerner's mouth, in essence sentencing everyone in the cotton-producing states, both black and white, to starve. If slavery were to be outlawed tomorrow, there would be chaos in the South. The whole economy would collapse."

"But it is an economy built upon an injustice to others."

"Ah ha, you have hit upon an important point. To Northerners, slavery is an abomination. But I have traveled through the great Northern cities. I have visited the factories that the Northerners are so proud of. And I have seen workers, children included, who live not unlike those on plantations run by the most cruel owners."

"Those factory workers toil hard, but at the end of the day they can go home to their families. They can walk the streets. They are free."

"A dubious privilege considering some of the conditions I have witnessed. Pay is so low for most of them they cannot afford the basic necessities. Many of them dress in rags. They suffer from consumption because they never get out to breathe fresh air. Their teeth are rotting because of improper diet. Their children, as soon as they are old enough, are sent to work in the same dark, dirty, noisy buildings. You call that freedom?"

"They are not whipped when they fail to perform up to expectations or because they have done something that displeases the foreman."

"Worse," said Fontenot. "They are fired. Tossed out on the streets. I'm not sure which is worse. If I were a worker, I'm not sure I'd rather not face a lashing than be forced to watch my family go hungry."

"Perhaps that's because you've never been lashed."

"*Touché*. But you see, we ourselves are falling into the same trap that threatens to snare everyone else. We are making this an emotional issue when, in reality, it is an eco-political one."

"I'm not sure I follow your reasoning."

"Then let me explain," Fontenot said. "Frau Schmidt," he said, looking around the room, "may we please have some more coffee? Your *apfelstrudel* was among the best I've ever eaten. Where and how you manage to obtain all the ingredients out here on the frontier I'll never understand. It is a real tribute to your skill that you have performed so diligently."

"*Danke*, Herr Fontenot," Holzbein beamed. "Your praise makes my bosom swell."

"*Heart*, Mutter," Inge whispered. "The word is heart, not bosom."

"It makes no difference," Frau Schmidt replied in German. "He knows what I mean."

"You were saying, senator," Kemp prompted.

"Oh yes," Fontenot said, shaking his leonine head. "The older I get, the more my attention starts to wander. What I was trying to do was explain how, largely through the efforts of the abolitionists, slavery has become the issue while, in actuality, it is the economic survival of our culture. We Southerners do not take kindly to suggestions that we should voluntarily destroy the system that has made us what we are simply to satisfy the whims of a few misguided souls."

"But the counterargument is that slavery is wrong no matter what attempt is made at justification."

"Let me put the shoe on the other foot," Fontenot said. "What if the Southern contingent in Congress were to say that it is cruel and unjust for people to have to work in factories? Would every owner run out to close his mill? I think not. But still, that is not the real issue."

"Then what is? I must be missing a point here somewhere," Kemp said, frowning.

"The point is, what right do Northerners have to tell Southerners how to run their enterprises? We Southerners feel that we have every right to continue to conduct our business as we have done in the past. In our view, the Constitution delegates authority to the individual states to govern their own affairs. We have developed an economic system that has proved successful for us. And we feel we should be allowed to keep it. This is where the term States Rights comes in. We feel that individual political jurisdictions, call them states if you will, have the prerogative to decide in their own best interest. The Northerners insist that if we are to remain part of the political whole—call it the Union—then we have to bow to the demands of the majority, which of course the North has because of its large cities. The Southern position, on the other hand, is that we do not wish to accede to these demands and if they continue we will have no choice but to withdraw from the political alliance. In a word, secede."

Kemp stared at his coffee, playing idly with the stump of his cigar. "Do you think," he asked after a long pause, "that it is going to come to that?"

Fontenot emitted a long sigh. "I hope not," he said softly. "Despite all the weak points in our current form of government I think it is fundamentally sound, that it is probably the best form of government existing in the world today. I would like to preserve that. Unfortunately, the decision will not be mine. I, too, am subject to the whims of my constituency. If Louisiana votes to secede, I will have no choice but to go along. But it has not come to that yet. In the meantime, I continue to applaud the benefits of a united country and hope that wisdom will prevail. Unlike some of my fellow lawmakers, I see the really dark side of a divided country."

"And what is that?" Grant interjected, no longer able to restrain himself from entering the conversation. "My uncle, Ulysses, is an extremely strong advocate of preserving the union."

"In my view," Fontenot said solemnly, "secession is tantamount to a declaration of war. And if it comes to war, the conflict will be long, unbelievably cruel, and forever divisive. Once a split comes, if it does, the damage may never again be repaired."

"This is all very grim," Kemp said, shaking himself. "I'm almost sorry I brought it up. Captain," he said, turning to Harrigan, "let's get to more practical matters. What are your plans?"

Harrigan, who had been mesmerized by the talk of a possible war between the states, cleared his throat. "Mr. Ashby says he's been told by some of his Cheyenne friends that a party of whites has set up camp in a small valley along the Niobrara at the juncture of a creek the Cheyenne call Icy Water. It's a good three-day ride north of here. I intend to leave an hour before dawn tomorrow and push straight through."

"And once you get there?"

"After we ascertain that it is the group of men we're looking for, I plan to try to open a dialogue which I hope will lead to the voluntary return of the prisoner."

"With all due respect, captain," Fontenot interjected, "I think you're dreaming. Those men aren't going to give up without a fight."

"You may be right, senator," Harrigan agreed with a nod. "But I feel I have to give them the chance."

"What if they take opportunity of that time to kill Congressman Couvillion?"

"I think that's a chance we have to take, sir. They have nothing to gain by killing him."

"And they have nothing to gain by *not* killing him. If

they give him up, they no longer have any leverage. They know they can't surrender or they will face the same fate as that boy you hanged last week."

"They can't possibly know Anderson was executed."

"Don't be a fool, captain. They're deserters, thieves, and murderers. They know what awaits them."

Harrigan looked pleadingly at Kemp. "I can't just ride in there and kill them in cold blood can I, sir? Don't I at least have to make an effort to avoid bloodshed?"

"The captain has a point, senator. Although he understands he is not obligated to accept your advice I'm sure he would be grateful for your opinion."

Fontenot grinned. "Colonel, if you ever decide to go into politics I hope it isn't in Louisiana. Why don't you make them an offer?" he suggested, turning to Harrigan. "Promise them the ransom and the opportunity to leave the camp unmolested."

"But they'll want the money right then."

"Well, hell, captain, use your imagination. Make up some story. Say you couldn't carry twenty thousand dollars in your saddlebags. There was not enough time to raise the money. It was too risky to travel with it. Something."

"And then what?" asked Harrigan. "What if they believe me and they turn over the Congressman?"

Fontenot's lips compressed to a straight line and his eyes glittered like chunks of coal. "Kill the bastards," he rasped.

Harrigan blinked and the color drained from his face. "Y-Y-Y-Yes, sir," he stammered.

Sad Bear watched Blizzard out of the corner of his eye, fearful that by looking at him directly he might incur his wrath, something the Miniconjou youth was loath to risk. Although he had known him only for a few short months, during much of which time Blizzard had lain incapacitated by wounds suffered at the hands of General Harney's men during the attack at Blue Water, Sad Bear had seen how quickly Blizzard's temper could flare and he had no desire to be the target of the warrior's ire.

One evening, not long after Blizzard was mobile again, the Brulé named Open Wound had dared to disagree when Blizzard spoke bitterly about the council members of the Wazhazha Band, calling them cowards and men with the hearts of women. Open Wound, who had been a junior warrior in the Wazhazhas before he joined the small group known among its members as Blizzard's Pack, took exception to the characterizations, telling Blizzard he was a fool for saying such things. While still so weak he could barely walk, Blizzard pulled himself to his feet and drew his knife, ready to attack the hale Open Wound. A fight was prevented when the old Arapaho, Big Hand, stepped between the two men.

That had been two months ago and, since then, Blizzard's condition, if not his hair-trigger temper, had improved remarkably. Except for a half dozen new scars and a fairly noticeable limp, Blizzard appeared as an imposing physical presence. A tall, well-muscled man in his mid-thirties with a great hooked nose and eyes as dark and cold as the inside of a cave, he could strike fear even in the hearts of the brave with a single, penetrating glare.

Even before the incident at Blue Water, Blizzard had carried his share of battle reminders. Across the upper left side of his chest was a large, raised scar, the result of a wound suffered in hand-to-hand combat with a Pawnee, who Blizzard had subsequently eviscerated. And on his thigh was a sunken purple circle the size of a baby's hand, the result of being shot during a raid on a group of emigrants a year earlier, the attack in which Frau Schmidt's husband, Hans, had been killed, along with four other German emigrants, including an eight-year-old girl. It was in that encounter that Frau Schmidt was wounded and the two Mueller boys, Werner and Wilhelm, had been taken captive.

Added to these scars were the ones that resulted from the wounds inflicted during the Blue Water fight: two small circular spots waist-high on the left side of his torso, one in front and one in back, like two sides of a coin. One of the soldiers had shot Blizzard with a small caliber handgun and the bullet, almost miraculously, had gone completely through his side without striking any major organs. But the most visible reminder was Blizzard's face. Exhibiting his preference for hand-to-hand fighting, Blizzard had attacked one of the mounted soldiers with his bare hands, trying to pull him off his horse so he could slit his throat with the knife he sharpened every night as a last act before he went to sleep. Remarkably, given Blizzard's fearsome demeanor, the trooper did not flinch. As soon as Blizzard got within arm's reach, the soldier swung his sabre, striking Blizzard flush across his right cheek, leaving a deep gouge that ran from his eyebrow to his jawline. Worse, it dislodged Blizzard's eye, plucking it from its socket like a raisin from a loaf of bread. As ugly as it looked, the wound was not mortal. Whimpering softly, blinded by blood and racked with pain, Blizzard had been able to crawl away. The soldier would have followed up his attack but his horse, hit in the shoulder by an arrow, reared abruptly, tossing his rider into the dust. While Blizzard was on his hands and knees, blinded by blood and pain, another mounted trooper fired into his back. Assuming he had killed him, the trooper turned to another target.

Crow Killer, a Miniconjou revered for his bravery, had dragged Blizzard out of the melee, threw him over the back of one of the horses that had been tethered in a nearby copse, and carried him to safety. When they got to a safe camp site, he tended Blizzard's wounds and nursed him back to health. It was, however, not in Blizzard's nature to show gratitude. Instead of thanking Crow Killer for saving his life, Blizzard scolded him for not rescuing his prized war club as well. A fierce-looking instrument about two-and-a-half-feet long painted in Blizzard's "power" colors of red and black, it had been left behind on the battlefield.

"You're an unappreciative man," Crow Killer had responded angrily. "I kept you from getting killed and you don't even have the courtesy to say thank you. Your wife, Trembling Pine, was murdered in the attack and you yourself have been horribly disfigured, but the only thing you care about is your war club."

If Blizzard had been able to stand, he might have attacked Crow Killer on the spot. But the anger between the two cooled during Blizzard's period of convalescence and the memory of the hasty words apparently was expunged. Crow Killer, in fact, became the only one among the group to whom Blizzard listened seriously.

"We are like starving wolves," Crow Killer remarked one evening when all they had to eat were two scrawny rabbits they had snared. "We are hungry, bedraggled, and homeless. The only thing, it seems, that keeps us going is our hatred for the white man."

When Blizzard began making cough-like sounds deep in his throat, Crow Killer looked up in alarm, certain the warrior was choking on a piece of the stringy meat. It took him a moment to realize that his friend was laughing.

"That's exactly what we are," Blizzard wheezed. "Wolves. We will operate as a pack, prowling the forests and the plains looking for white prey."

"We certainly look as repulsive as any pack of wolves I've ever seen," added Crow Killer, joining in the laughter. "Especially you."

It was not an exaggeration. Although Blizzard's wounds had healed, his appearance remained hideous. Where his right eye had been was an ugly, gaping hole that was only half covered by a draping, muscleless eyelid that never moved. The skin on his cheek looked like a piece of old buffalo hide that had been ripped and patched by an inexpert seamstress, and his lip, which had been sliced deeply by the sabre, was puckered by a thick scar and curled upward in a permanent sneer.

Sad Bear looked at Blizzard and inwardly trembled.

Minutes before, the Pack had killed a fat buffalo cow and Blizzard sat astride the animal's hump, carving thick portions from the recently removed liver and cramming them into his mouth. His mangled cheek was smeared with buffalo blood. More blood seeped out of the corner of his lacerated lip and trickled down his chin, dripping onto his scarred chest. As Blizzard ate, he emitted small grunts of satisfaction, seemingly reveling in epicurean rapture, oblivious to the others who were hovering over the carcass like so many buzzards anxious to begin their own feast.

"What are you looking at?" Blizzard roughly demanded of Sad Bear when he noticed the youth's covert glances.

"Noth . . . Nothing," Sad Bear stammered.

"Are you going to share that or do you intend to eat it all?" Crow Killer interrupted, diverting Blizzard's attention. Of the nine other members of the Pack, Crow Killer was the only one who could speak to Blizzard in that tone and get away with it.

"Here," Blizzard replied, passing the bloody lump. "All you had to do was ask."

"And that would further establish your authority, wouldn't it?" Crow Killer replied, cutting off a slice and handing the organ to Big Hand.

Slowly the liver went around the circle, from Big Hand to Four Wolves to Fat Bull to Broken Club to Open Wound to Red Chin and, lastly, to Sad Bear and Goose, the two youths.

Later, as they sat around the campfire with their stomachs full of fresh meat, Blizzard outlined his plan in further detail. Meticulously, he assigned each of the Pack members a specific role that he commanded they perform when they attacked the Crow camp.

"We haven't even *found* the camp yet," Fat Bull

protested. A short, rotund Brulé whose physical appearance reflected his name with uncanny accuracy, Fat Bull also was cursed with an exceptionally high voice that always made Sad Bear wonder if there was not a skinny woman hidden somewhere inside that corpulent frame.

"No, but we will," Blizzard replied emphatically. "It's just a matter of time."

"Why are you so determined to raid the *Kangi*?" asked Open Wound. "We should be devoting more effort to laying aside some meat. The winter is not that far away."

"You sound like a woman," Blizzard sneered. "If you're afraid why don't you go back to the Wazhazhas?"

"You know why not," Open Wound said petulantly. "Scalptaker is too willing to compromise with the white man; he's willing to trade our birthright for what he believes will be perpetual peace. I can't go along with that. After what happened at Blue Water, I don't understand how he could be so ignorant."

"It is the white man who is our true enemy," said Broken Club, whose entire family was wiped out by Harney's troopers.

"You will find no argument from me on that score," Blizzard replied, nodding.

"Then why are we going after the Kangi?" Sad Bear ventured. "Why don't we attack the whites directly?"

"Because we're too short of the supplies we need to take our war to the whites," Blizzard replied, adopting the tone of a parent explaining an issue to a thick-headed child. "We don't have anything to trade for supplies, thanks to the white soldiers, so we need to capture necessary items from the Crow: More horses, guns, powder, and provisions."

"It might not be a bad idea to grab a few Kangi

women, too," Broken Club proposed. "It would be very nice to have someone to share a bed with on the long nights that are coming."

Goose giggled, drawing a sharp look from Blizzard.

"As a matter of fact, that's not a bad idea," agreed Crow Killer. "We are just a group of warriors and we need women for a number of reasons, not the least of which is physical relief."

"If the opportunity presents itself," Blizzard said noncommittally, "but don't forget that we need to move quickly from place to place; we have no time for amenities. If you choose a woman, choose a very young one."

"Why do you say that?" asked Goose, who, at fifteen, was the youngest of the group.

"Because," whispered Sad Bear, "they don't have enough experience to nag at you like an older woman would."

"And you know what you're talking about?" Goose whispered back. "What suddenly makes you an expert on women?"

"Enough," growled Blizzard. "If you two pups want to gossip go into the woods. We have things we need to discuss."

"Is all this really necessary?" Four Wolves asked. "In the long run, what can ten men—make that eight men and two boys—hope to accomplish against such a large number of whites who have good horses and infinitely superior guns?"

"We can show that we are not intimidated, for one thing," Crow Killer responded. "We have to demonstrate our willingness to fight for our land."

"Crow Killer is right," Blizzard added. "If we can do this, other warriors will join us and our Pack will grow large and powerful. When that day comes we will have our revenge against the whites. It will not matter how many horses or guns they have because we are braver men and better fighters."

"Blizzard makes a lot of sense," said Red Chin, breaking his traditional silence. Of all the members of the Pack, Red Chin was the most enigmatic. He had shown up in the Pack's temporary camp one morning a week or so after the Harney attack and calmly taken a seat around the fire. Other than telling the others his name, he had hardly spoken a word since.

"And why do you think that?" Broken Club asked in surprise.

"Because I have seen first hand the white man's treachery," Red Chin replied.

"Would you care to explain that further?" Crow Killer asked.

Red Chin shrugged. "I was at Fort Laramie when the white soldiers opened fire on our camp because they thought we had tried to kill a solider. It wasn't true, but that didn't stop them from reacting violently. Also, I was at the camp along the Platte when that white man with hair the color of a June sunrise arrogantly decided that he and a handful of men could take Blizzard captive. They shot first, just as they had done at Fort Laramie. Both attacks were unprovoked. And that says nothing of what happened at Blue Water."

"Were you there also?" asked Fat Bull.

"No." Red Chin shook his head. "I had taken my wife to visit her people along the Cheyenne River and I was returning to Blue Water when the soldiers attacked. I was so outraged by what had happened that I decided that something needed to be done. When I heard about the Pack, I decided to join you."

"What about your wife?" asked Broken Club. "And children? I assume you have children."

"Two young sons," Red Chin replied with a grin. It was the first time any of the men had seen him smile.

"And they are with your wife?"

Red Chin nodded. "They are safe since they are so far to the north. I feel my duty is with you."

"They may be safe today," said Crow Killer, "but tomorrow the whites may be there as well. That is why we have to try to stop them now, send them back to the east where they came from."

"It's late," Blizzard announced with a yawn. "It is time to go to sleep so we will be refreshed tomorrow. Who knows. Maybe tomorrow we'll find the Kangi camp."

"He still tires easily," Broken Club whispered to Four Wolves. "I think he is not as fully recovered from his wounds as he pretends. We should discuss the possibility of postponing any action until then."

"I am almost as good as I ever was," Blizzard replied sharply.

"You weren't meant to hear that," Broken Club said, surprised.

"It was my sight that was damaged, not my hearing," Blizzard barked. "If you find that I can't keep up, you have my permission to kill me and leave me along the trail. If you're man enough, that is."

"No one is questioning your authority," Crow Killer said placatingly.

"Good,' said Blizzard. "In that case I command everyone to bed. All except Sad Bear and Goose. They will stand sentry until Open Wound relieves them. Fat Bull, douse the fire. My robe is beckoning."

Sad Bear's chin sank slowly toward his chest and his eyelids drooped as if weighted with pebbles. He was just beginning to dream that he was chasing Goose through a heavy forest in an impromptu game of catch-me-if-you-can when he realized the rustling in the bushes was not his friend. Jerking awake with a start, he strained to see through the blackness. "Who's there?" he asked nervously, notching an arrow. "Speak or you will soon be dead," he added with false bravado.

"I'm going to be dead soon enough," a deep voice replied with a chuckle. "There's no need for you to hurry me along."

"Oh, it's you, Big Hand," Sad Bear mumbled in relief. "You frightened me out of my skin."

"I was deliberately trying to be noisy so you wouldn't think I was trying to sneak up on you," the Arapaho said. "It's a good thing I wasn't a Crow. If I were, you would be lying in a pool of blood and your scalp would have be dangling from my belt. One of the first things you have to learn as a warrior," he said sternly, "is never to sleep on sentry duty."

"Please don't tell Blizzard," Sad Bear implored. "He would beat me with that new club he has been carving for the last month."

"Why would I tell that half-blind monster anything?" Big Hand whispered hoarsely. "I believe it's enough if I tell you."

"You're right, that's enough. You won't catch me sleeping on guard again."

"I hope you're right. When you sleep when you're supposed to be watching, you endanger everyone. Where's your friend?"

"Over there," Sad Bear waved. "I hope," he said, looking anxiously at Big Hand, "that he isn't sleeping too."

"I'm certain that he is," Big Hand grunted.

"Did you come out just to see if we were awake?" Sad Bear asked, trying to change the subject.

"No, I just got restless. When you get to be my age you don't sleep as much. And when I do nod off, my bad dreams haunt me."

"What do you dream about that's so terrible that it keeps you from sleeping soundly? I can't imagine anything that would make sleep unpleasant."

"When you get old and when you have seen as many people die as I have, the idea of surrendering your soul to the darkness becomes less appetizing."

"I've never seen anyone die," Sad Bear said quietly. "Not really. There was an old man in the camp . . ." he paused, looking at Big Hand in embarrassment. "I mean a really old man, much older than you . . . "

"Don't worry." Big Hand smiled. "I know what you meant."

"He got a fish bone caught in his throat and he choked to death while sitting around the council fire. Several men tried to save him but they couldn't pry it loose in time. It was very unsettling. He died making a terrible wheezing sound and his face was as purple as the sky at sunset. It made a very vivid impression on me."

"But how about your family?" Big Hand asked gently. "Aren't they also dead?"

"Oh yes," Sad Bear replied with a catch in his voice, grateful that it was dark and Big Hand couldn't see the tears forming in his eyes. "But I didn't *see* them die. Goose and I were not in the camp at Blue Water when the soldiers attacked."

"Oh?" Big Hand said, raising an eyebrow. "I thought you were there."

"No," Sad Bear said, shaking his head. "Goose and I were hunting. We wounded an elk and had been tracking him for almost a full day, following his trail through the pine forest. We finally caught up with him when he became too tired to run any more. My arrow was sticking out of his neck," Sad Bear said proudly, "but somehow it missed hitting a vital spot. He was so weak from loss of blood, he just couldn't run any more."

"So you killed him, butchered him, and returned to camp?"

"Yes." Sad Bear nodded. "By then we had been gone almost three days. We were sure our fathers would be furious and we would be severely punished. I wish that's what would have happened," he said sorrowfully. "I mean, I wish our fathers would have been alive. Instead we found their bodies. No one from my family or Goose's survived. My younger brother's head had been chopped off and my father's genitals had been removed and stuffed in his mouth. I don't know what they did to my mother before they killed her because they tried to burn her body. I just hope," he said, unable to hold back his tears any longer, "that she was dead by the time they put her in the fire."

"And what about Goose?" Big Hand asked quietly.

"Oh, his story is almost the same," Sad Bear replied, wiping his face with his forearm. "His father, mother, and sister were also killed. His mother and sister had been raped, too. We could tell from the way their dresses had been ripped. But at least they were killed quickly. His mother was shot in the back of the head and his sister had been stabbed in the heart."

"Is that why you joined up with Blizzard? To get revenge?"

"Partly," Sad Bear said, nodding. "Also, Goose and I had nowhere else to go. Our cousins had fled to the hills and it seemed better to join Crow Killer and Blizzard than to try to find our relatives. Besides, at the time Blizzard was still unconscious from his wounds. We did not know how evil-tempered he could be."

"He is not only evil-tempered," Big Hand commented, "he is evil as well. He wants to kill the whites—any whites he can find—not just because of what happened at Blue Water but because he truly likes to kill. In my time I have seen several men like that and they all came to a bad end. I feel certain that is what will happen to Blizzard, too, but maybe not right away."

"Why do you stay if you feel that way?" Sad Bear asked. "And why did you join us anyway? None of your people were killed in the attack."

"No," Big Hand agreed, "my family did not die violently, but they died at the white man's hands just the same."

"What do you mean?" Sad Bear asked curiously.

"They died of white man's disease."

"But how can you blame that on the white man? People get sick all the time."

"Not like my wife and two sons. They were stricken with a sickness brought by the white man in an attempt to kill the Indian. It was very bad," he said, shuddering. "My wife and sons took a long time to die. They begged me to kill them, but I couldn't do it."

"No," Sad Bear said slowly. "I can understand that. I don't think I could kill anyone I loved either. But how did you escape the disease? Didn't you get sick too?"

Big Hand shook his head. "No. For some reason I escaped. I don't know why I was spared. Maybe because I still have some important things to do."

"You mean kill the people who brought the disease to your family?"

"Not them specifically but those just like them. Other whites. Before the white man came we had very little disease. There was infection, of course, and some of the old people would get the fever and cough that would kill them, but that was understandable because they were old and it was their time to die. To them, death was merciful."

"But you're old too," Sad Bear blurted.

"Not *that* old," Big Hand answered sharply. I'm probably not much older than your father was."

"That's true," Sad Bear replied, looking closely at the warrior. "I've just always thought of you as being much older."

"Our lives were very tranquil until the white man came," Big Hand said, picking up the thread of his story. "We fought with the Crow and the Pawnee but that was the way things were supposed to be. Game was plentiful and the buffalo roamed in herds that stretched from horizon to horizon. Now the elk and deer are harder to find and most of the bears have retreated to the mountains. The buffalo herds have dwindled almost to the point of disappearing, all since the white man came in his home on wheels bringing his women and his diseases. If we are to survive as a people we have to stem this tide of emigrants. Otherwise by the time your children come there will be no meat for them to eat and no forests for them to hunt in. That's why I decided to join with Blizzard. His heart is as black as a grizzly's asshole, but he understands what must be done. Besides, I am like you. With my family dead I had no where else to go."

"That is a very unhappy story you have told," Sad Bear said. "I can understand your bitterness."

"But that doesn't mean you should be bitter as well," Big Hand cautioned. "Your family was killed by soldiers but if the attackers had been Crows they would just as surely have died and probably no less kindly. Believe me when I say that the Crows can inflict tortures that the white man has not imagined."

"What are you trying to tell me?" Sad Bear asked.

"That I should not seek revenge for what has happened to my father, mother, and brother? That I shouldn't want to kill as many whites as I can?"

"No, I'm not telling you that. What I'm saying is you should not kill for the wrong reasons. The white man has to be stopped because he is a danger to all our people—to me and you and even our enemies, the Crow and the Pawnee. We have always had enemies. We have always fought. Sometimes they killed us; sometimes we killed them. But even while we were killing or being killed it was not the same as what the white man threatens to do to us. If I die in battle against a Crow it is an act of bravery and I will be rewarded in the next life. My killer will gain stature with his people and he will hang my scalp proudly from his lance, in effect honoring me as a worthy opponent. That is the way that things were meant to be. It is the way our people have always lived. But if I die of the white man's disease it is a shameful death that brings no good either here or in the hereafter. The white man spreads death and destruction for their own sake, not because they bring him honor and respect."

"So what is your message?"

"My message is to keep your mind and your purpose clear. Do not let yourself become confused. It is an honorable thing to want to kill the white man because that is the only way they can be stopped. But do it because you love your people, not because you hate the white man."

"I'm not sure I understand," Sad Bear said, screwing up his face.

"Listen to me well," Big Hand said earnestly, looking deep into the youth's eyes. "It is, I think, a good thing that you want to drive the white man out but it ceases to be a good thing if you allow yourself to become infected with the same hatred that motivates Blizzard and Crow Killer. They are born assassins; they would kill you or me just as dispassionately as they would kill a white soldier. I have seen the fear in your eyes when you look at Blizzard, and that is good because it keeps you from becoming too confident. It is wise to fear him, but it is not wise to try to be like him. Do you see what I am trying to tell you?"

"I think so," Sad Bear said hesitantly.

"You think so what?" a squeaky voice interrupted from the darkness.

"That settles it," Big Hand said, slapping himself across the forehead. "I *am* getting old. Never in my prime would I have failed to hear your friend approaching."

"Maybe it's because I'm such a good stalker and not because you lack skills as a warrior," Goose said with a grin.

"You see," Big Hand said laughingly to Sad Bear, "your friend is much more of a diplomat than you. At least twice you have called me 'old' but Goose doesn't insult me, he compliments me although in a rather backhanded way."

"You're supposed to be watching to make sure no one approaches from that direction," Sad Bear said reproachfully to Goose, irritated that his friend seemed to have effortlessly won Big Hand's approval while he had prattled on like a child.

"A herd of buffalo could come running through the camp and you two would not hear them coming because you are too busy gossiping like women." Goose chuckled. "You make so much noise I couldn't even sleep."

"Speaking of sleep," Big Hand said, "I want you two to go find a nearby quiet place and curl up in your robes. Let me watch for awhile."

"But that isn't fair," argued Sad Bear. "It is our *duty* to be sentries."

"It is your duty to keep yourselves in good condition so you will be strong and ready when the time comes to fight. It may sound strange to you because you are so young, but the youth require more sleep than the old. Go and lie down. I will awaken you before the next man comes to relieve you so Blizzard will never know you have not been watchful the whole time."

"You would do that for us?" Goose asked in surprise.

"No," Big Hand replied. "I would do it for me. If I am not standing guard I will have to go to sleep and then I will be forced to confront my nightmares. Now do as I suggest. And you," he said, pointing at Sad Bear, "don't forget what we discussed."

"What is he talking about?" Goose asked, puzzled.

"I'll tell you later," Sad Bear said with a grin. "When we have more time and we're not so sleepy."

11

"How much longer we going to have to hang around this godforsaken place?" Unicorn Breedlove grumbled. "I'm beginning to recognize all the rattlers and horny toads by sight."

"I'm with him," agreed Jeb Wilkins. "I've had about all of this shit hole I can stand."

"Me too," echoed Frank Rigano, the short, dark deserter from Fort Laramie the others called "Wop." "Why don't we just take the money we got and head for California? No sense being greedy about it."

"If I've told y'all once, I've told you a hundred times," Notch Henderson replied testily, "this is the best place to be right now. Colonel Kemp's going to think just like Wop, that we're headed for California, and he's going to seal off the route. After a few days when we don't show up, he's going to send a detachment out looking for us."

"Well, we ain't exactly well-hidden, are we?" Breedlove argued.

"Look around," Henderson said, sighing. "See all them little caves? First time we get wind of somebody coming up, we just disappear in them and they'll go right by us. Never even know we've been here. That's why I'm so fired up about keeping a lookout. We'll see them long before they see us. Besides, they ain't going to come this way."

"What makes you think that?" Wilkins asked.

"'Cause I know how officers think," Henderson replied patiently. "They'll think we went north because it's easier to hide in the mountains. But if they're looking for us in the wrong spot, it don't matter anyway how easy it is to hide. They're never going to find us, I promise you that."

"What about him?" Breedlove asked, nodding at Clement Couvillion, who was rolled up in a blanket at the edge of the fire despite the fact that it was well past dawn and the sun was quickly warming the country.

"What about him?" Henderson asked, glancing over his shoulder.

"I mean we going to kill him or what? He's getting to be a real pain in the ass. Besides, he eats too much."

"Hell no, we're not going to kill him," Henderson said forcefully. "He's worth a lot of money."

"I don't understand this," Wilkins said, scratching his chin, which was sprouting a week-old growth of blond whiskers. "We're supposed to collect a good bit of ransom for that palm-presser. That right?"

"That's right," Henderson said, nodding.

"But how we going to collect the ransom if the Army can't find us to give it to us?"

"That's a good point." Henderson grinned. "The way I figure it, they don't have that much money available at Fort Laramie anyway. So we give 'em time to raise it, maybe bring it in from Leavenworth, and then we send word to 'em that we're ready to deal. In the meantime, the important thing is they don't find us."

Wilkins stared into his coffee cup, saying nothing.

"I got an idea," Rigano spoke up.

"Now *that's* unusual," Henderson said. "What's your brainstorm?"

"Why don't we divvy up the money we've got, all that payroll cash. Then those of us who don't want to wait around for another three or four weeks can take their share and head on out."

"Nope!" Henderson said emphatically.

"Why not?" Rigano insisted. "I think we ought to just put a pistol up to that sumbitch's head and forget about the ransom. He's more trouble than he's worth."

"Wop's half right about that," said Breedlove. "You ask me, that Frenchie's half-woman half-rainwater anyways."

"No one's asking you," Henderson shot back. "When we started out, y'all agreed we'd do things my way. And my way is we hold on to Mister Couvillion until we get paid."

"It's Couvillion," the captive said, rolling out of his bedroll. "COO-vee-yawn. And the title is Congressman, not Mister."

"Well, look who's showing some guts." Henderson chuckled. "You a little sensitive about your name, are you?"

"You may as well pronounce it right," Couvillion pouted.

"I like it better my way," said Henderson. "Coo-VILL-ion to rhyme with million. Reminds me of money."

"Seems to me everything reminds you of money," Couvillion said, rising. "I don't guess you mind if I have some coffee?"

"Man at the pot!" Wilkins yelled cheerfully when the captive lifted the battered metal container.

"Huh?" Couvillion said, looking blank.

"It means you got to fill everybody's cup." Henderson smiled. "It's tradition."

"You mean be your *servant*?"

"That's one way of looking at it."

"No," he said defiantly, replacing the pot by the fire. "I won't do it," he added, crossing his arms.

"Jesus, what a sorehead," Rigano mumbled, taking the pot and pouring coffee all around. "I'll bet when you was little your mamma had to tie a pork chop around your neck 'fore the dog would play with you."

"That isn't funny," Couvillion said, frowning. "And don't talk about my mother."

"An' what are you going to do about it?" Breedlove said, slipping his knife out of its scabbard and pointedly digging it under his thumbnail. "You maybe want to take it up with me?"

"N-N-N-No," Couvillion said, the color draining from his face. "I just meant that I didn't appreciate being the butt of your jokes."

"Well ain't that too fucking bad," Breedlove said, staring hard.

"Ease up," Henderson commanded. "We're going to have to be together quite awhile yet and we might as well be friendly about it. Jeb," he said, turning to Wilkins, "you ride out to relieve Will."

"It can't be my turn again already," Wilkins groused. "When are you going to take a turn as sentry?"

"The man's right." Breedlove chuckled. "I thought we was all in this together. That means you got to do some of the dirty work too."

"Okay, okay," Henderson said with a sigh. "Guess you're right. Jeb, you go on out now and I'll come take your place about midday. That suit you?"

"Suits me just fine," Wilkins replied, grinning. "The great thing about not being in the Army no more is we're all equal."

"Don't get the wrong idea," Henderson said, a touch

of warning in his voice. "I agreed to pitch in on the chores but that don't mean that some of us ain't more equal than others, if you get my drift."

"Whatever you say, boss," Wilkins replied agreeably, throwing the remainder of his coffee on the fire. "Don't forget to bring me a box lunch when you ride out."

The sun was just beginning its final plunge toward the horizon when Red Horse and White Crane plodded wearily onto the bluff overlooking the Arapaho camp at the junction of Crippled Elk Creek and the Republican River. Looking down on the valley, they paused to study the scene before them. Spread along both banks of the river were hundreds of lodges, all grouped in orderly fashion according to a plan neither of the Lakota warriors totally understood. In the center was a large open space, where most of the Arapahoes seemed to be gathered. Despite the fact that the late afternoon wind that was whipping at their backs and carrying the sounds away from them, they could clearly distinguish the beat of drums and the chants of the tribespeople.

"Looks as though we're arriving at a good time," Red Horse said, studying the scene. "Right in the middle of their Sun Dance ceremony."

"That means we'll eat very well tonight," White Crane added, hungrily licking his lips.

"Is that all you ever think about?" Red Horse said, somewhat peeved.

"Of course not," White Crane replied easily, ignoring his friend's mild censure. "I also think about counting coup, completing a successful hunt, and deflowering young maidens. What else is a man my age supposed to think about?"

"I wish that you would learn to take life a little more seriously."

"You mean like you?"

"Yes, if you want to put it that way. Like me."

"At times you remind me of my father," White Crane replied, some of the joviality gone from his voice. "He doesn't *enjoy* life; he looks at it as a trial to be endured. My feeling is that we're only young once and if we don't take advantage of it, the opportunity is gone forever. You know," he said, studying his friend, "you've changed a lot since your vision."

"That's because I now realize what a great responsibility I have to our people," Red Horse said. "You believe that life is nothing but one great adventure and that your main purpose in being here is to collect battle honors and garner respect as a great hunter."

"You're right about that," White Crane replied. "There will be time enough later, when my bones begin to get brittle and my mind soft, to let things weigh so heavily upon me that I cannot savor my experiences. Besides," he said, studying Red Horse out of the corner of his eye, "I think you're just jealous."

"Jealous?" Red Horse said in surprise. "Why would I be jealous of you? I have a loving wife, a strong, intelligent son, and a great ambition."

"You also have a crippled leg," White Crane replied, "and a tremendous burden that sits on your shoulders like a buffalo calf. Ever since your vision quest, you have come to believe that our whole band's future rests entirely in your hands. But you have let that rob you of your youth; you can't take life on its own terms. And," he added, "you are obsessed with finding Blizzard."

"You want to find him just as badly as I do."

"Yes," White Crane said, nodding, "but for different reasons."

"What do you mean?"

"I want to find him because *you* want to find him. You are my *kola,* my best friend, and what you want, I want. However, I have to confess that I have another reason as well."

"Oh?" Red Horse asked curiously, "and what is that?"

"*If* Blizzard is still alive—and that's a fairly large if, from my point of view—it is because he is some sort of superhuman."

"So?"

"So that means whoever kills him will win much honor and respect."

"You're looking for glory, then, while I'm looking for revenge for what he did to my brother."

"In the long run," White Crane pointed out, "there is not much difference. We both want him dead."

"Then you think he is still alive?"

White Crane shrugged. "Who knows? We've been searching for him much of the summer. The *Sihiyena,* when we visited their camp, said they had seen evidence of a mysterious group that had moved through their hunting ground, maybe as many as a dozen men. The Cheyenne are perceptive people; they didn't think the intruders were *Kangi* because Crow would have raided their herds. The same goes for *Padani.* If they had been Pawnee they surely would have attacked. Whoever this mysterious group is, they are at least half friendly."

"But we saw Blizzard's body."

"No. We saw the body of a man that *may* have been Blizzard. Neither of us was able to say for certain that it was him."

"Maybe this *thing* that is roaming the forests is a spirit. Maybe it is not Blizzard at all, but his ghost."

"And he has many other ghosts to keep him company?" White Crane asked sardonically. "Your belief in spirits is stronger than mine. I doubt that spirits need to kill buffalo and leave dead campfires behind them. The evidence that Blizzard is still alive, in my opinion, is strong enough to keep me going."

"Me too," agreed Red Horse. "But where do we go from here? We have been north to the Cheyenne and Belle Fouche Rivers. We've been deep into Cheyenne territory to Beaver Lake. The only place we have not been is into Pawnee territory, and that would be foolhardy."

"But it's a possibility," argued White Crane. "I think if we do not learn something here, from the *Mahpiyato*, we should consider it."

"We can't afford to get too discouraged," Red Horse said solemnly. "Let's wait until we've talked to the Arapaho."

"Your timing is perfect," Crooked Nose said, filling the red catlinite pipe with crushed sumac leaves, the mixture preferred by the Southern Arapahoes. "Today was the final day of our *Bayaawu*. Our People are now at total peace with themselves and with our friends."

"You'll have to forgive our ignorance," Red Horse said diplomatically, "but White Crane and I know very little about your customs."

"That is nothing to be ashamed of," Crooked Nose replied with a grin. "I enjoy the role of teacher."

While Crooked Nose launched into a history of his tribe, White Crane studied him carefully, interested more in the man's demeanor than the tales he was telling. A sturdy-looking man in his mid-forties with a broad forehead and short, stubby fingers, the village chief impressed the Lakota warrior as reliable and trustworthy.

"Whatever he tells us will be the truth," White Crane whispered to Red Horse when Crooked Nose excused himself to go outside to urinate. "I sense that about the man and my instincts are rarely wrong."

"I agree," Red Horse replied as Crooked Nose reentered the lodge.

Known throughout the Plains as the "Tattooed People" because of their fondness for body decoration, Crooked Nose was a prime example. As he fiddled with the pipe, the muscles across his chest rippled in the firelight, calling attention to the symbols etched permanently on his upper body. Although Red Horse was unable to tell exactly what the marks represented, he remained fascinated by their presence: three fist-sized indelible emblems placed symmetrically in a line, one over each nipple and one in the exact center of his chest.

"What exactly is a bayaawu?" White Crane asked. "Is that just your term for Sun Dance?"

"Oh, no," Crooked Nose replied. "It is more expansive than that. 'Bayaawu' means 'all the lodges' because that is a time when all of the *Kananacich* come together to celebrate. A Sun Dance is only one of the ceremonies. The Buffalo Lodge, for example, is another bayaawu."

"Again, we are but uninformed wanderers," Red Horse interrupted. "What is a Buffalo Lodge?"

"I can't believe you've never heard of the Buffalo Lodge!" Crooked Nose replied in honest disbelief.

Red Horse gave an elaborate shrug. "Please enlighten us."

"A Buffalo Lodge," Crooked Nose began in a singsong voice, "is the only ceremony I've ever heard of that is performed solely by women."

"Women?" White Crane exclaimed in disbelief. "They have their own sacred ceremony?"

"Among the Kanbanacich, indeed they do." Crooked Nose laughed. "Like a Sun Dance, it is pledged by a woman who feels the need for a religious experience. Usually, the pledger is one who has prayed for the recovery of an ill or wounded relative. If the prayers are answered, she convenes a Buffalo Lodge."

"Is it as elaborate as the Sun Dance?" asked Red Horse.

"Not quite. The Sun Dance continues for seven days, a Buffalo Lodge for only four. But is just as important symbolically."

"Why do you call it a Buffalo Lodge?" Red Horse inquired, deeply interested in anything of a religious nature.

"According to tradition, when the ceremony is over all the participants, including the few men who are allowed to help with the drums and chanting, turn into buffalo and disappear. Except for the pledger. She remains as a white cow."

"That's very interesting," Red Horse interjected. "Do you have ceremonies besides the bayaawu?"

"Oh, yes," Crooked Nose nodded. "The most important is the Wrapping of the Wheel."

Laughing at the puzzled look the two Lakotas exchanged when he mentioned the ceremony, Crooked Nose launched into a detailed explanation.

"A long, long time ago," he said, "the Wheel, the *Hehotti*, was given to our people by Man-Above. It is our most sacred object."

Then it is a physical thing," Red Horse said, "like that pipe in your hand."

"Yes, very much so. My cousin, Broken Tooth, is the Keeper. He guards it with his life."

"May we see it?" White Crane asked.

Crooked Nose hesitated. "Maybe," he said slowly. "I will ask Broken Tooth about that. Usually, it is brought out only during the special ceremony."

"Well, can you describe it to us?" Red Horse persisted.

"That's easy enough," Crooked Nose said happily. "It is about this big," he said, folding his arms into a circle about eighteen inches in diameter. "Basically, it is a branch bent into a wheel shape. One end is tapered, like the tail of a snake, and the other end is lumpy, like a snake's head."

"That's all? Just a branch bent into a circle?"

"It is elaborately carved," Crooked Nose continued. "There are two crosses that represent the Morning Star and two marks that symbolize the Thunderbird."

"Oh," Red Horse said excitedly. "You recognize the Thunderbird as well?"

"We believe," Crooked Nose said with a nod, "that the thunder is caused by the Thunderbird flapping his wings and lightning is the flashing of his eyes. This is all detailed symbolically on the Wheel. Also attached to the wheel are forty-eight eagle feathers, which are the most important part of the device since the eagle is a very powerful bird; its medicine is extremely effective."

"But what's the meaning of the snake shape? Does that have special significance?"

"You are very clever," Crooked Nose said, smiling. "Not many outsiders would ask that question. Yes, it is a water snake that is meant to represent the oceans that surround the earth."

"Oceans?" White Crane said skeptically. "Have you ever seen an ocean?"

"No, but I know they are there," Crooked Nose said with conviction. "Man-Above has told us so."

"What does this wheel *do*?" White Crane asked. "Besides rest in a lodge under guard?"

"Don't be rude," Red Horse said angrily, striking White Crane across the shoulder with the back of his hand.

"I apologize," White Crane said meekly. "I did not intend to be impudent."

"No offense," Crooked Nose said tightly. "You are an outsider and you do not know any better. Worse, you are young and the young are naturally irreverent."

"My friend often speaks before he thinks," Red Horse told Crooked Nose quietly. "He meant no insult."

"Maybe if he had his mouth full of food, he would be less likely to speak in haste," Crooked Nose said. "There is a large feast being prepared to celebrate the end of the Sun Dance. A number of fat puppies have been butchered. You two will be my guests. We will eat well and then tomorrow we will talk about the business that has brought you here."

"What a wonderful idea," White Crane said enthusiastically. "I could eat an entire puppy all by myself."

"You see what I have to put up with," Red Horse said to Crooked Nose, rolling his eyes. "My friend is not only thoughtless, he is a glutton as well."

"But you haven't actually seen him?" Red Horse asked excitedly.

"No," said Frozen Eye, shaking his head. "But one of our warriors, Big Hand, went to join his group and he has not returned so I assume he made contact."

"Why would he do that? Doesn't he know that Blizzard's a murderer."

"Big Hand heard, from what source I do not know, that the man you're looking for, Blizzard, was forming a group to attack the whites. Big Hand's family died of cholera last spring and the deaths made him a little crazy. He got it into his head that the white man was responsible for the deaths and he vowed revenge. I guess he thought that could best be accomplished by teaming up with the outcast Blizzard."

"But you have no idea where he might be right now?" Red Horse asked, his exhilaration dimming.

"No," said He Swims the River. "The only report of strangers we have received is that one of our Coyote Men, Long Leg, sent word that a group of white men was camped west of here, near the big river."

"White men?" said White Crane. "You mean soldiers?"

"No, not soldiers. Maybe they were soldiers once but they no longer wear uniforms or appear to be engaged on any military mission. They aren't doing anything, in fact, except sitting around a campfire arguing with each other."

"Arguing?" Red Horse asked, surprised.

"You'd argue, too, if all you had to eat was buffalo bull," laughed Elk Ear, the youngest man among the group of six Arapahoes gathered in the tight circle convened by Crooked Nose. Because it was such a beautiful day the group abandoned the chief's lodge and spread out among the cottonwoods on the riverbank, luxuriating in the cool breeze that blew down from the hills to the west.

"Are you joking?" asked White Crane. "They're actually eating bull at this time of year?"

"It just shows their ignorance," said Elk Ear. "Everyone knows you don't eat bull during the summer because the meat is too tough."

"Apparently they don't know it." Frozen Eye grinned.

"Why are they there?" Red Horse asked suspiciously. "Have they been there long?"

"They were in the same campground earlier," said Frozen Eye. "Then they left for several days but they came back. Two of the men who were in the original group were not with them when they returned, but they had a stranger with them, probably a captive from the way he's treated. This information comes from Long Leg, who has been watching them closely."

"Are you going to do anything about them?" asked White Crane.

"No," said Crooked Nose. "They show no hostile intentions toward us so their purpose in being there is none of our concern. There are only five of them, not counting the captive, so we could conquer them any time we want."

"No one agrees with me," said Elk Ear, "but I think we should kill them. Their presence in our territory makes me uneasy. If they were Crow or Pawnee, we'd attack without a second thought."

"It would only be starting more trouble with the whites," Crooked Nose said sharply. "We've been over this before. As long as they show no hostility toward us, we will leave them alone. We don't want the white soldiers to come after us like they did against the Brulé and the Miniconjou at Blue Water."

"See," Elk Ear said, raising his hands. "I can't convince anyone in the council that the only good white man is a dead one."

"Let's get back to Blizzard," Red Horse said determinedly. "It is very important to me that we find him and kill him."

"He killed your brother?" Frozen Eye asked. "A member of his own band?"

Red Horse nodded.

"Then he deserves to die."

"But not Big Hand," Frozen Eye said. "He is a good warrior, a respected man. He is no outcast. Nor is he a criminal."

"If he joins in the company of criminals, he has to be prepared to meet the consequences," Crooked Nose pointed out. "At some point the white soldiers will go looking for the group, at least if they persist in their promise to kill every white they can. The soldiers will not know that Big Hand is a good man who just happens to be a little crazy from grief. My hope is he will come to his senses and return before it's too late."

"If we find the group, we will not harm Big Hand," Red Horse promised.

"Unless he tries to hurt us first," White Crane added.

"If you have to act in self defense you have no other choice," Frozen Eye said. "That is understandable."

"The problem," said Red Horse, "is we have no idea where to look. We have searched the Cheyenne country and we found no sign of Blizzard's group. So White Crane and I think he must be somewhere in your territory."

"We are sitting virtually in the middle of our land," said Crooked Nose. "You came in from the north and you saw no sign of him."

"That still leaves us a lot of territory to cover," Red Horse said dejectedly.

"I have an idea," Crooked Nose said.

"And that is?"

"I suggest you two split up. One go east, one go west, then circle toward the south and come back to the camp here."

"But neither of us is that familiar with the country," said White Crane.

"Then I will send a guide with each of you," Crooked Nose proposed. "Bear Claw has a son who is anxious to become a warrior. His name is Flint Shaper and he has a lot of promise. He would be a valuable companion."

"And the other?" asked He Swims the River.

"I would suggest Cut Neck," Crooked Nose said. "He, too, is anxious to test his wings."

"It sounds like a good plan to me," agreed Red Horse. "We can leave in the morning."

"What if one of us finds him?" asked White Crane.

"That's true," said Red Horse, rubbing his chin. "We began this search together and we should end it together. Let's do this. If either one of us spots Blizzard's group, we will return here immediately, then together we will go back and challenge him."

"That sounds fair enough," said White Crane.

"It is agreed then. We will meet back here in no later than . . . what?" he asked, turning to Crooked Nose.

"Five days?" Crooked Nose shrugged. "Seven days?"

"Seven days to be on the safe side," Red Horse proposed, looking at White Crane.

"Seven days it is." He smiled. "With luck, maybe our search is almost over."

"You trust to luck," Red Horse said. "I'll cast my providence with the gods."

"Can you believe our good fortune?" Blizzard asked, leaning carefully over the edge of the cliff. "This is more than what we could have hoped for!"

"It seems too good to be true," Open Wound replied, grinning broadly. "Are you sure it isn't a trap?"

"How could it possibly be a trap? There are only five of them. What could five men possibly do against a force of any size?"

"That's true," agreed Open Wound. "I just can't decide what they could be doing there."

"Who knows why men do anything," Blizzard replied. "They are crazy. But this group has made a big mistake. They are as good as dead. Let's go tell the others," he said, backing slowly away from the edge. "We need to make plans. I want to attack at dawn."

"What about the Crow? I thought we were going to raid a Crow camp so we could lift some prime horses and maybe," he added with a grin, "some prime maidens as well."

Forget the horses and the women for right now," Blizzard replied. "This is more important."

"Will the others agree?"

"Of course they will agree; they have no choice."

"Why did you bring me with you? I was just getting accustomed to the campsite," Couvillion whined.

"Will you quit crying," Henderson said in exasperation. "You sound like a little girl. Besides, I thought you'd want to get away for awhile, what with the way Breedlove is always taunting you."

"I'm glad to get away from him all right, but spending the night in a cold camp doesn't sound like a welcome alternative."

"It's safer for you to be with me," Henderson explained. "If I left you alone back there, the men might kill you just for the hell of it. Unicorn would slit your throat as soon as look at you."

"How do you know they won't leave while you're gone? Just take the money and run?"

"Because they don't know where it is," Henderson said, grinning. "I hid it."

"Really?" Couvillion asked in surprise. "When did you do that?"

"One night when all of you were asleep. I figured it was good insurance."

"That's very clever," Couvillion said, nodding his head. "Maybe you have more brains than I gave you credit for."

Henderson looked at him and grinned. "More balls, too. And don't you forget it. There's Wop. Let's go tell him he's relieved."

"Hi, Notch," Rigano said when he saw the horses approaching. "You're my relief? I thought you were just shitting us when you said you'd take your turn on sentry duty."

"I'm a man of my word," Henderson said, slipping to the ground. "One thing I learned in the Army: You want your men to respect you, never ask them to do anything you wouldn't do yourself. Coovey," he said, turning to Couvillion, "unsaddle our horses while I finish taking Wop's report."

"Jesus," Rigano said, nodding in appreciation. "I can't believe you've got that little turd following your every order."

"Goddamnit, I just love it," Henderson said with a grin. "When would I ever have the chance to boss around a real live Congressman. I'll bet if I told him to suck my dick he'd do that too."

"He might even enjoy it." Rigano smiled.

"Well, I reckon I'll never learn the answer to that one since I ain't inclined that way. Hell, I was in the Army, not the damn Navy. You see anything this afternoon?"

"Nary a thing. Not even a damned buffalo. Sure wish we could bag us a nice cow, though. That bull meat is tougher than saddle leather."

"That's for fucking sure, but it's better'n going hungry. You can go on back to camp now. Me and Coovey can handle things until tomorrow morning."

"Okay," Rigano said, throwing his saddle over his mare's back. "See you in the morning."

"I wish you wouldn't humiliate me like that in front of the others," Couvillion said as soon as they were alone. "I may be your captive but I'm not your damned nigger."

"Goddamn," Henderson said, sighing, "all you do is moan. You don't know what humiliation is and you'd better hope you never find out."

"What do we do now?" Couvillion said, sinking to the ground. "I mean, what does one do on sentry duty?"

"You keep your eyes open is what you do." Henderson chuckled. "You watch that area over there, the big flat valley, and you wake me up if you see anything."

"You mean you're going to sleep?"

"Sure am. That's one of the reasons I brung you out here."

"You mean, I have to sit up all night and stare at nothing while you snore away?"

"Not *all* night, Coovey. I'm going to take me a little siesta and when I wake up, you can stretch out. But I'll tell you one thing. If I wake up and find you sleeping, it's going to be your ass. If you got any *cojones* at all, I'll cut 'em off and feed 'em to you. You get my drift?"

Couvillion stared at Henderson. "You're a terrible person, do you know that? Once I get out of here you're going to be sorry for the way you've treated me."

"Yeah, yeah, yeah," Henderson said, pulling his hat over his eyes. "You keep thinking about how much you hate me because that'll probably keep you awake."

12

White Crane struggled to conceal his excitement. "Look," he said to Flint Shaper, pointing to the tracks along the creek bed, "a large party has been this way only hours ago."

As Flint Shaper slipped off his pony and dropped into a squat to examine the prints, White Crane scurried upstream for a dozen yards, looking for more evidence.

"I'd say at least a half dozen horses," Flint Shaper said after studying the ground.

"More like nine, maybe ten," White Crane added with a professional air. "Headed south."

"Those white men Crooked Nose was telling you about are camped in that direction, maybe two hours away."

"These tracks were made by Indian ponies, not white men's horses," White Crane pointed out.

"Do you think they know about the white men?" Flint Shaper asked, suddenly making the connection.

"Of course they know about them." White Crane grinned. "That's where they're going. I *knew* my hunch would pay off," he said, slapping Flint Shaper on the shoulder. "Those white men are like bait in a trap. Once

Blizzard got the scent he would not be able to resist. He's going after the camp."

"I think you're right," Flint Shaper said, nodding. "In that case we should get back to my village and wait for Red Horse."

"Oh, no. Not yet. We've only been gone two days and Red Horse isn't going to be back for another five. By that time Blizzard may have disappeared again."

"Then what are we going to do?"

"Follow them, naturally. My guess is Blizzard will attack the white men's camp as soon as he finds them, which may be while we're standing here talking. It won't last long; the white men won't be any match for Blizzard and his men. After he kills them, he'll be on the move again and I don't want to lose him."

"But what about Red Horse? You promised that you wouldn't take any action until both of you were there."

"I can't take the chance of losing Blizzard's trail. We'll follow him to the white men's camp and see where he goes from there. Then you can go back to your village and wait for Red Horse. As soon as he arrives, you tell him where you last saw me and he can catch up. I'll be following Blizzard and I'll be careful to leave a clear trail for Red Horse."

"I don't know," Flint Shaper said doubtfully. "I think maybe we should go back right now."

"Are you afraid?" White Crane asked, studying the boy carefully.

"A little," Flint Shaper replied honestly. "What if Blizzard finds *us*?"

"Don't worry about that," White Crane said. "He's going to be too interested in the white men. He's not even going to think about looking behind him. Besides, we're not going to be very close. I only want to get close enough not to lose his tracks. I won't take any action without Red Horse."

"If you say so," Flint Shaper said uncertainly.

"I say so!" White Crane said emphatically. "Come on, we're wasting time. Blizzard may already be collecting those white scalps."

"Goddamn that buffalo meat," Unicorn Breedlove cursed, throwing back his blanket and struggling to his feet.

"What's wrong?" Jeb Wilkins groused sleepily. "It ain't time to get up yet."

"That fucking buffalo meat always gives me the squirts," Breedlove complained, pulling on his boots. "It's bad going down and it's worse coming out. If we ever get back to civilization there's one thing I ain't never going to do again and that's eat buffalo. I've et enough to plumb last me a lifetime," he added, staggering toward the bushes on the edge of the camp.

"Don't make so damn much noise," Wilkins said angrily. "Some of us are trying to sleep." Pulling his blanket over his head, he rolled heavily onto his side.

"It ain't healthy," Breedlove said to himself, fumbling for the buttons on his trousers. "Having to get up in the pitch black night to . . ." he said half aloud, stopping in mid-sentence, startled by a sudden movement nearby and to his left. Looking up, his eyes widened in horror. Barely visible in the predawn gloom was the most frightening thing Breedlove had ever seen, an apparition that brought all his childhood nightmares to life. Looming out of the blackness was a huge manlike form painted in vivid colors that seemed to catch the fading moonlight and glow with a mysterious luminescence. As the creature turned to face him fully, Breedlove found himself staring into a single gleaming eye. Where the other eye should have been was only a black hole that Breedlove was certain was the gateway to hell. Involuntarily, his bowels emptied, soiling his trousers and letting loose a stench that smelled like death.

Breedlove opened his mouth to scream, but the cry was cut short when Blizzard's well-honed knife slashed across the deserter's throat, sending his blood flying into the air in a dark stream that spurted like an erupting volcano.

"What the hell?" Wilkins said, popping upright. "Uni . . ." he began, his words ending abruptly when an arrow loosed by Crow Killer thudded into his left eye. It hit with such force that it went almost completely through his head, burying itself up to the feathers. Wilkins emitted one loud, piercing scream before he pitched backward, dead before his shoulders touched the ground.

"Injuns!" Wop Rigano yelled, coming suddenly awake. It was a credit to his military training that he acted instinctively. Instead of panicking, he rolled swiftly to his left, grabbing his rifle as he turned. He was still on his back when he raised his weapon and found himself staring into the hideously-painted face of the stolid Brulé, Fat Bull. Remembering to squeeze the trigger rather than jerking it, he let off an unaimed round that hit Fat Bull squarely between the eyes. Rigano's eyes widened in wonder as he watched the Indian's head erupt in a cloud of blood and brain matter. "Got that fucker," he mumbled to himself as he reached for his handgun. His fingers were just closing on the scarred wooden grip when Broken Club's lance severed his spine just below his shoulder blades. For the last three seconds of his life, Rigano flopped wildly about like a chicken whose head had just been chopped off.

Will O'Quinn, who had been sleeping at his sentry post two dozen paces away from the campfire, jerked rudely awake when Rigano screamed his warning. Lifting his rifle, he fired a quick shot that buzzed two feet over the head of Four Wolves, who was galloping toward the center of the camp atop his piebald pony.

"Over there," the Miniconjou warrior screamed, trying to turn his animal.

Alerted by the flare of O'Quinn's rifle, Goose dug his heels into his pony's side and urged the high-spirited animal onward, anxious to beat Four Wolves to the enemy.

Dropping his rifle, O'Quinn pulled his pistol and aimed at the closest target: Goose.

Squeezing the trigger, he stared as the shot hit Goose's pony in the jaw. The animal reared in pain, toppling over backwards with his rider underneath. The boy uttered a barely audible grunt as his chest collapsed under the weight of his dying mount.

Grinning broadly, Four Wolves hopped to the ground and quickly closed on O'Quinn, both of whose weapons were now empty. The former private from Fort Kearny was scrambling for his knife when Four Wolves pivoted and levered his stone-headed club in a huge roundhouse swing. The heavy weapon caught O'Quinn on his left side, instantly crushing five ribs and sending him sprawling. Screaming in pain and terror, O'Quinn struggled to his knees and was trying to regain his feet when Four Wolves swung again, this time an overhead blow. The club hit O'Quinn squarely in the face.

"It sounded like a melon being dropped to the ground," Four Wolves laughed a few minutes later as he removed O'Quinn's scalp.

"What was that?" Couvillion squeaked, coming suddenly awake.

"Shut up!" Henderson barked, straining to hear.

"What—" Couvillion persisted, still half asleep.

"Goddamn you," Henderson repeated, "I told you to shut up. Now do it."

Chastised, Couvillion slumped back against his bedroll, trying hard to control the shaking that convulsed his body like a violent fever. With his hands tightly gripping the blanket that he had pulled to his chin, the congressman watched Henderson through eyes the size of silver dollars, unaware that his teeth were chattering loudly enough to cause the horses thirty yards away to shift nervously in response to the unfamiliar noise.

"Three shots," Henderson said, as much to himself as to Couvillion. "Two rifle, one pistol."

"What does that mean?" Couvillion asked, fearing to hear the answer.

"Can't mean but one thing," Henderson replied grimly. "Injuns. They're attacking the camp. Get up!" he said sharply, turning to Couvillion.

"Get up?" Couvillion replied, afraid that his quivering legs would not support him and unwilling to let Henderson see that he had urinated on himself.

"What is this? A fucking echo? I said get your ass up. We have to get out of here." Already, Henderson was lifting the saddle that he had been using as a backrest and was moving toward his horse.

"We . . . we . . . we're just going to run off?" Couvillion mumbled weakly.

Henderson looked at him and smiled grimly. "You got a better idea? You think maybe we should go back to the camp and try to talk them injuns into being nice?"

"Aren't you going to help your men?"

"Help 'em?" Henderson chuckled humorlessly. "I reckon by now they're already dead. And we're going to be too if we don't get moving. I don't want to have to tell you again, get up and get saddled."

"I d-d-d-don't think I can move," Couvillion stammered.

"I'll get you moving," Henderson replied, hurriedly, returning to where Couvillion was cowering. Lifting his right leg, he kicked the congressman viciously on his hip. "This ain't no joke," he said, leaning forward until Couvillion thought he would faint from the odor of the deserter's sour breath. "If we don't get out of here *right now* we're as good as dead. Maybe you want your scalp to be dangling from an injun's lance, but I don't. If you ain't ready to go in thirty seconds, I'm leaving without you."

"Yes . . . yes . . . yes," Couvillion blurted in panic. Despite his fear, he scrambled to his feet.

Belying the seriousness of the situation, Henderson could not help laughing as he watched Couvillion struggle to get his horse saddled. "Come on," he said, swinging aboard his own mount, "we ain't got a second to lose."

"That didn't take very long, did it?" White Crane whispered dispassionately.

He and Flint Shaper were sprawled on their stomachs on the edge of the bluff that overlooked the site where the white men had been camped, buffalo robes pulled over their heads as camouflage.

Even though they were looking almost directly into the sun as it rose over the eastern horizon, they could easily see Blizzard and his men as they went about the grim task of cleaning up the battle site.

Blizzard, Broken Club, Four Wolves, and Crow Killer, whose arrow had been the one that killed Wilkins, were claiming their victims' scalps. It was the first time White Crane had seen Blizzard since before he killed Badger and fled the Wazhazha camp many months before. He was shocked by the change in the warrior's appearance.

"Finally, he looks like the monster he truly is," White Crane mumbled.

"Just the sight of him makes me tremble," Flint Shaper whispered, staring at Blizzard as he cleaned his bloody knife on Breedlove's shirt. "Look at that smile! He's really enjoying what he's doing!"

While the four were busy with their grisly tasks, Red Chin was wrapping Fat Bull's body in a blanket he had recovered from the campsite. Off to the side, Big Hand, Crow Killer, and Sad Bear struggled to remove the pony off Goose's lifeless body.

"We could use some help," Big Hand grunted breathlessly, struggling for a handhold. Sad Bear, smeared with the pony's blood, was using a piece of firewood to try to lever the pony's form upward. As he struggled, tears streamed down his cheeks and dripped onto the ground, making small puddles in the dust.

"Here," said Red Chin, coming to help them. "I'll work from this end." Straining mightily, the three shoved the pony's body a foot to the left while Sad Bear grabbed Goose's arms and pulled backward, throwing all his weight into the effort. Slowly, like a badger being dragged from a hole, Goose's body wiggled free. Except for thin streams of blood that trickled out of his nostrils and the corners of his mouth, the youth's body was surprisingly unmarked.

"Get up, Goose," Sad Bear urged plaintively. "Open your eyes and look at me."

"He's dead," Big Hand said, placing his hand on Sad Bear's shoulder. "He can't hear you."

"He had no time to suffer," Crow Killer remarked, "and he died a warrior's death. What else can a man hope for?"

"Come on," Blizzard said, approaching the group. "We need to be on the move."

"What's the hurry?" Sad Bear asked, turning his tear-stained face toward Blizzard. "I would like to tend my friend's body."

"There may be soldiers in the area," Blizzard replied. "They would have heard the shots."

"What about the bodies of our men?" asked Big Hand.

"Leave them," Blizzard replied coldly. "It is an honor for a warrior felled in battle to be left where he dropped."

"No," Big Hand said stubbornly. "I am an Arapaho. We believe in burying the dead."

"Bury them, then," Blizzard said curtly. "But the rest of us are leaving."

"Sad Bear will stay and help me," Big Hand replied. "We will catch up with you by nightfall."

"All right," Blizzard replied. "But don't take too long. The dead don't care what you do with their remains. They aren't," he added with what was intended as a smile, "likely to complain one way or another."

After watching Blizzard and his men for a few minutes, White Crane and Flint Shaper wiggled backward like crabs away from the edge of the bluff. Once they were far enough away so that they no longer worried about being seen from below, they rose into a crouch, then slowly stood completely erect. Never taking their eyes off the edge of the bluff, they walked slowly backward until they reached the spot where they had tethered their horses.

"Do you remember the plan?" White Crane whispered.

"Yes," Flint Shaper answered softly. "I go back to my village and wait for Red Horse to return. Then I bring him back here and we look for your trail."

"That's right," White Crane said, nodding. "I'll follow Blizzard and leave marks that even Red Horse will be able to see. I'll stay on their heels until you catch up with me."

"But what about the others?" Flint Shaper asked, frowning. "You and Red Horse can't fight eight men."

"We won't try to," said White Crane. "We'll explain that our argument is with Blizzard, that it is a personal matter. Once we do that, they will not interfere."

"If you ask me, that's taking a pretty big chance," Flint Shaper said.

"Nothing is without risk," White Crane replied with a smile. "If you intend to be a good warrior that's one lesson you have to learn early."

"There are so many things to learn." Flint Shaper sighed. "I wonder if I will ever be a man."

"You will," White Crane said kindly. "I felt the same when . . ." Pausing, he stared into the distance, off to the north.

"What is it?" Flint Shaper asked anxiously, his heartbeat quickening.

"Look over there," White Crane said, pointing.

Flint Shaper stared in that direction, surprised to see twin trails of dust heading rapidly away.

"Who *is* that?" Flint Shaper whispered.

"It must be two more white men. They must have been lookouts posted away from the camp. It was very careless of Blizzard not to know about them. His lust for white man's blood must have been great for him not to thoroughly scout the area before ordering an attack. It just goes to show," he added, shaking his head, "that no one is perfect. Not even the great Blizzard."

"I think they're going to get away," Flint Shaper said, half in surprise.

"I agree," said White Crane. "Blizzard doesn't know they're there and by now they have a good lead. You see," he said, turning to his companion, "that's still another lesson for you to learn. *Always* scout the area before an attack. Never commit yourself without knowing what you are facing. Now, we have wasted enough time talking. We have to leave before Blizzard stumbles upon us. I'm going to ride to the north, out of Blizzard's probable path and give him and his men a chance to leave. Then I'll fall in behind them. You travel swiftly. I'll see you soon when you return with Red Horse."

"I think we're in the clear now," Henderson said, reining his horse to a stop. "It's almost noon," he said, checking the angle of the sun. "If they aren't chasing us by now, we got away in time."

"Were we lucky?" Couvillion asked innocently.

Henderson laughed. "Damn lucky. Maybe you'll never know just how lucky. Whoever those Indians were, they were damn careless. Otherwise, they would have known where we were and kilt us, too."

"What now?" Couvillion asked worriedly. "We don't have any supplies or anything."

"Well," Henderson drawled, "I reckon we'll mosey over there to that cottonwood grove. Then we stretch out in the shade and take a little siesta."

"You mean just calmly go to sleep? How can you do that?"

"What do you mean?"

"I mean, your men have just all been killed and you've barely escaped with your own life. Now you want to go recline in the shade and take a *nap*?"

"Well what else would you suggest? I'm just trying to kill a little time before we go back to the campsite."

"Oh, God!" Couvillion said, shocked. "You mean go back to where all those men were killed? Their bodies will probably still be there."

"Of course they'll still be there, you numskull. What you think's going to happen? They going to get up and walk away?"

"Why do you want to go back there? Why don't we just keep going?"

"Go where? Fort Laramie? You just want me to ride in there and say, 'Hidy, colonel. Guess who's back?'"

"Well, maybe not exactly like that."

"Are you fucking crazy?" Henderson asked, staring at Couvillion. "You think I'm going to surrender or something? They'd hang me quicker'n you can say 'Pass the salt.'"

"I could speak up for you. Say how you've treated me well."

"And you think that's gonna make up for those people killed in the raid on the wagon train? Not to mention that I'm a deserter?"

"Well, maybe not," Couvillion said. "But maybe you won't hang."

"And maybe the buffalo won't shit on the ground," Henderson replied. "If they ever catch me, they're going to stretch my neck. And I don't aim to give 'em the chance."

"I haven't stopped to think about it," Couvillion

conceded. "I guess you have a point. But why do you want to go back to the campsite?"

"To get the money, you fucking idiot. You think I'm just going to ride away and leave all that payroll loot? You think maybe the injuns is going to take it?"

"Oh, my. I'd completely forgotten about the money."

"A man in my position don't ever forget about money," Henderson said bitterly. "Only rich guys like you can afford not to think about cash. And that brings up the subject of your ransom."

"Oh dear," Couvillion said, paling. "What about that?"

"Damn good question. Way I see it, I don't have much choice. I ain't in no position any longer to hang around waiting to collect. I got to get moving."

"And me?"

"Well," Henderson said, looking closely at Couvillion. "I could kill you."

"Kill me!" Couvillion gasped. "Why on earth would you want to do that?"

"It's either that or leave you here. You can't come with me, that's for sure."

"Leave me!" Couvillion urged. "I'll be fine. You go on. Go wherever you have to go. Do whatever you have to do. I can find my way to Fort Laramie."

"What if you stumble on them injuns?" Henderson grinned. "That happens, you'll wish I killed you nice and quick-like."

"Are you trying to frighten me? If you are, you're succeeding."

"Just joshing with you, Coovey," Henderson replied. "But you do have a point. I got a lot of time and interest invested in you. And I could rightly use that ransom money. Come to think of it, there ain't no reason why I still can't get something out of this shambles."

"How's that?"

"Say I don't kill you. In fact, say I even point you on the right trail that'll get you nice and safe back to Fort Laramie."

"And?"

"And then sometime in the not-too-distant future I come ask you for a loan."

"You mean extortion!" Couvillion said indignantly.

"Guess that's one name for it. Better than being dead out here in the middle of nowhere though, ain't it?"

"How do you know I'll pay you? That I won't just have you arrested?"

"Give me some credit, will you," Henderson said slyly. "I ain't going to be stupid about it. I'll figure a way to get the money without you and me having direct contact. Besides, you know me by now. You know what'll happen to you if you don't pay up."

"How much do you want?" Couvillion said, sounding resigned.

"I don't know yet." Henderson smiled. "Depends on how much I need. Right now, I need to think on it just a bit more. I want to make sure I ain't leaving you room to double-cross me. That would make me right disagreeable. So why don't we go on over yonder and stretch out in the shade for an hour or two and then we'll work out the details."

"You're a devil, Henderson," Couvillion said angrily.

"Yeah, I guess I am," Henderson agreed amiably. "But a damn clever one."

"Goose was my best friend," Sad Bear said, sobbing. "He was the closest thing I had left to family."

"The death of a loved one is never easy," agreed Big Hand, adding a rock to the pile atop the shallow grave where Goose and Fat Bull had been laid side by side. "But he is in a better place now, well on his journey along the Milky Way. There are some Arapaho who believe the dead turn into owls but I don't think so. I think the dead go beyond the mountains to the land of the rising sun where they live comfortably forever on a vast plain where game is plentiful."

"Goose was a Miniconjou, not an Arapaho, but our views on the afterlife are much the same."

"We all die sooner or later," Big Hand said. "Goose was lucky because he died a warrior's death. He will get special treatment in the next world. Usually, when an Arapaho dies we kill his horse so he will have a mount to accompany him on his journey."

"We Lakota do the same thing," Sad Bear added.

"But this is a very unusual circumstance. His horse also was killed."

"Perhaps the pony is already waiting for him," suggested Sad Bear.

"That is true," agreed Big Hand. "Come. We have done all we can. Now we need to go. Blizzard will be wondering what happened to us."

"Did they go this way?" Sad Bear asked, pointing toward the northwest. "I was so upset I didn't notice."

"Yes. But I know an easier path. Remember, this is my territory. If we go my route, we can save much time."

Leading the way, Big Hand led Sad Bear through a narrow canyon that split the southeastern wall of the cliff, then turned sharply back toward the north, bringing them out on the top of a large, flat mesa.

"See," he said proudly, "we have saved many steps by taking this route. And much time, too."

"What is this?" Sad Bear asked, staring at the ground. "Single pony tracks."

Big Hand slipped to the ground and pored over the indentations in the hard dirt. "You have very sharp eyes, my young friend. I probably would not have seen these."

"What do you make of them?"

Big Hand shrugged. "A single horse. An Indian pony, not a white man's animal. Fresh. The rider is in no hurry, but he's going in the same direction as Blizzard and the others. I would say he's following them."

"Following them? Why would he want to do that? Could he be one of the Pack who's lagging behind?"

"No, I don't think so," Big Hand replied. "These tracks are fresher than those of the Pack would be. "But two can play at this game. If he can follow Blizzard, we can follow him."

It was mid-afternoon before Big Hand and Sad Bear caught up with White Crane, who had stopped along a stream to allow his pony to drink.

"Hello, stranger," Big Hand yelled, emerging unexpectedly from the underbrush, his bow at the ready with an arrow already notched.

White Crane looked up in surprise, immediately deducing that Big Hand was one of Blizzard's men. He was reaching for his tomahawk when Sad Bear yelled from behind him.

"Don't do that," he cautioned. "You are one against two and we have the advantage of position."

Cursing himself for not being more careful, White Crane let his arm relax. I should have counted the tracks, he said angrily to himself. Then I would have known that two men were trailing.

"My name is White Crane," he said, forcing himself to be calm. "I am from the Wazhazha band of the Brulé and I mean you no harm."

"Then what do you want?" Big Hand asked without lowering his bow.

"My business is with Blizzard, not with you," White Crane replied.

"If you know whose tracks you are following you must have been at the campsite when we killed the white men," said Sad Bear.

"Yes, I was there." White Crane nodded. "But you did not see me. I was hidden."

"Why would you want to do that?"

"Because I have been looking a long time for Blizzard."

"You haven't said why."

"It's a long story," said White Crane. "It has to do with an incident that happened many months ago at the Wazhazha winter camp. Blizzard killed my kola's brother and I vowed to help him find him."

"Before Blue Water?" asked Sad Bear.

"Long before then. We were looking for Blizzard at Blue Water but we got there too late. We thought he had been killed by the soldiers, but obviously we were wrong."

"He *was* badly wounded," Sad Bear. "We did not think he was going to live but he proved to be remarkably strong."

"Why have you joined with him?" White Crane asked. "You do not seem like evil men."

"We agree with Blizzard that all white men should be killed," Sad Bear explained. "I lost my entire family at Blue Water and my thirst for revenge is great."

"And your companion?" White Crane asked, nodding at Big Hand. "He's an Arapaho. He must be Big Hand. We were at his village and Crooked Nose told us his story, how he had lost his family to disease and he blames the white man."

"The white men are devils," Sad Bear said harshly.

"One of them saved my life once," White Crane said. "So I don't think they're all bad. But Blizzard is a murderer; he is wicked. He even killed a fellow member of his band over nothing."

"I can believe that," Sad Bear said. "I can see the evil in him."

"Then why do you follow him?"

Sad Bear shrugged. "I have nowhere else to go."

Big Hand had been studying White Crane carefully. Finally he spoke. "And you wish to confront Blizzard?"

"Yes and no." White Crane shrugged. "It is my kola, Red Horse, who has the grudge with Blizzard. I promised I would help him find him."

"Then where is Red Horse? We found only your tracks."

"We agreed to split up to broaden our search. We were supposed to meet back at your village. But I found Blizzard first and I sent word back for Red Horse to come. I was to follow Blizzard and leave a trail for my friend."

"We can't pretend we never saw you," Big Hand pointed out. "I think you had better come with us. We will take you to Blizzard."

"I understand," White Crane replied, thinking fast. Although he wanted to wait for Red Horse to arrive, there was no chance of that now unless he could somehow overpower the man and boy. But to resist would be foolish; he would not stand a chance under the present circumstances. Besides, he had no fight with these two. It was better, he decided, to go along and let the situation unfold. If they intended to kill him, they already would have done so. Let them take him to Blizzard, since that was what he wanted anyway. If it meant that he must challenge Badger's killer before Red Horse arrived, there was nothing he could do about it. On the bright side, he had much to gain. If he killed Blizzard, it would be a great honor. Fate had put him in an unexpected situation and he was in no position to change it. Do not squander the opportunity, he told himself.

"If you're going to join Blizzard, then it would be my pleasure to join you," he said, trying to sound good-natured.

"Very well," Big Hand said slowly. "You will come with us. But you will have to travel as our prisoner. Sad Bear," he commanded, "bind his hands."

Jim Ashby leaned forward and spit a long stream of tobacco juice at his pony's feet, watching in apparent fascination as it disappeared almost immediately, leaving only a small, damp mound in the tan-colored dust.

"I got an idee, cap'n," he said.

"What's that?" the flush-faced Harrigan replied, taking off his hat and fanning himself.

"We ain't fer from where the 'hos usually make their summer camp. Whyn't I meander down there and see if they seen any trace o' those bastards we been lookin' fer."

"Why don't we all go?"

"Think it'd be better if I were to go on my lonesome," Ashby explained. "I'm afeared if we all go runnin' in it's gonna spook the 'hos, considering what happen'd at Blue Water an' all. They see a bunch o' soljers headin' their way, they might just panic. 'Sides, I got connections with the tribe. I used to be married to a 'ho."

"How long you talking about?"

Ashby shrugged and looked up at the sun. "It's almost midday now. Couple or three hours to the 'ho camp, an hour to smoke Crooked Nose's pipe and jabber a li'l. Couple hours back. You can start lookin' for me around dusk."

Harrigan raised in his saddle, studying the surrounding territory. "We crossed a stream 'bout an hour back. There's water and shade there. We'll go back there and wait for you. Can you find us okay?"

Ashby made no attempt to hide his offense. "Cap'n, you got seventeen white men awandering around the plains leaving a clear enuf trail for a ten-year-ol' injun to follow. I reckon I could find you even if you was tryin' to hide."

"Don't be so touchy, Ashby. I wasn't trying to insult you. But we've been gone from the post for eight days now and you haven't been able to find even a trace of those deserters."

"Wail," Ashby drawled. "I been thinkin' 'bout tha' too. I reckon they didn't head north as we figured they would, otherwise we'd afound their trail. The fac' that we didn't fin' 'em there or off to the east inclines me to believe they's either south or west, an' west ain't likely 'cause there's nothing out there for quite a ways. Tha' leaves south, which is 'ho country. If they be somewhere in 'ho country, ol' Crooked Nose is gonna know about it. If he can point us in the right direction, it'll save us a passel o' trouble."

"Well, go on then," Harrigan replied in exasperation. "I'll take the detachment back to the creek and we'll wait for you to get back. If you aren't back by noon tomorrow, we'll come looking for you at the Arapaho camp. I figure I just might be able to find that even without an uppity guide."

"I wouldn't bet your life on it," Ashby replied with a grin, digging his heels into his pony's side and galloping away before the red-faced Harrigan could respond.

Ashby could see the smoke and smell the camp long before he could see it, the scent of roasting meat spreading across the vast open land like a beckoning hand. By the time he approached the group, his mouth was starting to water in anticipation of a hot meal.

"See, cap'n," he began as he strolled up to the fire, "I'm back an' there's still an hour o' light left. I tole you . . ." he continued, stopping in surprise when he saw who was sitting next to Harrigan. "I'll be dipped in horseshit," he added, coming to a halt as if he'd seen a ghost. "Whar in hell did you come from?"

"Surprised, are you, Mr. Ashby?" Harrigan said, satisfaction dripping from his voice. "While you're off hobnobbing with your ex-in-laws we've been pretty busy on our own."

"Whar in tarnation did you fin' him?" Ashby asked, still in shock.

"I sent Privates DeLuca and O'Malley out to get some fresh meat. They came back with a young antelope and the congressman. Quite a catch, eh?"

"Well, I can't deny it ain't a revelation to me, considerin' what Crooked Nose tol' me an all."

"Sit," Harrigan ordered. "Help yourself to some food, then tell me what the Arapaho thinks occurred."

"Not two hours 'fore I got there," Ashby said, taking a large bite from the chunk of antelope flank he had impaled on the end of his knife, "this boy named Flint Shaper came hustlin' back to the 'ho camp. He had been out with a Brulé named White Crane looking for an outcast injun named Blizzard when . . . "

"I don't care about all that," Harrigan interrupted. "Tell me what you heard about the deserters."

"I was gettin' to that, cap'n. While Flint Shaper and White Crane was lookin' for this Blizzard, who Red Horse wants to kill on account . . . "

"Goddamnit, Ashby, will you stick to the point?"

"They seen the shootin'," Ashby said, glancing angrily at Harrigan.

"Tell me about the shooting."

"Ain't much to tell. Blizzard and his band o' killers found the deserters' camp and cleaned their clocks. Murdered evr' last one o' 'em, the boy Flint Shaper said."

"Except for me and Mr. Henderson," Couvillion interjected.

"Oh, it's 'Mr. Henderson' is it?" Ashby asked, giving Couvillion a curious look. "You suddenly gone all respectful for your kidnapper? How come you ain't croaked?"

"*Mister* Henderson," Couvillion replied, emphasizing the title, "and I were standing watch some distance from the camp when the attack occurred. The hostiles apparently were not aware of our presence."

"So you jus' skedaddled?"

"Well, yes," Couvillion said slowly. Even in the dusk Ashby could see him blush. "What else were we supposed to do?"

"You mighta gone back an' helped."

"By the time we were aware of the attack, it was too late. We decided that escape was the better part of valor."

"I jus' reckon you did."

"Henderson turned the congressman loose and then he took off for parts unknown," Harrigan said. "He had intentions of making his way back to Fort Laramie when O'Malley and DeLuca found him."

"Them deserters was camped southwest o' here," Ashby pointed out. "If he was makin' his way to the fort, he was goin' the wrong way."

"He was, uh," Harrigan coughed delicately, "lost."

"Tha's a good un." Ashby laughed. "Ain't but two directions to go, east or west, an' the congressman picks the wrong one."

"It's easy to get confused on the Plains," Couvillion said hotly. "There is a disturbing lack of distinguishable features . . ."

"An honest mistake," Harrigan said quickly. "It isn't difficult for someone unfamiliar with the Plains to get turned around. But that isn't the important thing. What I need to know is can you lead us to the deserters' camp?"

"Reckon I can do that," Ashby said, nodding. "Crooked Nose gave me good directions. Is that where you suggestin' we go?"

"That's what we were debating when you arrived," said Benoit, who had been following the exchange in silence.

"What do you mean 'debate?'"

"I think we should go after Henderson," Benoit said. "From what Cle, uh, Congressman Couvillion, has told us Henderson returned briefly to the camp to recover the payroll money he had hidden in an attempt to keep the others from taking it. I believe we should track him down and get the money back."

"He could be halfway to Californy by now," Ashby said.

"I think that's what he wants us to think," Benoit said. "Personally, I believe he's headed back east."

Ashby's eyebrows rose. "How come you say that? Iffen it were me, I'd go west."

"It's because of what he told me," Couvillion interrupted. "He said he was turning me loose and abandoning the plan to collect the ransom only because he planned to contact me some time in the near future and extort an appropriate sum."

"Or what?" Ashby wanted to know.

"Or he'd kill me. And I believe he would. I didn't doubt it for a second when he said it."

"Um," Ashy said, staring into the fire, pondering the new information. After a pause he looked up at Harrigan. "You want my opinion?"

"Why the hell not?" he replied. "I've heard everyone else's."

"I think we oughta go after them injuns."

"That Blizzard and his men?"

"Yup."

"That's an interesting thought," Harrigan said, rubbing his chin. "After all, they did kill—what was it?" he asked, turning to Couvillion. "Four?"

"Four is correct."

"They did kill four white men even if they were killers and deserters."

"I forbid it," Couvillion said adamantly.

"Huh?" said Ashby, swivelling to look at the congressman.

"How's that?" asked Benoit. "You *forbid* it?"

"What's the matter with us going after the injuns?" Harrigan asked Couvillion. "I could detach a couple of men and send you back to the post . . . "

"A *couple* of men? What good would that do if Blizzard decided to attack? He probably has twenty or twenty-five . . . "

"Five and him according to Flint Shaper," interjected Ashby. "He lost two in the attack hisself."

"Even so, that would be six against two."

"I would imagine he's a long way from here by now," said Harrigan.

"My point 'actly," said Ashby. "We need to get after that sumbitch soon's we can."

"Blizzard and his men aren't going anywhere,"

argued Benoit. "The Plains is their home. We need to cut Henderson off before he disappears in some city somewhere with the Army payroll."

"The government will replace the payroll," said Couvillion. "I personally will see that it is expedited."

"There ain't no whites really safe on the Plains long's as Blizzard's roamin' 'round," persisted Ashby.

"It probably took Henderson a couple of hours to double back and dig up that money," said Benoit. "That means he doesn't have much of a . . . "

"Gentlemen!" Harrigan said loudly, cutting off the argument. "I'm commanding here and the decision is ultimately mine."

"Well," said Benoit, "what is your decision, captain?"

"Yeah, cap'n, what's it gonna be?"

"I'm all ears," added Couvillion.

"There are other considerations here," Harrigan began portentously.

"Uh, oh," said Benoit.

"Shit, damn, hellfire," Ashby mumbled under his breath.

"Political ones," Harrigan said, glancing at Couvillion out of the corner of his eye. "In my opinion there are three things to consider. They are," he said, lifting his hand and raising a finger, "looking for Henderson would be like searching for a needle in a haystack. We have no idea which way he's gone and even if Mr. Ashby can pick up his trail, he can run us ragged. We cannot afford to be gone from the fort that long. Two," he added, lifting a second finger, "the same holds true for the injuns. They are skilled evaders. They can continue to elude us almost indefinitely, or at least until we run out of supplies. That leaves the third issue."

"And that's Cle," said Benoit.

"Precisely," Harrigan said firmly. "The congressman

has been subjected to a harrowing ordeal. It is my obligation as a military man to return him to the bosom of his friends and loved ones . . . "

"Bosom is a very apt word," Benoit said, unable to restrain himself.

"Jean . . ." Couvillion began angrily.

"Enough!" Harrigan said. "I made a bad word choice. No one meant anything offensive. Benoit, you will keep your mouth shut unless spoken to. Congressman, I beg you not to be so quick to jump. This is the West; we're a little more outspoken out here than in Washington. But as I was saying, I feel a duty to return Congressman Couvillion to the *safety* . . . does that word suit everyone? . . . to the safety of Fort Laramie at the earliest possible time. That means as soon as we march to the site of the attack to verify the casualties and bury the dead we will proceed back to Fort Laramie. We leave at sunrise tomorrow. Understood?"

"Jon . . ." said Benoit.

"That's Captain Harrigan."

"Okay. Uh, yes, sir. Captain Harrigan. I implore you to reconsider . . . "

"Implore all you want, Benoit, I'm not going to change my mind. Now let's all get some sleep. We have a long day ahead of us tomorrow."

White Crane let his gaze sweep around the circle, meeting the hostility that radiated from the men with disciplined aplomb. Of the eight pairs of eyes staring back at him, only those of Big Hand and Sad Bear were not openly antagonistic. Let them think what they want, White Crane told himself, but I will not let myself be cowed into submission. Nothing would please Blizzard more than sensing that I am afraid.

"I can understand why you might be suspicious of my motives," he said as calmly as he could, "but let me repeat that I have no argument with anyone here except Blizzard."

At the mention of his name, Blizzard's lone eye flashed briefly, but the look faded to one of watchful disbelief.

"I know about you even though we are not of the same band," said the Brulé Open Wound. "I have heard that you are a brave young warrior but one perhaps with too much affinity toward the white man."

White Crane paused, taking his turn with the pipe that was passed by Broken Club. "Whoever told you that," he said, exhaling the smoke, "does not know me very well. It is true that I once spent time in the white man's fortress but I was unconscious the entire time. As soon as I regained my senses, Red Horse and I left to return to our people."

"Didn't you play host to that white soldier? The one who was wounded by one of his own during the massacre at Blue Water?" persisted Open Wound.

"No, that was Red Horse. I helped him carry the soldier from the battlefield, but he did not stay in my lodge."

"But you are very close to Red Horse, are you not?" Four Wolves asked.

"He is my kola," White Crane said simply. "I would do anything for him. And he for me."

"Including die for him?" Blizzard said, speaking for the first time. His voice, deep and reverberating, cut the air like a distant thunderclap.

Willing himself to be calm, White Crane turned to face his questioner, trying hard to ignore the unsightly disfigurement. "It is for Red Horse that I am here now," he replied, sidestepping the question. "He seeks revenge against you for murdering his brother. I promised him I would help find you. And that is what I've done."

"Since Red Horse isn't here to speak for himself, can you speak for him?" Blizzard asked in a voice that made the hair rise on the back of White Crane's neck.

"Speak, yes," White Crane said. "But if you can be patient for two or three more days Red Horse will be here to speak for himself."

"Why should we wait for this half-cripple to hobble his way across the Plains?" asked Crow Killer, entering the conversation. "We have things to do."

This is a mean one indeed, White Crane thought, turning his attention to the Miniconjou. There is hardly a shade of difference between him and Blizzard.

"I'm not asking you to wait," White Crane said. "I'm just presenting you with the facts."

"You have a very nimble tongue," Broken Club said belligerently. "It might be less so if Blizzard were to cut it out."

White Crane blushed as a wave of laughter swept around the group, but he was reassured when he looked up and saw that neither Sad Bear nor Big Hand had joined in the merriment.

"I'm not trying to play word games with you," White Crane replied evenly, struggling to keep his temper under control. "I'm only explaining why I'm here."

"I think you came to try to kill me yourself," said Blizzard in a voice as cold as a January wind. "Is that not true?" he asked when White Crane did not immediately reply.

He's run me into a corner, White Crane told himself. If I say no, I will be branded a coward and the rest will turn on me like wolves on a wounded elk. And if I say yes we will have to fight to the death. "I did not follow you from the scene of the white man's slaughter with the intention of challenging you," White Crane said evenly, "but neither do you frighten me. It is Red Horse that has the real grievance and I would prefer to let him face you directly."

"The two of you could try to overpower me," Blizzard said.

"No," replied White Crane, forcing himself to laugh. "How could we do that when you have so many men at your command?"

"My men will not interfere in any personal disagreement I have. I can promise you that."

"And what good are your promises? You're a murderer, a thief, and a man who has been banned by his own people."

"You have gone too far," Blizzard hissed, his countenance turning to stone. "You have insulted me in front of my men."

He's right, thought White Crane. I let my mouth run away from me again. Now I have no choice. I have to fight him. "No," he said with unfelt bravado, "It is you who insult me. You offend me by breathing the same air. Nothing would make me happier than to impale you on the end of my knife."

"Then let us see who will impale whom," Blizzard said, rising and tossing off his blanket. "I will wait for you outside," he added, slipping out of the lodge.

"What did you do that for?" Sad Bear whispered as the others rushed to join Blizzard under the cottonwoods. "You had just about made your story convincing."

"No," White Crane whispered back. "From the first Blizzard had decided that he wanted to taste my blood. I read it in his face. Nothing I could have said would have distracted him; he would have kept after me until he got the fight that he wants."

"Aren't you frightened?" Sad Bear asked, awed.

"Me?" White Crane asked, throwing out his chest. Looking around to make sure they were alone, he added: "Yes. Blizzard is very skilled at hand-to-hand combat. He has experience and the desire to kill. I have only my agility and my wits. That's why I said what I did to him. I hoped it would make him angry enough that he might get careless."

"What if he kills you?"

"That's a chance I have to take," White Crane said with a shrug. "At least I will die a warrior's death, which is better than living to be old and toothless. But look at the other side. What if kill him? I will gain much renown. My name will be known among all the tribes."

"A lot of good that will do you if you're dead," Sad Bear said softly.

Red Horse trudged wearily up the trail. As soon as he returned to the Arapaho camp and heard what Flint Shaper had to tell him about White Crane finding Blizzard, he had thrown a few provisions into his parfleche and set off to the northwest. Rounding a bend where the trail descended a steep hill, he was surprised to find two men sitting on the side, under a towering pine. Looking closely, Red Horse saw that one was an elderly Arapaho, and the other was not a man at all but a Miniconjou youth.

"Are you the man called Red Horse?" the youth asked when Red Horse halted his pony.

"Yes," he replied, surprised. "How did you know my name?"

"We've been waiting for you," the youth said. "What took you so long to get here?"

Red Horse looked at the pair carefully, letting his

hand slip to the knife he carried in his belt. "How did you know to expect me?" he asked suspiciously.

"White Crane said you would be here," said the elderly man, speaking for the first time.

"White Crane!" Red Horse said in relief. "So you know my kola. Where is he?"

The two looked at each other, then back at Red Horse.

"My name is Big Hand," said the old man, "and this is Sad Bear."

"I have heard of you," Red Horse said to Big Hand. "Crooked Nose speaks highly of you. But he said you had run off to join the group headed by the Brulé called Blizzard."

"I did. In fact, both of us did," Big Hand said, correcting himself.

"I don't understand," Red Horse said warily. "If you are members of Blizzard's group, why are you here. And where is White Crane?"

"White Crane is dead," Big Hand said softly. "Blizzard killed him."

The look of shock on Red Horse's face turned to one of grief. Leaping off his pony he threw himself onto the ground and began wailing. Yanking his hair, he turned his face toward the sky and began chanting the Wazhazha death song. Tears streamed down his cheeks, cutting trails through the dust. Finally, a long time later when his energy was spent, he sagged exhausted to the ground.

"Where is his body?" he whispered. "I want to see my friend."

"We performed the customary rites," said Sad Bear, "and hoisted him on a scaffold in the Lakota fashion. It is only a short walk down the hill if you want to go."

"Soon," said Red Horse. "Let me gather my thoughts. In the meantime, tell me what happened."

"It is partly our fault," Sad Bear said, explaining how they had captured White Crane and made him accompany them to the outlaw camp.

"Do not blame yourselves," Red Horse said. "I am sure that White Crane did not find you at fault. Secretly, that may be what he wanted anyway: to meet Blizzard face-to-face. Although he knew I felt it was my duty to challenge Blizzard I suspect that deep in his heart he wanted the opportunity to kill him himself. Tell me," he said, "did White Crane conduct himself well?"

"Oh, yes," said Sad Bear. "Despite Blizzard's advantage in experience and cunning it looked for awhile as if White Crane would be the victor."

"He wounded Blizzard with a cut along his neck," said Big Hand.

"But when he severely wounded him with a deep slash across his right forearm, Blizzard had to switch his knife to his left hand," added Sad Bear. "That's when we thought he might defeat the monster."

"What happened to turn things around so drastically?" asked Red Horse.

"White Crane slipped on a loose stone. While he was momentarily off balance, Blizzard butted him with his head, which sent him staggering. Then Blizzard got his knife into his groin and it was all over."

Red Horse sighed heavily. "I hope he died quickly."

"More quickly than Blizzard hoped," Big Hand said uneasily. "Blizzard wanted to prolong his death but White Crane was bleeding too heavily from the wound. He died without calling for mercy."

"Is that all?" Red Horse asked. "I feel there is something you are not telling me. What you have said so far does not explain why you're here."

"Do you want to tell him?" asked Sad Bear, looking at Big Hand.

The older man sighed. "After White Crane died, Blizzard was angry because he had not been able to torture him so he mutilated his body," Big Hand said in a rush.

"What do you mean 'mutilated?'" Red Horse asked, lifting his head. Sad Bear saw his eyes flash and noticed the ripple of the muscle along Red Horse's jaw.

"He cut off his fingers and his genitals," Big Hand said softly. "He said he was going to string them on a necklace."

"This, of course, was in addition to taking his scalp?"

Sad Bear and Big Hand nodded. "It was the mutilation that we could not stand," Big Hand explained. "White Crane fought well and honorably. We felt it was an insult to his honor to cut up his body that way."

"Is that why you're here?" Red Horse said, making an effort to control himself.

"Yes," said Big Hand. "We were very upset about that."

"Even Crow Killer disagreed. He and Blizzard exchanged sharp words."

"Who is Crow Killer?"

"Blizzard's second-in-command," explained Big Hand. "He is almost as bloodthirsty as Blizzard but even he felt that was unnecessary."

"What happened then?" asked Red Horse.

"The boy and I," Big Hand said, inclining his head toward Sad Bear, "felt we no longer wanted any part of what Blizzard calls his wolf pack. We told him we were leaving."

"And he let you go? Just like that?"

Big Hand nodded. "He sensed the mood of the others. When men like Crow Killer find your actions distasteful, that is something that not even Blizzard can ignore."

"But he did not protest when you left."

"Oh, no," said Sad Bear. "He told us he had no need for a boy and an old man in the pack anyway and when others heard about his accomplishments, they would be clamoring to join him. He insisted we go and said we would not be missed."

"He may be right about others," Red Horse said heavily. "Just before I left Crooked Nose's camp he said another of his warriors, a man named Elk Ear, had told him he was going to join Blizzard because of what he did to those white men."

"I know Elk Ear," said Big Hand. "I know he has great hatred for the whites. So I'm not surprised by what you tell me."

"But how about you?" Red Horse asked. "Crooked Nose said you, too, are very bitter toward the whites because of the deaths of your wife and son."

"I *was*," Big Hand said. "After White Crane's death I built a sweat lodge because I felt so unclean. On the second day I had a vision in which I was told that I was too old to be so bitter, that if I did not change my ways I would die a lonely old man and there would be no one to mourn my passing."

"And you believe this was a true vision?"

"Oh, yes, I have no doubt about that. The voice was that of my wife's and she would never lie to me. She said she was saddened to see what had happened to me because of her and our son and that if I wanted to make her spirit happy I needed to mend my ways. And that is what I intend to do. I will go to Crooked Nose and beg him to accept me back in his camp."

"I think he will be very glad to see you," Red Horse said with a tired smile. "He told me he hoped that something like this would occur. What about you?" he asked, turning to Sad Bear.

"All my family was killed at Blue Water. I have nowhere to go."

"I have told him he is welcome to come with me," said Big Hand. "He would be accepted among Crooked Nose's people."

"I am grateful to know that he thinks so highly of me," Sad Bear said, "but my instincts tell me this may not yet be the time."

"Why don't you come with me?" said Red Horse. "I would like the companionship. The only thing is you know of my desire—now it has become what White Crane called an obsession—to find and destroy Blizzard."

"I have no objection to that," Sad Bear said. "I agree that Blizzard must be killed. Although I lack your personal determination, I think your quest is just. I have to add, though, that I am no replacement for White Crane."

"No one could ever replace White Crane," Red Horse said, the tears starting to flow anew. "But that does not mean that you would not be welcome to ride by my side."

"It is good to have the time to stop and eat a decent meal again," Blizzard said, digging another chunk of fat hump meat out of the fire.

"We've been watching our trail carefully," said Crow Killer. "No one is following us."

"Not since I took care of the last one," Blizzard said with a humorless grin. "I have to admit he slashed me good. He was a lot better fighter than I expected."

"We feared for awhile that it might go the other way," Open Wound mumbled, barely understandable since he spoke with a mouth jammed with food.

"And what would you have done if it had?" Blizzard asked coldly, fixing him with a one-eyed stare.

Open Wound spit his food into his hand, the better to talk. "We would have killed him, of course."

"You say that because I'm the one sitting here now. I don't think you would have had the courage," Blizzard added.

Open Wound turned his eyes downward and kept them averted.

"You're playing games," said Crow Killer. "What has happened has happened. We can't change it with speculation."

"That is true," Blizzard agreed. "All in all, even with this troublesome wound, this has proved to be a good summer."

"Does that mean that there will be no more raids?" Broken Club asked, surprised.

"Not until next spring," Blizzard said. "We need to find a secure place in the mountains where we can winter. We need to prepare food to carry us through the cold months."

"No raids?" asked Four Wolves. "Not even against the Crow?"

"Well," Blizzard considered smiling. "Maybe against the Crow. We could always use more horses."

"And a couple of women, too," added Red Chin.

"And a couple of women," Blizzard agreed, laughing.

"Do you regret letting Big Hand and Sad Bear go so easily?" Crow Killer asked, turning serious.

Blizzard paused. "No," he said deliberately. "They were a drain on our energies. An old man and a boy. When word of our exploits spreads we will have ten volunteers for each of them. We will be able to pick and choose among them, to find the most skilled and the most dedicated. By the time next summer comes, we will be feared and respected throughout the Plains; the whites will regret they ever came."

"Do you know where we're going to winter?" asked Red Chin.

"I have an idea," said Blizzard. "There is a valley I remember from many years ago when the Wazhazhas were passing through the area looking for buffalo. It is so isolated that none of the tribes go there. We would not have been there either if that had not been a particularly difficult year that made the buffalo hard to find. And," he added with a smile, "there is another advantage as well."

"What is that?" Crow Killer asked solemnly.

"To get there we need to pass close to a favorite Crow summer camp. At this time of year, the Kangi will certainly be there, collecting berries and making preparations for the winter. Their horses will be fat from summer grazing and their women will be ripe for the plucking."

"Then what are we waiting for?" said Open Wound. "Why don't we leave tomorrow?"

"Soon," Blizzard said craftily. "I want to wait just a little longer to make sure Red Horse is not riding his pony into the ground trying to catch up with us."

"You mean Jace isn't up and around by now?" Benoit asked disbelievingly. "Last I saw of him, he was trying to walk across the room."

"He took a turn for the worse," Inge replied. "A couple of days after you left his fever came back stronger than ever. He figures it's pneumonia."

"Whew," Benoit whistled. "That can be deadly. What are you doing for him?"

"Ellen's been spending day and night with him. She refuses to leave. I spell her every now and then so she can run her errands and take care of her chores."

"Is he lucid?"

"From time to time. Every now and then he wakes up and gives instructions on medication. Ellen's been raiding his medical stores and dosing him with quinine, powdered willow bark, and foxglove. I can't see where they're doing much good but no telling what would happen without them."

"I'm going to go see him," Benoit said, rising wearily.

"It's almost dinner time," Inge protested. "Aren't you hungry for a home-cooked meal?"

"I'm famished. I've been dreaming about your

mother's cooking for the last week. But I want to visit Jace first. Don't let the others eat everything; I'll be there as soon as I can."

"Prepare yourself first," Inge warned.

"What do you mean?"

"He looks like hell, what with the way the fever has ravaged him and his broken nose. Just don't expect to see the same old Jace."

"Hi, Jean," Ellen O'Reilly greeted Benoit warmly when he entered the room Dobbs had set aside for a hospital. "I heard the horses coming in and I figured y'all were back. Was anyone hurt?'

"No," Benoit replied. "We never fired a shot in anger. It was a hard trip, though. We've been eighteen hours in the saddle just so Harrigan could hurry back and lick Kemp's boots. He didn't want to make a command decision so he decided to push it off on Kemp."

"Was the foray successful?"

"Yes and no. We got Cle back. He's fine. The injuns got to the deserters before we did and killed 'em all except Henderson, who got away with the payroll. So you could say we had our ups and downs. From what Inge tells me, Jace has had his own problems."

"He's sleeping right now," Ellen said, nodding toward the cot where Dobbs was buried under a pile of blankets. "He comes awake every now and then. Sometimes he knows what's going on, sometimes not. For the last couple of days he's been calling me Colleen. Was that his wife?"

"Yeah. She died of some kind of fever while Jace was off in Mexico. About six or eight years ago, I reckon."

"He must have loved her a lot. He speaks real sweet to me when he thinks I'm her."

"I imagine he speaks real sweet when he knows its you, too," Benoit said, forcing a smile.

"He's a good patient," she agreed. "But I'm real worried about him. I've never seen anyone have a fever like that for this long and come out of it."

"That bad, huh?" Benoit asked, frowning.

"By God," he said, leaning over the cot, "he does look like hell. Speaking of which, you don't look so good . . ." He began only to be interrupted by a croaking noise from Dobbs.

"*Agua . . . agua,*" he rasped.

"'Our'," said Benoit, crossing to the cot. "What the hell's he talking about?"

"Not 'our,'" Ellen corrected. "Agua. Means 'water' in Spanish. He thinks he's in Mexico most of the time. Speaks to me in Spanish and I don't have the slightest idea what he's saying. One of the troopers who was in Mexico comes in to help me change the sheets and he's been here a couple of times when Jace starts rattling off his Spanish. He doesn't understand much of it either, but he knew what agua was."

"Jesus," Benoit said, looking down at his friend, "he *does* look like death warmed over."

Dobbs's nose, still red and misshapen from the fall, looked as large as a cantaloupe, its size undoubtedly exaggerated by the way his cheeks had caved in upon themselves, giving him a death's-head look. His skin was as white as the bed covering and looked as fragile as tissue paper. Also, he had lost considerable weight during his illness and the hand that extended from under the covers looked more like a claw than an appendage that should be attached to a human. As Benoit stood staring at him, Dobbs's eyes flickered open and roamed unfocused around the room.

"Hi, Jace," Benoit said as heartily as he could. "How you feeling?"

At the sound of Benoit's voice, Dobbs turned his head and squinted as if he were looking into the noonday sun. "Pepperdine!" he said excitedly. "Don't just stand there looking stupid. We've got to get ready for the casualties. The messenger said there were a lot of wounded."

"He thinks I'm someone from his unit during the war," Benoit said lamely.

"Don't take it personal."

"Colleen!" Dobbs said shrilly at the sound of Ellen's voice. "What are you doing here? Get the kids to safety! We're expecting a shelling."

"I don't know what to say when he gets this way," Ellen said sadly. "I'm not sure he even hears me."

"Don't argue about it," Dobbs said, sounding peeved. "We don't have time for that. I *told* you you should have stayed home. An army on the march is no picnic. I hope today isn't going to be like yesterday. That boy from the Third died under my hands. Nothing I could do to stop the hemorrhage. Goddamn," he said, tears starting to form in the corners of his eyes, "I don't even know his name. There are so many of them," he sobbed. "So damn many. I feel so powerless."

"It's okay, Jace," Benoit said soothingly, patting his friend's shoulder.

"Okay my ass, Pepperdine. Too many are dying! We need two more surgeons at least. Why don't those dumb generals in Washington understand that? How do they expect us to keep these boys alive when we don't have the manpower or the medicine? ¡*Que cabrones*! ¡*Que pendejos*!"

"Don't get yourself all worked up, Jace," Benoit said gently as Dobbs began thrashing around, swinging his skinny arms from which the skin drooped in sallow folds. Saliva flecked with blood began collecting in the corners of his mouth and running down his chin.

"Oh, God," Ellen said, reaching for a damp cloth, "I hate it when he starts getting excited like this. "It takes forever to get him calmed down."

"*¿Donde estan las carretas*? Don't those dumb fuckers know we need transport? The quicker we can get the wounded here the better. *¿Donde estan las* fucking *carretas*?" he screeched excitedly.

"Take it easy, Jace," Benoit said firmly, clamping his hands on Dobbs's shoulders and pinning him to the bed.

"The hell you say, Pepperdine. How did you ever get to be a lieutenant? Use your brains, man. Didn't God give you . . . "

As abruptly as the outburst started, it subsided. As Benoit watched in horror, Dobbs's eyes rolled back in his head. "*No puedo ver*," he mumbled. "*Yo oigo música*." In seconds, he was snoring softly, his emaciated chest rising and falling in an irregular pattern.

"This is very frightening," Benoit said, turning to Ellen.

"Sometimes he's worse," she said, shrugging. "Sometimes he's better."

"You know," Benoit said, studying her, "you don't look very good yourself. Why don't you let me sit with him for a spell while you go get some sleep."

"I'm alright," she insisted. "I manage to sleep when he does."

"Still, you need to get away for awhile. I have to go to the dining room. Harrigan is going to be making his report to Kemp after dinner and he will expect me to be there. As soon as the meeting breaks up, I'm coming back here and I want you to get away for a few hours. Don't argue with me, please."

"Okay, Jean. Go to your meeting and then come back. Maybe you're right; maybe I do need a few hours away from the sickroom."

"Of course I'm right," Benoit said with a feeble smile. "I'm always right. That's why I'm given so much responsibility."

"Sorry I'm late, sir," Benoit said apologetically, slipping into his chair at the end of the table. Across from him, in the spot normally occupied by Dobbs, was Clement Couvillion.

Clockwise around the table, from Couvillion, were Marie Fontenot, George Teasley, Senator Emile Fontenot, Kemp, Harrigan, First Lieutenant Harry Grant, and Second Lieutenant Zack Adamson.

Tucking a napkin into his collar, Benoit glanced at Couvillion, who had his head bent over his plate and was shovelling food into his mouth like coal into a furnace.

"It's been a long time since I had a good meal," he said between mouthfuls, looking only slightly embarrassed.

"I'm glad you could join us, Ben-oight," Kemp said with mild sarcasm. "Captain Harrigan has been telling me you two had a bit of a disagreement over what course of action to take."

"It wasn't exactly a disagreement, sir," Benoit said, spearing a large chunk of venison from the serving platter that Frau Schmidt had been holding in reserve. "I just tried to explain to the captain that I thought we should pursue that deserter, Henderson, and try to recover the payroll money. Captain Harrigan, however, thought it would be better if we returned immediately to the post."

"Harrigan was quite correct," Kemp said, nodding toward the captain. As Kemp spoke, Harrigan leaned forward and turned to Benoit, shooting him a smug I-told-you-so look. "The detachment's first priority was securing the safe return of Congressman Couvillion."

"But what about Henderson, sir?" Benoit asked, pausing to savor the aroma of the roast before popping it into his mouth.

"Forget Henderson for the moment," Kemp said agitatedly. "I'm much more concerned about that group of Indians. I had a nice talk with Mr. Ashby, who explained to me exactly what is going on. From what he learned in the Arapaho camp, the group that killed the deserters is made up of what amounts to murderous thugs. Their sole *raison d'être*, it seems, is to bring a halt to white emigration."

"Isn't that in violation of the Fort Laramie Treaty, sir?" Lieutenant Harry Grant offered, anxious to play a role in the debate.

"Seems that way to me," Kemp replied, nodding. "How about it, Mr. Teasley?"

"Definitely, colonel," the Indian agent replied, lifting his napkin from his lap and wiping his mouth, camouflage for what his hand had really been doing under the table to Marie. "Under the terms of the treaty, the emigrant road is to be kept open and the travelers are not to be molested. However, the rub comes in trying to enforce it."

"Why can't we just withhold the annuities?" Grant asked.

"And punish the law-abiding tribesmen?"

"Make it *their* responsibility to bring the renegades under control," Grant countered.

"It isn't as if these men are operating with the sanction of the tribes, Grant," Kemp explained. "From what

Mr. Ashby tells me, they have been murdering Indians as well as whites."

"Then it clearly becomes our responsibility to track them down, sir," said Grant. "We must avenge the white deaths."

"To hell with the white deaths," Kemp said. "Excuse me, ma'am," he said, bowing slightly to Marie. "I mean I'm not going to get very upset about the deaths of those deserters. As far as I'm concerned, the Indians did us a favor getting rid of those scalawags because I certainly would have hung 'em if they had been caught. But Grant's right that the issue of a concerted campaign against whites is an important one. The Indians didn't know those men were outlaws in their own community. As far as the Indians were concerned, the deserters deserved to die simply because they were white. Next time—and I'm firmly convinced there will be a next time if we don't do something about it—the victims might be a group of emigrants."

"If that happens, you certainly will be hearing from Washington," added Fontenot. "I can guarantee you that."

"My point exactly, Senator," Kemp said, smiling tightly. "There's no question in my mind but those outlaws have to be tracked down and killed."

"You mean murdered?" Marie said daintily.

"No, ma'am," Kemp said. "Killed. Either killed or captured and brought back here and hung. I have no reason at all to believe these men would surrender. So if we find 'em—make that *when* we find 'em—there's going to be a shoot-out. You can bank on it."

"Are you absolutely . . ." Marie began.

"That's enough, Marie," Fontenot said sternly. "You may be accustomed to having your way when you're dealing with men, but you can't tell the colonel how to run his post."

"Yes, father," she said meekly. "You're absolutely right. My apologies, colonel."

"Nothing to apologize for, ma'am," Kemp said, smiling gallantly. "We were just having a spirited debate."

"Who's going to track them down, colonel?" Grant asked hopefully.

"I am, lieutenant."

"*You* are?" Benoit gushed, almost choking on his water.

"You see something wrong with that, Ben-oight?" Kemp asked icily. "You find it astounding that your commanding officer might actually go out in the field?"

"N-N-No, sir," Benoit stammered, trying to recover. "It's just that you've never done it before, sir. You don't know anything about Indians . . . "

"I don't, eh? Need I remind you that I've been in this man's army for more years than you have been breathing . . . "

"Yes, sir," Benoit said, turning bright red.

". . . and that I've done three previous tours on the frontier . . . "

"You're right, sir."

". . . and that I've probably forgotten more about Indians than you'll ever know . . . "

"Absolutely, sir."

"And besides, I have insurance."

"Insurance, sir?" Benoit asked, looking puzzled.

"Yes," Kemp replied. "Insurance. You. You're going along."

"Yes, sir," Benoit said, his face falling.

"You don't look too happy about it, lieutenant."

"It isn't that, sir. I'd welcome the opportunity to operate with you under field conditions."

"Then what is it?"

"It's, uh, that I just got back, sir. I was hoping, uh, to spend a little time getting, uh, reacclimated—that's it, *reacclimated*—to life on the post before being sent back out."

"Your love life will wait, lieutenant. Absence makes the heart grow fonder, you know."

"That's not all, sir," Benoit said, his face crimson, "I'm very worried about Lieutenant Dobbs as well."

"We're all worried about Dobbs, lieutenant. But he's getting the best care available. There's nothing you could do that isn't already being done. You're going. That's all there is to it."

"Yes, sir," Benoit replied, looking dejectedly at his plate.

"Colonel?" Grant interjected humbly.

"No need to ask, lieutenant. You're going as well. You need some seasoning."

"Yes, *sir*!" Grant replied, beaming.

"Captain Harrigan will be in charge while I'm gone. Lieutenant Adamson is going to be out with a wood-gathering detail. Have to start thinking about winter, you know. Mr. Ashby will go with us."

"How about Legendre, sir?" Benoit asked.

"It seems that after a few months of celibacy he's decided that he would like a new wife to keep him company during the coming winter. He asked for a few days off to go and fetch his late wife's sister. I didn't feel it proper to tell him no. He won't be back for another week or so. Anything else? Any more questions?"

"Just one, sir," Benoit said tentatively.

"Yes, Ben-oight," Kemp sighed heavily. "What is it?"

"How come, sir, with all due respect, since you apparently have no trouble with the senator's Gallic surname, or with the congressman's for that matter, you can't pronounce my name correctly?"

Kemp grinned. "Just one reason," he said benignly. "Sometimes you just gripe my ass. Begging your pardon, ma'am."

Carefully Benoit arranged the items in front of him, placing each precisely in its place on a small table he'd found in a storeroom and lugged into Dobbs's hospital quarters. To his left, within easy reach, was his favorite coffee cup, a chipped piece of his mother's discarded china that he had carried lovingly from Louisiana. Just below that was a copy of a new book sent to him by his sister, Marion, that had been identified in an accompanying note as "the latest rage." Benoit picked it up and read the title one more time: *Walden*. Never heard of it, Benoit said to himself. Or of Henry David Thoreau. Giving the tome a last, dubious glance, he gingerly replaced it.

On the right side of the table, symmetrically aligned with the coffee cup, was an inkwell filled almost to overflowing. And below that was a new quill pen he had bought from Bertrand Sevier, the sutler, just before he had left on the mission with Harrigan and never used. Precisely in the center was a stack of linen writing sheets, also obtained from Sevier's store at a dear price.

"Why don't you hurry and wake up," Benoit said jovially to Dobbs's inert form. "I'm going to put some coffee on to brew and if that aroma doesn't arouse you I may have to pour some of it down your throat."

Sighing despondently when there was no response from his friend, Benoit crossed to the woodstove and fired it up. Once it was going, he filled a heavy pot with water and put it on the stove to boil. While that was heating, he wiped off his long-necked coffee pot and shovelled ground beans, also sent to him by his sister, into its maw. Then he poured two inches of water into an iron skillet, which he also set on the cooking surface with the coffeepot in the center. When the water in the skillet began to boil, he patiently transferred it, a spoonful at a time, to the coffeepot, pouring it gently over the grounds. After a few minutes, he lifted the coffee pot and poured the thick dark liquid into his cup, conscientiously stopping when it was half full. Then he topped off the cup with water from the heavy pot, in effect diluting his brew neatly by half.

Leaning close to the steaming cup, he inhaled deeply, smiling in ecstasy. "Nothing like it," he said half-aloud. "A Cajun without his coffee is worse than a fish out of water."

Delicately placing the cup on the corner of the table, he pulled up the rickety chair that also had been salvaged from the cobweb-filled room and sat erectly, his shoulders perfectly square, his feet flat on the floor at precise ninety-degree angles as he had been taught in penmanship class when he was a child. Lifting the pen, he dipped the point in the ink and moved it slowly over the paper. In his meticulous hand, he began to write:

17 August 55
Fort Laramie
Dear Mamman,

It has, indeed, been a long time since you have heard from your wayward elder son. Mea culpa. I would have written earlier but I have been away on a mission for a number of days and I leave again soon on another. No rest for the weary, I imagine. It goes to show, though, how much we must accomplish during the summer because once winter gets here almost nothing moves for months and months. It is hard to believe that I am already approaching my second win-

ter; it seems like only yesterday that I was leaving from Missouri.

I realize it must seem that the only news you get from me is bad, but you have indicated you are interested in les affaires de militaire, particularly as they apply to Fort Laramie, and that requires the recording of all events, both agreeable and unpleasant. First the disagreeable. My good friend, the one who you enquire about every time you write, Jason Dobbs, lies at death's door, struck down by the evil pneumonia. He is being well cared for, but there is nothing more that can be done. His recovery now lies in God's hands. I know it may seem a strange request coming from me, but the next time you are visiting the St. Louis Cathedral, please say a prayer for his recovery. He is a good man, a good friend, and a good physician. It would sadden me deeply to lose him.

Turning to a different issue, speaking of affairs, please tell Marion (although I am sure it will come as no surprise to her), that her friend, Marie Fontenot, is carrying on the most torrid affaire de couer with the resident Indian Agent, a man named George Teasley. It is no business of mine and I am trying my best to keep my nose out of it, but in a place as small and close-knit as the post, it is hard if not impossible to keep a secret. For reasons too complicated to explain Cle Couvillion has not yet learned of the situation. I recently had occasion to spend a little time with Cle and I must confess that I find him rather a strange duck. I do not know him well enough to predict how he will react when he learns of Marie's dalliances, but I suspect he will not take it well. I hope I do not get dragged into the muddle that will certainly result.

And speaking of women, let me prepare you for what may be still another shock. To get to the point immediately,

I am considering marrying Inge Schmidt, the young woman about whom I have written many times. For some reason I have not been able to fathom, she seems to think I would make a good husband although you and I both know that I would be the winner in such a match. She is a wonderful person, Mamman, a lot like you must have been when you were her age: beautiful, clever, and very feisty. Her mother approves wholeheartedly of the situation and I am sure you would, too, if you could but meet her, which of course you will at some point. Please do not run to the New Orleans Picayune or Le Machacebe as yet since this does not constitute a formal announcement. There will be plenty of time for that in the future. Once we decide to take this large step (tell me honestly, Mamman, do you think seventeen is too young for a woman to be married?) I must get permission from my commanding officer, Colonel Kemp. Unfortunately that may not be as perfunctory as it sounds. I don't know why, but I seem to irritate him almost to the point of disbelief. One reason I am always receiving assignments that carry me away from the post may be that he is overjoyed to get rid of me. In any case, his approval is the first step. I will inform you forthwith once I get up enough courage to put the question before him.

As usual, this will be fairly brief. It is almost time for Jace's medicine so I must awaken him to make him take it. That always seems so strange to me, but it is a procedure he insists upon even when he himself is the patient. On the other hand, I have a surprise for him. I have prepared a pot of your coffee, which he dearly loves, and if I can keep him awake long enough I intend to let him drink as much as he can consume.

I eagerly await your next letter with news of yourself, Marion, and Theophile. Please know that I love all of you dearly and I count the days until I can see you again. Maybe when next we get together I will have a new bride on my arm.

Your loving son,

Jean

P.S. Please do not forget the prayer for Jace.

"What do you mean keep my hands to myself?" Couvillion asked angrily. "You have never told me that before."

"Well, this is different, Cle," Marie said soothingly. "You've been away quite a while. I have to get used to you all over again."

"'Get used to me?'" Couvillion said indignantly. "I'm the same person you have known since you were a child, the same person whose ring you agreed to wear."

"It must be the air in the West, Cle. Somehow things seem to be in a different perspective now."

"It's that bastard Teasley, isn't it?" Couvillion said, rising from the couch and stomping across the room. Opening a cupboard he removed a bottle and poured himself a drink.

"Now why would you say something like that?" Marie said innocently.

"Do you think I'm blind? Or stupid? I could see the way you were looking at each other at dinner. And I noticed, too, the way he always had his right hand below the table. Your hand was also out of sight a good bit of the time. What were you doing, feeling each other up?"

"Cle, that's a terrible thing to say," Marie replied angrily.

"But it's true, isn't it? I can tell by the way you're blushing."

"I wish you wouldn't be like this, Cle. I really do. You're going to embarrass everyone."

"Embarrass my ass. I'm going to demand satisfaction is what I'm going to do."

"Oh, Cle," Marie said as she giggled, "don't be so provincial. No one except a swell in New Orleans 'demands satisfaction' anymore. That is so old-fashioned, not to mention stupid. Someone can get killed that way."

"They certainly can," Couvillion agreed, "and it won't be me."

"Cle, I'm begging you, don't make a fool of yourself."

"A fool," Couvillion shouted, dashing his glass to the floor. "Is it better to be a cuckold?"

"You can't be a cuckold!" She laughed. "We're not even married."

"You know what I mean. How do you think this looks for my reputation? I'm a rising young Congressman and my fiancée is diddling some man old enough to be her father. A married man at that."

"Cle, he's married only in the strictest sense of the word. He hasn't seen his wife in months and months. They no longer even share a bed."

"You see," he said, pointing a finger at her. "I *knew* I was right. I *knew* he was diddling you."

"Don't be so crude, Cle. 'Diddling' is such a common word."

"Oh, my, aren't we getting prissy? Maybe you'd prefer if I said 'fucking.' It's the same thing."

"George is thinking about divorcing his wife," Marie said, trying to change the subject.

"And that makes it all right? Just because he tells you he is *thinking* about a divorce that gives you the right to run off in the woods and copulate like rabbits?"

"I wish you wouldn't get so upset, Cle. Why can't we sit down and talk about this like two adults?"

"I was off in the wilderness," Couvillion said, pulling a fresh glass out of the cabinet and filling it from the same bottle. "You didn't know if I was ever going to come back. For all you knew I was already dead. And here you were humping away with the first virile-looking man that crosses your path."

"It isn't just his looks, Cle. He's a very kind, gentle man."

"A kind, gentle man, eh? Maybe you'd like to see the copies of his military record. See how he performed when he was in uniform."

"You have that, Cle?" Marie asked in surprise. "How in the world did you get that?"

Couvillion laughed. "Being a congressman does have some privileges, you know. As a precaution I pulled the records of all the important people at the posts we were planning to visit. I believe in planning ahead."

"But how did you happen to pick him, for goodness sake?"

"I didn't pick *him* exclusively," Couvillion explained. "I knew that you would never become involved with anyone who wasn't important—except for that lust thing you had with Jean Benoit . . . "

"You know about that?"

"Of course I know about that. Would you like me to tell you the others that I know about as well?"

"No," she said, shaking her head. "That won't be necessary. But tell me this: If you mistrusted me so much why did you ever ask me to marry you?"

"Ambition, my dear. Pure ambition." Couvillion smiled. "Your father is a very important man. It certainly couldn't hurt my career if my wife was Senator Fontenot's daughter. Besides, you're very beautiful.

And you perform in bed better than anyone I've ever known."

"There you go, getting crude again."

"I'm not being crude, I'm being truthful. When it comes to sucking and fucking, you have no peer."

"You're just trying to make me angry, Cle, and it isn't going to work."

"No, you misunderstand, my lovely. I'm the one who's angry. I'm the one who's been wronged. Even if I did not consider your action a tremendous personal insult, which I do, I couldn't let you two get away with it. It would ruin my chances for reelection."

"No one need ever know, except you and me."

"'Need ever know?' Don't be ridiculous. Everyone west of Columbia probably knows about it. Do you think you can keep any secrets in a place like this?"

"We've been very discreet."

"Sure you have. Like tonight at the dinner table, eh? No, my love. Unfortunately you have left me no alternative. I must call Mr. Teasley out."

"Stop and think about what you're saying, Cle. George is a former career Army officer, well trained in the use of firearms, inured to the threat of death."

"And you think I'm not skilled? Tell me one New Orleans blue-blood you know who has not received extensive professional instruction in the art of dueling."

"Don't do it, Cle. It's a big mistake."

"Mistake or not, I have to do it. Actually, I'm rather looking forward to it. I've always wondered what it felt like to kill someone."

"You sound like a crazy man."

"Yes," he said, smiling broadly. "I do, don't I? Now that my mind is made up, it isn't as frightening as it seemed in the abstract. Actually," he said, refilling his glass, "I have only one regret."

"And what is that?" Marie asked nervously.

"That I can't call *you* out," Couvillion replied with a chuckle. "There's no doubt in my mind that you initiated the whole sordid affair but poor George Teasley must pay for it. I think that's a shame."

The men huddled around the dining room table, fortified with several pots of Frau Schmidt's strong, black coffee, poring over maps that covered the territory from Fort Kearny on the east to Sublette's Cutoff on the west, south to the Ute country and north almost to the Canadian border, a flat, desolate, windswept chunk of topographic uncertainty that sprawled over some four hundred thousand square miles.

"That's impossible!" Benoit breathed in disbelief when he fully grasped the enormity of the area. "We can't cover all that."

"Of course we can't," Kemp said, looking at Benoit in exasperation. "I just want all of you to see and appreciate what we're faced with. Since we can't be everywhere we have to use our heads and try to anticipate where this group of outcasts might be. Let's start off with Mr. Ashby, who knows this part of the world better than anyone here. Assuming you were a renegade injun trying to hide from me and my men, where would you go, Mr. Ashby? Where would we be likely to find your camp?"

"It ain't all that easy to say, colonel," Ashby drawled.

"It's like looking for a needle in a haystack. But mayhaps I can narrow it down a little."

"Please do."

"Firs' thang," Ashby drawled, "is you got to consider the makeup of this party. Except for a smidgen of 'hos, they's all Lakota."

"And what does that tell you?"

"That they ain't gonna be welcome in territory where the tribes ain't friendly to the Lakotas."

"That makes sense," Kemp said with a laugh. "I guess that was kind of a dumb question. But all right, show us where you're talking about on the maps."

"Over here," Ashby said, plunking down a stained, gnarly finger with a thick, dirty nail, "to the east, up above Kearny, is Pawnee stompin' grounds. They ain't gonna be there."

"Okay," said Kemp, gathering and rolling three of the maps. "We don't need these. "How about west?"

"You can forgit 'bout these, too," Ashby said, shoving aside maps depicting the area west of the junction of the Sweetwater and North Platte Rivers. "Tha' be Shoshone and Crow country. They ain't thar neither."

"We're making progress," said Kemp, rolling several more maps and handing them to the ever-present Harrigan.

"South ain't too likely since that ain't good country to hide in. Too flat, no trees. An injun can hide *anywhar* for a li'l while, but this is a winter camp we're talkin' 'bout since I'm assuming these redskins gotta spen' some time gettin' ready for the snows. They ain't far off, you know, specially to the north. Tha's sumthing you gotta keep in min'."

"How long do you figure we have?" asked Kemp.

Ashby stared into the distance, unconsciously scratching his privates. "Damn body lice," he mumbled. "They been real bad this year."

"How long," Kemp prompted, rolling his eyes.

"Four weeks minimum in the mountains," Ashby calculated. "Six weeks you don' mind walking through drifts up to your waist. After tha', plan on spendin' the winter with the grizzlies."

"We got off track," Kemp said, reaching for a cigar. On cue, Harrigan leaned forward and scratched a match. "Where do you think this Blizzard is likely to be?"

"Iffen I were him," Ashby said, tapping one of the maps, "I'd be up 'bout here, up in the Black Hills. Tha's right rugged country, a hunner', no a thousand, places to hide, and it's right plumb in the middle of Sioux territory. Iffen I were him, and I wouldn' want to be tha' mangy pissant, not fer all the beaver in th' west, I'd fin' me a nice li'l valley up thar tha's protected from the north wind, where there's a stream that don' freeze solid and some trees fer the horses to nibble on when the groun' gets covered with snow. Tha's where I'd hunker down. Then I'd wait til spring when I could come out all refreshed and rarin' to go. Tha's what I'd do."

"Okay," Kemp said. "That narrows it down to fifteen or twenty thousand square miles. Now where do you think he is?"

"Shit, colonel," Ashby said, smiling crookedly, "iffen I could tell you tha' I'd move back east and set up shop telling politicos wha' to do 'bout the gov'ment. Your guess is as good as mine. I'd bet you next year's wages, though, tha's where he is, but gettin' any closer than tha' is plumb fortune tellin'."

Kemp sighed, dropping his cigar butt in what remained of his coffee. In the silence, the sizzle sounded like someone ripping a sheet.

"Here's what we're going to do, men," he said at length. "We're leaving early tomorrow. Me, Grant, Benoight, Mr. Ashby, and two dozen enlisted men. Grant and Ben-oight, you get together and decide who goes. I want good marksmen and at least two seasoned NCOs. And make sure everyone has plenty of ammunition. Understood?"

Grant and Benoit looked at each other and nodded.

"No more than two dozen men. I can't afford to strip the post, not with winter just around the corner and all the preparations that need to be made here. Grant, you take care of the provisions. Plan on us being gone three to four weeks. Ben-oight, you make sure we have sound horses; I don't want to get out in the middle of nowhere and have my mount collapse. Although I've been forced to eat it several times, I'm not real fond of dead-horse stew. Now where we're going—Mr. Ashby, you speak up if you see some fallacy in reasoning here—is east . . ."

"East?" Benoit asked in surprise. "I thought we figured they'd be in the north."

"You didn't let me finish, lieutenant."

"Sorry, sir." Benoit blushed.

"We're going to go east along the Platte for about a day on the chance we might be able to find their trail. The spot where they killed the deserters is here," he said, pointing to the map, "south of the Platte. So they had to cross the river to get to the Black Hills. Maybe we'll get lucky and find their tracks."

"We'd have to be more'n lucky, colonel," Ashby interjected. "This be the rainy season and we've had a couple good storms."

"Nevertheless, I reckon it's worth a try. It might save us days of wandering around. I guess that about sums it up. You have anything you want to add, Senator?" he said, turning to Fontenot, who had been sitting silently on the side during the planning session.

"A couple of things, colonel, if you don't mind,"

Fontenot said, clearing his throat. "First, I know all of you have heard the adage that typifies current thinking in Washington: 'It's cheaper to feed them for a year than fight them for a day.' I think that's poppycock, a simplistic slogan coined by someone who's never been west of the Potomac. These bloodthirsty bastards need to be *killed*, not coddled. And I know you men are the ones to do it. In my limited time out here I've come to appreciate the obstacles you men are facing and I want you to know that you have my sympathy and my support. God knows what's going to happen to this country in the near future. Far as I can tell, it's going to hell in a handbasket. But until that day comes, men like you are holding everything together, doing what you have to do under very trying circumstances. I think you're doing a hell of a job. I'm proud of you. Now go get those sonsabitches."

"Hear, hear," Kemp said enthusiastically. "Frau Schmidt," he called loudly, "please break out that bottle of cognac you've been hiding in the linen closet. I think it's time for a toast."

"Well, Mr. Ashby," Kemp said, shaking his head. "I guess you were right. We've been a day's march to the east and haven't found a sign of tracks heading north."

"It's the rains, colonel. I was afeared o' tha'."

"Then I reckon it's time we turned north to try our luck. After the noon break I'm going to turn ninety degrees."

"Sounds good—" Ashby began, only to be interrupted by a cry from Private Bianchi, who had been riding a hundred yards in front of the column. "Rider coming, sir," he yelled loudly. "A lone civilian."

Kemp called a halt and watched as the speck in the

distance grew to a life-sized image of a man approaching quickly, whipping his horse as if he were racing for a gold cup. When he was almost there, Kemp could see that it was a skinny emigrant, dressed in worn work clothes, atop a raw-boned gelding that looked as it were ready to be put out to pasture. Attached to his saddle, Kemp noted, was a scabbard with the butt of a rifle sticking out. In addition, the man had a pistol strapped to his waist—a lot of armament, Kemp figured, for an emigrant farmer.

"Morning, stranger," Kemp said when the man had reigned to a stop. "What can we do for you?"

"Hidy, captain," the man said, gulping to catch his breath.

"It's colonel," Grant informed him. "This is the commanding officer at Fort Laramie."

"That's okay, Grant, we don't have to be formal. I'm Aloysius Kemp," he said, touching the brim of his hat. "What seems to be the problem?"

"Jebediah Adkins, cap'n. An' the problem is them fuckin' injuns."

Kemp's pulse quickened. "Have you been attacked by hostiles?" he asked excitedly.

"Nah." Adkins shook his head. "But they stole one of my horses."

Kemp slumped in his saddle, disappointed. "Exactly what happened, Mr. Adkins?"

"I'm with the train about ten miles back," he said. "We been camped in a cottonwood grove for a couple days, resting up after a hard trip out from Missouri. We let our horses wander a little, seeing as how grass is getting hard to find and all."

"Get to the point please, sir," Kemp said impatiently. We're on a mission of some urgency."

"I was helping round up the stock this morning when

I noticed my mare was gone. I figured she'd wandered off so I started looking for her. Found her in an injun herd a couple miles away. When I tried to talk to their chief he brushed me off. Looked right threatening and I got scared for my life. That's when I seed your dust column and figured it might be soljers. Reckon I was right, huh?"

"What do you expect us to do, Mr. Adkins?" Kemp asked, anxious to get the men headed north.

"I expect you to get my fucking horse back," Adkins said angrily. "That's what you're out here for, ain't it? To protect us from them redskins?"

"I can't see where this rightly falls under the protection clause of my orders," Kemp said, irritated.

"Well, goddamnit," Adkins continued, "I expect you to do *something*. You may think we ain't nothing but poor white trash, but by God we do got some rights, don't we? And ain't one of 'em the freedom from having our horses pilfered?"

"Doan sound right to me, colonel," Ashby interjected. "If injuns were raidin' horses they ain't gonna take jest one."

"I don't know how many they might of took," Adkins said. "But I know them sonsabitches got my mare. And I want her back."

Kemp sighed. "Tell you what I'm going to do, Mr. Adkins. We're on a mission that can't be interrupted by a minor transgression like the one you're describing . . . "

"Goddamnit . . . "

"*But,*" Kemp added, holding up his hand to signal Adkins to silence, "I'll send a man with you to see if the problem can't be worked out."

"That'd be appreciated, cap. You got someone who speaks injun?"

"I can't spare my scout right now, but I have a man with considerable experience among the Indians. He's resourceful; he can come up with something." Turning to the column, Kemp searched the faces. "Ben-oight!" he called loudly, "front and center!"

"Lieutenant," he said when Benoit galloped forward, "I want you to go with this man and see if you can help him resolve a certain situation. It doesn't sound complicated, so try to work out a quick solution. We're turning north and you know our route. Help this man and then catch up with us. It shouldn't take you more than a day at most."

"Yes, sir," Benoit said reluctantly, sizing up the man and not liking what he saw. "My name is Ben-wah," he said, watching Kemp out of the corner of his eye. "It's a French name and I'm kind of sensitive about it."

"Ben-wah, huh?" Adkins said, rubbing his finger along his nose. "I thought your colonel said it was Ben-oight."

"There they be," Adkins said, pointing into a shallow valley.

Benoit raised in his saddle to get a better view. Spread along a clear, fast-running creek that travelled southward toward the Platte was a well-organized Indian camp with several dozen lodges. Benoit recognized the markings immediately.

"Those are Cheyenne," Benoit said to Adkins. "They're friendly, good-natured people. They aren't horse thieves."

"I don't give a shit who they are," Adkins said. "Injuns is injuns. But these 'uns got my mare. She be over there, in their herd."

"Well," Benoit said, sighing, "let's go down and see what we can do."

As they rode into the camp, the men began filing out to greet them. Benoit smiled and waved, recognizing Short Hair, Long Chin, Rock Forehead, White Wolf, and several others.

"You're right friendly with them savages," Adkins grumped. "How do I know you ain't going to take their side?"

"I'm not here to take sides," Benoit said sharply. "I'm here to adjudicate a dispute. These people are fair and honest and I don't want you giving them any shit, understood?"

Adkins gave him a hard look and didn't reply.

Benoit and Adkins were approaching the center of the village when a large white man with shoulders as wide as an ax handle is long emerged from one of the lodges and began waving happily.

"'Tienne!" Benoit cried joyfully. Jumping off his horse he ran forward and embraced the man, slapping him on the back.

"What a pleasant surprise," he said in French. "You're the last person I expected to run into out here."

"The pleasure is mine," Etienne Legendre replied, also in French. "I want you to meet my new wife, who is too bashful to come out of the lodge. After she gets accustomed to you, we will kill a puppy and have a feast."

"That's the best invitation I've had all day," Benoit said with a laugh. "But what are you doing here?"

"I came to get married," Legendre said, grinning. "And then I just decided to accompany the Tsis-tsis-tas southward. Short Hair is living up to his promise. He's bringing the two white boys to the fort as he said he would."

"Speaking of boys," Benoit said, "where's David?"

"He's out hunting rabbits with Puma and Magpie, the two Germans. They have become fast friends. You wouldn't recognize them, they've gro . . . "

"What are you two talking about so much in Frog?" Adkins asked sourly. "You plotting against us white people?"

"Who is this imbecile?" Legendre asked, looking Adkins up and down.

"I heard that," Adkins said. "I know what imbecile means. Who the fuck you think you're talking to, you squaw lover?"

"Calm down, Mr. Adkins," Benoit said soothingly. "I suggest you talk pleasantly to Mr. Legendre if you want your mare back. He's like family to these people."

Turning back to Legendre, Benoit explained in French Adkins's contention that his horse was stolen.

Frowning, Legendre turned to Long Chin. After a long discussion in Cheyenne, the Canadian told Benoit what the situation was. Benoit explained it in English to Adkins.

"The horse you're talking about was found wandering across the plains by one of the young warriors, a youth named Carries the Otter. He claims the horse was a stray and therefore belongs to him. I suggest you make an offer to buy her back; it wouldn't take more than a token."

"I ain't paying for my own fucking horse," Adkins said angrily.

Benoit sighed. "You don't understand, Mr. Adkins. You're not back in Ohio any more. Things are done differently out here. You're going to have to learn to adjust."

"I ain't paying for my own fucking horse," Adkins insisted.

Benoit looked at Legendre and rolled his eyes.

"Is that the thief there?" Adkins said, pointing to a young warrior standing on the side.

"No," Legendre said. "That's One-eyed Bear. He knows nothing of the affair."

"He's the one," Adkins said. "I know he is and you're lying for him."

"Can't we talk about this sensibly, Mr. Adkins?" Benoit asked as calmly as he could. "Losing your temper isn't going to accomplish anything."

"He's the fucking thief," Adkins said, pointing at One-Eyed Bear.

"He's *not* a thief," Benoit said, losing his patience. "Now quit acting like a spoiled child. You want to resolve this, don't you?"

"I'll show you what we do to horse thieves in Ohio," Adkins said, pulling his rifle from the scabbard.

"No!" Benoit yelled, reaching for the weapon. When he grabbed it, it twisted in Adkins's hand and went off. The slug struck White Wolf at the base of his throat, in the hollow where the collar bones meet. He dropped to the ground, gripping the wound and coughing, choking on his own blood.

"You dumb fucking cracker," Benoit exploded. "Look what you've done."

Legendre threw his arms in the air and began dancing around, yelling in Cheyenne. "Don't shoot! Don't shoot! It was an accident. Don't shoot."

Sliced Nose, who had been standing next to White Wolf, picked up a piece of firewood and swung it, intending to hit Adkins. Instead, he struck Legendre on the side of the head, toppling the Canadian into the dust.

"Who you calling a cracker, you goddamn Carpet Knight?" Adkins said to Benoit. Discarding his rifle, he reached for his pistol. He had the weapon out and was levelling it at Benoit's chest, when Benoit fired. His round caught Adkins dead center, the impact catapulting him backward out of the saddle. He jerked twice and then lay still, his blood making a pool around his body.

"Oh, Jesus," Benoit cursed. "What a fucking mess."

It was several minutes before he realized he was the only one standing at the spot. Legendre was motionless at his feet. Adkins, too, lay without stirring, the fist-sized wound in his chest staring at the sky like a bloody third eye.

Turning, he watched as the Cheyenne quickly dismantled and loaded their lodges. In what seemed a matter of minutes, they were packed and moving silently into the distance, crossing a low hill to the north and winding out of sight. No one spoke to Benoit during the process or even glanced in his direction; he was treated as if he did not exist.

The Cheyenne had been gone for almost an hour when Benoit willed himself into action. It took him another hour to gather enough wood to make a travois. Then he loaded the still unconscious Legendre onto the device and tied him in so he wouldn't slip off. Grunting, he hoisted Adkins's body and threw it belly down across the horse he had ridden to the campsite.

Dejectedly, he swung himself aboard his own mount, the large gray gelding he favored, and pointed the animal westward, toward Fort Laramie.

"Goddamn, Benoit!" Harrigan said in exasperation after Benoit straggled into the post thirty-six hours later, leading his pathetic procession. "How do you manage to get yourself in such situations?"

"Legendre's still alive," Benoit said without emotion. "He took a terrible whack on the head, but his pulse rate is strong and his breathing is regular."

"Then let's get him into a bed," Harrigan said. "There's an empty one in the hospital."

"Oh, my God," Benoit said, his knees buckling. "Don't tell me that Jace died."

"No," Harrigan said, smiling slightly. "That's the good news. His fever broke an hour after y'all pulled out. He's still weaker than hell, but he's managing to get around pretty much on his own. Miss Ellen has gone back to her business."

"What a relief," Benoit said, his voice trembling. "God, it will be good to see ol' Jace. Those prayers must have worked."

"You'd better start praying for yourself," Harrigan said, grabbing Legendre's feet. "Grab his shoulders, will you?"

"What do you mean?" Benoit asked, "It wasn't what you think."

"We'll talk about that in a little while," Harrigan said. "Right now let's take care of Legendre."

"I've got ice packs on his head and he's immobile," Dobbs explained. "That's about all I can do for him. Now we just have to wait and see if he comes to."

"What do you think the chances are?" asked Benoit.

"Who knows." Dobbs shrugged. "Remember that Indian we had awhile back that was unconscious from a head injury? What was his name?"

"White Crane," Benoit replied quickly. "He and Red Horse rescued me at Blue Water. Saved my life, actually."

"I'm so bad with names," Dobbs said. "Maybe it's partly the aftereffects of pneumonia. I wonder how he's doing these days?" he asked pensively, almost to himself. "Anyway," he said, shaking his head, "Remember how he was unconscious for days and days? Then one day he woke up and it was as if he'd never been hurt?"

"You think that's going to happen with Legendre?" Benoit asked encouragingly.

"You just can't tell with head injuries," Dobbs said. "All you can do is hope."

"And pray. It worked for you. But I have to admit you look like hell."

"I'll get better." Dobbs smiled. "The fever's gone and my lungs are clear. I'm sleeping about twenty hours a day. Just awake long enough to eat and I do that like a man who's never seen food before."

"*Ja,* that's truth," said Frau Schmidt, reaching over Dobbs's shoulder to refill his plate. "You be strong soon, you eat my fixing."

"*Cooking,* Mutter," Inge whispered. "'You eat my cooking.'"

"*Ja, ja,*" Frau Schmidt said, shrugging. "He knows."

"You'd better hope he recovers," Harrigan said, "and the sooner the better."

"What do you mean?" Benoit asked, halting his fork halfway to his mouth.

"Look, Benoit," Harrigan said, "you're in a lot of trouble. I've got a dead emigrant out there in the ice-house—shot with your pistol, I might add—an unconscious employee, and a whole bunch of mad Indians. All because of you."

"It was self-defense," Benoit said angrily.

"That's what you say."

"What do you mean, that's what I say. I'm an *officer,* for God's sake. I'm not going to lie about something like that."

"I don't care if you're a preacher. We've got a dead man we have to consider. You claim it was self-defense but the only people who can substantiate that are either unconscious or off in the mountains somewhere. If I were you, I'd pray real hard for Legendre's recovery because if he dies, you might be facing a murder charge. Maybe two."

"That's not fair," Benoit said indignantly.

"This is the *Army*, lieutenant," Harrigan said. "Do I have to remind you that we have strict standards? Until Legendre wakes up or one of those Indians comes wandering in, which ain't very likely considering the mood they're in now, I'm going to have to put you under house arrest. After dinner, you'll go to your quarters and stay there pending further developments. If necessary, I'll put a guard outside the door."

"You're pushing your authority, Harrigan . . . "

"*Captain* Harrigan . . . "

"You're being unreasonable, *Captain*. Colonel Kemp knows . . . "

"The colonel isn't here. I'm acting C.O. And you will do what I damn well tell you. Is that clear, *lieutenant*?"

"No. Goddamnit," Benoit said, staring to rise.

"Calm down, Jean," Dobbs said, putting a hand on his arm. "Captain Harrigan's right. He's the commanding officer. You can appeal to Colonel Kemp when he gets back . . . "

"*If* he gets back," Harrigan said. "If he doesn't," he added, grinning at Benoit, "your ass is mine. Think about that for awhile."

"I don't believe it!" Benoit said, staring at Dobbs. "That's actually what happened?"

"Cross my heart," the surgeon replied. "If I hadn't been there, I wouldn't have believed it myself."

"Tell me again."

Dobbs sighed. "We were sitting at the dinner table, having coffee and strudel . . . "

"No, the other part."

"Okay. I'll make it terse. Couvillion, who's been taking his meals in his room, walked in as cool as an icicle. Strode right over to Teasley and slapped him across the cheek."

"An open-handed blow? A slap, not a slug?"

"A slap. Very definitely a slap."

"Then what?"

Dobbs shrugged. "Not much. He said something like, 'You have insulted my honor by your behavior with my intended. I want you to know that is totally unacceptable and I demand satisfaction.' Or something like that. That's close enough."

"I'll be damned," Benoit said. "He challenged Teasley to a *duel*. But certainly it won't come to pass . . . "

"*Au contraire, mon ami*. Tomorrow morning at sunrise."

"Son of a bitch," Benoit said, slapping his forehead. "But Harrigan was there. Didn't he say it couldn't be done?"

"He started to but Couvillion deflected that. He reminded the captain that he and Teasley were civilians and not under his authority."

"But this is a *military* post and Harrigan is acting commanding officer. He has the power to dictate what happens on the post."

"He brought that up. But Couvillion said if he prohibited it, he and Teasley would just go off post to settle their differences. Then he told Harrigan, again I'm paraphrasing, 'If you force us to do that and I survive I'll go back to my congressman's job in Washington and sooner or later you'll come up for promotion.' "

"A blatant threat!"

"That's the way I interpreted it."

"What did Harrigan do?"

"He turned the brightest red I've ever seen anyone. I

thought he was going to have a stroke. He coughed and wheezed and then allowed he had no jurisdiction over civilians."

"Wasn't the senator there, too?"

"He was. But he looked as if he wanted to climb into a hole."

"And Marie?"

"Her too. You'll love this," Dobbs said. "She fainted dead away. Just keeled over."

"Of all the damn times to be stuck in my room," Benoit cursed. "Damn Harrigan anyway. I don't guess Legendre has regained consciousness?"

Dobbs shook his head. "I can't believe that we're so excited about this. Tomorrow morning one man is going to try to kill another and we're accepting it as a matter of everyday occurrence."

"It happens in New Orleans all the time," Benoit said. "I've been involved myself . . . "

"You!" Dobbs said, shocked.

"It's a long story," Benoit said, waving his hand. "I just can't believe that prissy little Cle would have the balls to do it. I misjudged him considerably. To be realistic, though, I don't imagine he stands much of a chance. Teasley has a lot of experience. *Military* experience. A side arm is like a third hand to him. He's a cold, calculating bastard . . . "

"Maybe you're underestimating Couvillion."

"Maybe," said Benoit. "I've been wrong once or twice, I reckon."

The action was over in a flash, Benoit learned later. It was the aftereffects that took longer.

George Teasley, perhaps anxious to bring the entire experience to a speedy conclusion, fired first. It may have been that the flat, early-morning light was deceptive, or maybe he had been distracted by the cawing of a crow. In any case, his aim was off a fraction. His round zipped by Couvillion's head, tearing a long, ugly gash in his left cheek. Couvillion blinked, wobbled slightly at the thought of the close call, then deliberately levelled his pistol and fired. Teasley was struck in the lower abdomen, just below his belt buckle. The impact drove him back a few feet, where he collapsed in considerable pain, groaning loudly enough to spook the horses in the stables thirty yards distant.

For two days he lingered while Dobbs tried to save him. But, as Dobbs told him later, stomach wounds are extremely unpredictable. Despite the surgeon's considerable skill, Teasley died without regaining full consciousness.

The wound in Couvillion's cheek looked worse than it was. "You'll carry a scar for the rest of your life to remind you of this incident," Dobbs told him. "Maybe if you grew a beard, it would help hide it."

"Really?" Couvillion said, sounding more excited than sorry. "I really don't look good in a beard."

"I still can't believe you actually did it," Marie said, packing the last of her trunks for the trip back to Washington.

"I can't believe I was that far off," Couvillion said, shaking his head. "I was aiming for his gonads."

"You can be a real son of a bitch," Marie said, spinning to face him angrily.

"Can't I though?" Couvillion grinned. "I think that's something you probably should remember."

"And you're really going to make me go through with this wedding?"

"Of course I am, my dear. You've put me through a lot of strain. I expect you to be worth it."

"How can you expect me to go to bed with you after all of this?"

"Who said anything about us going to bed? That's what mistresses are for."

"I don't understand," Marie said, pausing in the middle of folding a dress. "If you don't intend to consummate the marriage, why are you going through with it?"

"That's simple enough," Couvillion said with a laugh. "As I said before, you're beautiful, intelligent, charming, and you already know everyone in Washington. What else could a rising young congressman ask for? And," he paused, "there's one other thing to consider, too."

Marie stared at him. "And what is that? Although I think I already know."

"Of course you do, my dear. It's your father. He's getting very close to retirement. Can you think of a more suitable successor than his dashing young son-in-law?"

"It's been more than a week now," Benoit said, pacing nervously around the small room. "No change in Legendre's condition?"

"None," Dobbs said, shaking his head. "But I do have some news."

"I hope it's good," Benoit said. "I'm about to go crazy in here."

"You decide," Dobbs said. "A trapper came in this morning to get supplies. He's been up north, working his lines. Said a Brulé warrior who begged some tobacco from him told him there had been a skirmish in the Black Hills. There were some casualties, but he didn't know who or how many."

"Damn!" Benoit said. "If the Indians got Kemp and Legendre doesn't come around, I'm really in trouble."

"Look on the bright side," said Dobbs. "If there was a fight, everything may be over with and the detachment is probably on its way back."

"That's true," Benoit conceded. "At least it gives me something to look forward to."

"One other thing," Dobbs said, turning to the door.

"What's that?" Benoit asked, frowning.

"Marie Fontenot. They're packing up to go back to Washington. She got special permission from Harrigan to visit you to say good-bye. She's waiting outside now."

"Oh, Jesus," Benoit said, his eyes growing wide. "Please, please, Jace," he begged, "don't leave me alone with her."

Ken Englade is a bestselling author of fiction and nonfiction whose books include *Hoffa, Hotblood,* and *Beyond Reason,* which was nominated for an Edgar Award in 1991. He lives in Corrales, New Mexico.

NEW YORK TIMES
BESTSELLING AUTHOR

TONY HILLERMAN

"Hillerman's novels inject fresh urgency to the age-old questions about good and evil that lie at the heart of all detective fiction."
—*Baltimore Sun*

MAIL TO: **HarperCollins Publishers**
P.O. Box 588 Dunmore, PA 18512-0588

Yes, please send me the books I have checked:

❑ Finding Moon 109261-4	$6.99 U.S./ NCR
❑ Sacred Clowns 109260-6	$6.99 U.S./ NCR
❑ A Thief of Time 100004-3	$6.99 U.S./ $7.99 Can.
❑ Coyote Waits 109932-5	$6.99 U.S./ $7.99 Can.
❑ Dance Hall of the Dead 100002-7	$5.99 U.S./ $6.99 Can.
❑ Listening Woman 100029-9	$5.99 U.S./ $6.99 Can.
❑ People of Darkness 109915-5	$5.99 U.S./ $6.99 Can.
❑ Skinwalkers 100017-5	$5.99 U.S./ $6.99 Can.
❑ Talking God 109918-X	$5.99 U.S./ $6.99 Can.
❑ The Blessing Way 100001-9	$5.99 U.S./ $6.99 Can.
❑ The Dark Wind 100003-5	$5.99 U.S./ $6.99 Can.
❑ The Fly on the Wall 100028-0	$5.99 U.S./ $6.99 Can.
❑ The Ghostway 100345-X	$5.99 U.S./ $6.99 Can.

SUBTOTAL .... $________
POSTAGE & HANDLING .... $________
SALES TAX (Add applicable sales tax) .... $________
TOTAL .... $________

Name ____________________
Address ____________________
City ____________________ State ________ Zip ________

Order 4 or more titles and postage & handling is **FREE!** For orders of fewer than 4 books, please include $2.00 postage & handling. Allow up to 6 weeks for delivery. Remit in U.S. funds. Do not send cash. Valid in U.S. & Canada. Prices subject to change. H06211

Visa & MasterCard holders—call 1-800-331-3761